Richard Crompton is a former BBC journalist and producer. He moved to East Africa several years ago with his wife, a human rights lawyer who worked on the Rwanda genocide trials. Richard won the *Daily Telegraph* Short Story Award in 2010 and his first novel, *The Honey Guide*, was published to great popular acclaim in 2013. He lives in Nairobi.

www.richardcrompton.com

HELL'S GATE

RICHARD CROMPTON

WEIDENFELD & NICOLSON

For Katya
without whom there would be no books

And our children
without whom there would be many more

First published in Great Britain in 2014
by Weidenfeld & Nicolson
This paperback edition published in 2015
by Weidenfeld & Nicolson
an imprint of Orion Books Ltd,
Orion House, 5 Upper St Martin's Lane,
London WC2H 9EA

An Hachette UK company

1 3 5 7 9 10 8 6 4 2

A CIP catalogue record for this book
is available from the British Library.

ISBN 978-1-7802-2273-8

Typeset by Input Data Services Ltd, Bridgwater, Somerset

Printed and bound in Great Britain by Clays Ltd, St Ives plc

The Orion Publishing Group's policy is to use papers that
are natural, renewable and recyclable products and
made from wood grown in sustainable forests. The logging
and manufacturing processes are expected to conform to
the environmental regulations of the country of origin.

www.orionbooks.co.uk

i-Loikop *(noun,* **Maa***): murder*

*Murder can only occur between Maasai. Only when a
Maasai kills another Maasai do we speak of murder.
Should disputes between Maasai culminate in death,
then this establishes a new relationship between the par-
ties involved whereby those responsible for any deaths are
referred to as* il-oo-ikop: *the-ones-who-hurt.*

Frans Mol, *Maasai Language and Culture*

*They cannot be made slaves, they cannot even be put into
prison. They die in prison if they are brought there, within
three months, so the English law of the country holds with
no penalty of imprisonment for the Masai, they are pun-
ished by fines. This stark inability to keep alive under the
yoke has given the Masai, alone amongst all the Native
tribes, rank with the immigrant aristocracy.*

Isak Dinesen (Karen Blixen), *Out of Africa*

1

THEY HAVE TAKEN THE SKY AND BOUND IT.

He is this: a pair of flip-flops, a pair of baggy shorts. A matching tunic in black and white stripes. In his arms he carries a grubby foam mattress – a half-mattress, cut down its longest axis, no wider than his shoulder blades. A scratchy woollen blanket is folded on top. In the pocket of his tunic sits a little yellow card, which bears, in handwritten letters, his name, his number, his crime.

He is this, and nothing more. Just another one of the four thousand or so inmates of the place. He looks like them. He even walks like them – a shallow, defeated shuffle, thanks to the oversized flip-flops.

He looks like them, but he is not one of them. They know it, too: the very first group he walks past stare at him with seven pairs of sullen, hostile eyes.

—Policeman! one of them hisses.

Many times he has entered prison. Many times he has smelled that scent of stale, confined humanity; felt air, thick with the heat of hundreds of bodies, burn the back of his throat.

Every time, panic threatens to rise within him. Every time, he shudders to suppress it. Reminds himself that unlike these others, he gets to walk out.

But not this time.

The guard behind him chuckles.

—You're not going to find many friends in here, Maasai. You'd better learn to sleep with your eyes open.

—Look out! comes a voice. And two white-clad prisoners thunder past, bearing a huge steaming aluminium cauldron of grey mush dotted with pink, fleshy beans.

The cooks deposit the cauldron with a clatter in the middle of the courtyard. On that signal the disparate clusters of men morph into a line, plastic plates and spoons in hand.

—You can get yours later, the guard instructs him. First to your cell.

They approach an ash-block wall with a narrow doorway in it. Above the doorway is painted the word *Remand*. With a jangle of keys the barred gate is opened and they pass through. Beyond, a second gate. The gates never seem to stop. This place is gate after gate, door after door, each of them opened and locked in turn. They step inside. The vinegary smell of the food had been bad, but the ripe, choking stench of the cell block immediately banishes it from memory. It is the smell of sweat, of urine, of shit, of humanity. They walk past open cells, catching a glimpse at each doorway of dark interiors, mattresses scattered on concrete floors. Meagre possessions tied in ragged bags to the bars of the high, narrow window through which grey light trickles in.

Now he is within the very heart of the gaol, and the denizens look up at him from their cots as he passes. Lassitude prevents most of them from stirring, but emotion flickers in their eyes. Amusement. Anger. Hatred. Pity.

A curious face rolls out and leers as he passes another door: a hand makes a slashing gesture across the throat.

The guard lets out a short, hard laugh and a baton in Mollel's ribs keeps him shuffling forward. His cracked flip-flops are hard to walk in, and he wishes he could kick them off. But bare feet, like shoes, are forbidden here. A simple precaution: you can't run in flip-flops. And needle-sharp granite gravel covers the ground all around these walls.

A barked order to stop. Mollel turns to face a cell door that is hanging open before him.

—Welcome to your new home, says the guard.

He counts six half-mattresses on the floor. Alongside a plastic tub crusted with flies, there is space for one more.

—New arrivals sleep next to the slops, says the guard, and he walks off jangling his keys.

Mollel pushes the tub as far as he can with his foot, and rolls out his mattress in the space that remains. Something stirs at the other side of the cell. What he had taken for a heap of blankets turns out to be the skeletal figure of a man. He can barely raise his head but his eyes, half open, roll in the direction of the newcomer.

—I'm Mollel.

—I know who you are, says the sick man. We all do. We heard you were coming.

His eyes now adjusting to the gloom, Mollel can see that the man's ears are looped just like his own.

—*Supai*, Mollel greets him in Maa. The man does not reply.

—What's wrong with you? says Mollel. Have you seen a doctor?

—There's no *mganga* can cure me, replies the man. Don't you know this is the fate of all Maasai in prison?

It is said that a Maasai never lasts more than three months inside. In the old days, it was believed they simply died. When the English sat in judgement, they wouldn't even put a Maasai behind bars for anything less than murder. Imprisonment was a death sentence to a people who believed that the whole world was their home.

Over the years, Mollel has seen plenty of Maasai serve out their time. He's even put a few of them there himself. They didn't die. But they may as well have. After a few weeks, they became apathetic, listless. Clouds descended upon their eyes and an ashen pallor upon their skin. The elegant Maasai frame, unaccustomed to lying on a cot for twenty hours of each day, became hunched and crabbed. These broken figures seldom spoke and never offered resistance. Their spirit was gone.

—How long have you been here?

—Two years, three years.

3

—On remand? asks Mollel. He knows the backlog of cases is huge, but even so, he is shocked. —Let me talk to the guards. Let me find you a doctor, a lawyer. I might be able to help.

—You just look after yourself, *Ole* Mollel, replies the man. No one's going to want your help in here.

The guard returns with a greasy plastic plate and spoon which he thrusts into Mollel's hand.

—Go get your food before it's all gone, he says.

Back in the courtyard, Mollel casts his eyes around the space. Prisoners stand in groups or sit on the ground, grazing like zebras from their bowls of slop. Around and among them prowl the guards, in their khaki uniforms, berets and shoulder braids, twirling their batons nonchalantly.

High walls run all around, dotted here and there with blank, gated doors. Atop the walls, the sky is bound with rusting curls of barbed wire.

A splash of warm liquid hits him in the face. The spit, full of chewed beans, slides down his cheek and he shakes his head to keep it from his mouth.

Laughter greets the bullseye.

—How'd you like that, *policeman*?

He casts his eyes down, but he cannot escape the mocking hostility as he takes his plate over to the cauldron, no longer steaming, in the middle of the yard.

He senses all eyes are on him as he approaches the tin cooking pot. There is nothing left. Two or three beans are smeared across the sides, otherwise all has been devoured.

As he absorbs this, the laughter returns. First, a sneer, then a catcall, then a tumultuous, clamorous cackling. What started haphazardly becomes rhythmic, vibrating: the prisoners are now stamping their feet in unison.

The guards do nothing for a minute. They are enjoying this, it seems. Then, suddenly, they've had enough. The batons are out, and the mob calms down. The prisoners are ordered back to their cells.

Mollel is held back, but only long enough for the others to reach their cells. There is no favouritism for him: the guards just don't want a fight in the corridors.

When Mollel gets to his cell, the dying Maasai is no longer the sole occupant. A chorus of groans greets him.

—Why do we have to have him? protests one voice.

—You get him, Oweno, because you've had floor space for another mattress ever since your cellmate hanged himself. While the other six of you were supposedly sleeping.

Oweno smiles. —We're heavy sleepers here. Aren't we, lads?

The man rises up, grabbing the plastic pot from its place on the ground and thrusts it into Mollel's hands. The smell hits him in the face. A half-inch of viscous piss sloshes at the bottom.

—Better get used to it, says Oweno. You're on slop duty.

—Behave yourselves, boys, warns the guard. This one isn't a mule thief from Kericho. If anything happens to him, people are going to ask questions.

—It's not us you need to worry about, replies Oweno. We're all big supporters of the *polisi*, here.

Another guard comes, and murmurs something to the first. The pair of them look at Mollel with interest.

—Well, well, Maasai. You're honoured. The boss wants to see you.

—The governor? Mollel asks.

Laughter rings out around the cell. Even the guards snigger.

—Come on.

They lead him past the gate to the Administration Block and onward to the dispensary. There, one of the guards respectfully knocks on the door.

It is opened by a tall man with a pleasant, plump face. Boyish eyes, which turn up at the corners. He looks as innocent as a child. Which is totally at odds with what Mollel knows of this man, and what he does.

He is Mdosi. This current stretch in prison has done nothing to diminish his power or influence. He stands aside to invite Mollel in, dismisses the guards with a nod and closes the door.

The dispensary is a single room which has evidently been converted into Mdosi's private residence. Curtains hang at the window. A rug is on the freshly painted concrete floor, next to the unavoidable piss-pot. A calendar showing scenes of a snow-capped Mount Kenya hangs on the wall. A small television flickers silently on a stool. And, perhaps most enviable of all, there is a bed. A proper full-sized bed, on legs, with the twisted bridal veil of a mosquito net hanging from a hook on the ceiling above it.

Mdosi's eyes dance with amusement.

—Have you anything to tell me, Maasai?

—About what?

—About why my men keep disappearing. About what is happening to them. They're not just retiring from the business, putting their feet up. They're being killed. And I want to know who's doing it.

—I've got nothing to tell you, Mollel says.

Mdosi smiles. Slowly, carefully, he removes one of his flip-flops. It has a line scored across the sole. Deftly he cracks it in half.

Next, he crosses to the piss-pot. He dips his fingers into the liquid, gingerly moves them around, searching for what the eye would miss, then pulls from it a four-inch shard of glass. He sticks the shard into the heel of the broken flip-flop, which Mollel sees has a notch in it for just that purpose. Mdosi handles the shank almost lovingly, watching it gleam in the low light.

—This, Mdosi says to Mollel, is for you.

It must have been the sound of the chair falling to the floor which made the guard open the door. Mdosi's shank is in Mollel's hand.

Blood drips from it.

The guard looks down at the body of Mdosi, lying in a rap-idly growing pool of blood on the concrete floor, then back at

Mollel. Mollel opens his hand and lets the shank fall to the ground, where it shatters. Finally, the guard manages to speak.

—*You've done it, you crazy bastard*, he cries. *You've killed him!*

2

—We might as well get a few things straight, says the young man, waving a bony finger in his face. Just because you used to be a Sergeant, doesn't mean you outrank me now. We're both Detective Constables, and since this is my patch, I have seniority. Got it?

—Got it, says Mollel.

He resists the temptation to tweak Shadrack Kitui's somewhat pointy nose. How old is this pup? Twenty-four, twenty-five? That makes him closer in age to Mollel's own son – now a rapidly growing twelve-year-old – than to Mollel himself. If Adam should ever grow up to be like this . . . thinks Mollel, and then shakes the thought from his mind. Adam has more decency and common sense right now than this upstart. And he's yet to hit puberty.

—Good, says Shadrack. We don't need any Nairobi rejects stepping on our toes down here. We do things our own way in Hell.

It must have been Otieno's idea of a joke. Too many offended egos back at headquarters; too many influential people unhappy with him in Nairobi. And yet, with his record, he was almost impossible to dismiss.

Mollel had gained an awkward reputation for solving crimes – or, as his boss had so elegantly put it: —I don't need to know

8

which dog keeps shitting on my doorstep, Mollel. I just need it cleared up. The Superintendent had held his face in his huge hands and kneaded his thumbs into his forehead when saying this. Mollel had not expected plaudits – he'd solved the case of a murdered prostitute, but managed to outrage some of the most powerful people in the city along the way – although a word of thanks would not have gone amiss.

But it was a time of death. They were still tallying up the figures. Some speculated whether they would ever truly know how many had died. A lynching here, a *panga* attack there. Whole families, whole communities, facing the fallout of a stolen election. Kikuyu, Luo, Kalenjin. Tribe against tribe, neighbour against neighbour. What was one dead *poko* amid all this carnage?

—You're a good detective, Mollel, Otieno had sighed. You believe in the law. But Nairobi doesn't need the law right now. It needs order. And I need you, Mollel, to be somewhere else. Somewhere far from here.

So Otieno had sent Mollel to Hell.

In fact, the tiny township which had grown up along the thin strip of land between Lake Naivasha and the National Park officially languished under the much less dramatic name of Maili Ishirini – signifying nothing more than the fact that it is twenty miles from the nearest administrative centre, Naivasha town. But in common parlance, the dusty, flyblown settlement had long since taken on the name of the National Park whose high, wire fence it bordered. Hell's Gate – the park – was a place renowned for its beauty, and the deep gorge that gave the Park its name. Hell – the town – was not. The police post, originally intended as little more than a checkpoint for traffic, had struggled to keep up with the demands of a surge of incomers. In recent years, as the flower farms clustered around the lake had blossomed, those employed on the gruelling task of picking the flowers within their polythene tunnels – and those in search of easier pickings outside – had built an ever-expanding informal settlement of breeze-block and tin-shack structures. So much so that Hell, today, has become home to a couple of thousand people, half a dozen sleazy bars and barbecue joints, a similar number of churches, a handful of shops, a twice-weekly flea market, one crumbling police post and four policemen.

Five policemen, Mollel corrects himself. He's one of them now. And Shadrack – however irritating – is his colleague. He has a job to do.

They stand before one of the polythene arcs right now. It describes a perfect semicircle, at its height about twice that of a man. In the centre, a double doorway of black rubber with a small, streaked window in each panel. A sign shouts its *ONYO – WARNING* in Swahili and English: *Danger. Pesticides in use. No unauthorised entry.*

—What are we supposed to do? asks Shadrack.

—I don't know. You're in charge.

—We should go in. We haven't got all day.

—After you, says Mollel.

Shadrack looks nervously at the sign. —Maybe we should wait for someone.

At that moment, they hear the word: —*Supai.*

The speaker is a warrior. He has come up behind them, silent in his tyre-tread sandals. His anklets and bangles have none of the small steel discs which villagers love for the jangle they make: he needs no sound to betray his movement. Lean legs rise into his red-chequered *shuka*, bound tightly at the waist by a leather belt decorated with cowrie shells. A long, straight dagger hangs sheathed on one hip, a polished *rungu*, or club, on the other. Between the two, clipped to the belt, is a cellphone. His arms, wiry but muscular, bear copper bands across the biceps. His neck is adorned with a white, tight-fitting beadwork collar. His hair, shaved to the skin at the temples, falls behind him in tightly bound dreadlocks, meticulously dyed with henna.

He is magnificent.

—*Ippa*, replies Mollel: the correct response to a greeting in Maa.

This had been him, once. A warrior. He keenly remembers

the sense of pride that used to swell inside his chest every time he presented himself in his full splendour. This warrior must be about the same age as Shadrack, but there could hardly be more difference between the two. Shadrack, with his stooped shoulders, baggy, shapeless clothing and cynical, resentful attitude. The warrior, eyeing them with relaxed self-confidence. Mollel even has the fleeting thought that he'd be proud to see Adam grow up like that – before dismissing it as ridiculous. The last wish of the boy's mother had been that he'd be raised in the modern fashion, and Mollel had spent the last twelve years fulfilling it. Adam hardly even spoke a word of Maa. Repulsive as the thought was, he was more likely to be a Shadrack than a warrior. And what of it? Mollel had turned his back on that life himself. He could hardly regret the loss of it for his son.

The remembrance of Adam forces him to focus on what is around him: let the immediate present take precedence. After all, there is nothing he can do about the fact that his son is far away in Nairobi: the job demands it. And the boy is in good hands with his grandmother. Yet a pang remains, and Mollel resolves to call him later.

The warrior sees Mollel glancing around the exterior of the greenhouses, taking in the scene. He gives a half-nod, one which tips the head back and chin up, rather than down.

—Welcome home, says the warrior.

Shadrack looks at Mollel with suspicion.

—You know each other?

By way of explanation, Mollel raises his right hand to his ear and taps his lobe. It hangs, looped and low; stretched, just like those of the warrior. The only difference is that two brass earrings glimmer from the warrior's lobes, whereas Mollel's are unadorned.

—This land is home to all Maasai, says the warrior, wherever they may be from. When my clan, the Il-Mutekoni, arrived here, generations ago, they said the Maasai need wander no further. They named the lake Naivasha: *that-which-glitters*.

—A lot of good it did you, replies Shadrack. Look at your

land now! Sliced up, fenced off. We can't even see that precious lake of yours for all the flower farms in the way. And what have you Maasai got to show for it? You're the best-dressed security guards in town.

Mollel, in his time, has heard enough jibes against the Maasai to ignore the young man's scoffing tone. He has come to expect such barbs, especially from his Kikuyu colleagues. He can't help wondering whether there isn't a note of envy underneath it all, somewhere. After all, the Maasai may have lost their land, but the Kikuyu, so eager to wear suits and ties and lace-up shoes, have lost their culture.

The warrior's fingers twitch on his *rungu*. Hastily, Mollel puts out his hand and the warrior makes a fist. Their knuckles touch in greeting.

—Mollel, says Mollel.

—Tonkei, replies the warrior. You're Il-Molelian?

—I was. As you can see, my clan is Il-Polisi these days.

The warrior laughs.

—I'm Detective Kitui, butts in Shadrack. I'm in charge here. We got a call about some kind of disturbance?

The warrior gives his head-up nod. —Come with me.

—What about the poison? asks Shadrack, nervously.

—The pesticide? It's harmless. We just put that up to stop people bothering the pickers. And he holds open one of the doors for the policemen to walk through.

Mollel's immediate reaction on setting foot inside the poly-tunnel is to flinch: all his senses rebel at once in reaction to the strange new environment. The heat causes his skin to prickle instantly with sweat. The sound of the three men's footsteps on the gravel path is deadened by the air, so heavy with the sweet, sickly perfume; a perfume which you smell breathing in and taste breathing out. Almost as overwhelming is the intensity of colour: block upon block of reds, here ember red, there sunset red, further on, blood red, further still, wine red.

Roses. Each one a spiral, a vortex. Each one unique – and identical to the hundreds, thousands growing alongside it. All the same height, all the same shape, a million teardrops furled.

Women move among the flowers, baskets on their backs, like strange grazing animals. Their arms are a blur of movement, selecting blooms with unhesitating precision, slicing them with a curved blade in one hand and tossing them into the basket with the other. Mollel has no idea whether they are picking perfect specimens or removing flawed ones: they are too distant, and the action is too swift, for him to tell. But he suspects he would not know the difference anyway. Cut flowers have always been a mystery to him, and he remembers marvelling at seeing them sold by the roadside the first time he came to Nairobi. They seemed so pointless: something alien and impractical. One of the many madnesses that infected non-Maasai, such as hunting for sport, keeping a pet or worshipping in a church.

As though reading his thoughts, the warrior says to him:

—*They have taken the sky and bound it.*

—What? barks Shadrack. To his evident annoyance, the warrior continues talking to Mollel as though the younger policeman were not even there.

—You know the old saying? Of course you do.

—*They fenced our land with wire* . . . begins Mollel, dragging the words with some difficulty into his mind. It is something his mother used to incant.

—So we grazed our herds in the scrub. They walled our lakes with stone . . .

—So we watered our cattle in the streams.

—And when they dammed the streams, we said: they can never take the sky.

The warrior says this with a flourish of his outstretched arm, which reaches up and follows the arc of the roof above them. The plastic sheeting is opaque, bright, white. The rays of the sun are diffused, scattered, the very shadows thwarted in this even, flat light.

—But they did it, says the warrior. They have taken our sky, and bound it.

—You Maasai talk some nonsense, says Shadrack.

The warrior smiles and shares a look with Mollel, which he interprets as: *What can you expect from a Kikuyu?*

There is something about the young *moran's* way of speaking and his way of holding himself that reminds Mollel of Lendeva.

His brother, Lendeva. He had the same posture, straight as a spear planted in the earth, and the same implacable self-assurance. Mollel always rued that self-assurance. It was supposed to be the other way around: the elder brother was supposed to be the one who taught the younger, guided him, formed him. But Lendeva always gave the impression of having arrived in the world fully formed, like Ntemelua, the trickster of Maasai legend, who stunned his parents by possessing, as a newborn, the full faculty of speech.

By contrast, it was Mollel whose path in the world seemed studded with the jagged rocks of self-doubt. There was nothing that Mollel could teach Lendeva. The younger boy made that perfectly clear by going out and finding teachers of his own.

Among those teachers had been the Samburu, who came one dry season and camped on the outskirts of the *manyatta* where Mollel, Lendeva and their mother lived with a handful of other families. The villagers were not happy about the new arrivals – particularly the camels they drove instead of the more familiar rangy, high-hipped cattle. Unlike cattle, these tall, ugly creatures were not docile or biddable, looking down their haughty noses at the Maasai who, reluctantly obeying the demands of hospitality, gave over space in their thorn-branch *boma* for night-time protection against lions. Sometimes the beasts' great heads would lunge on their snake-like necks to snap and bite, or they would project the inside of their cheek from the side of their mouths in a wobbling, fleshy bubble, working up a mouthful of spit, which they would propel in an unerringly accurate flume of stinking froth onto any person unfortunate, or unobservant, enough to get in their way.

But they provided prodigious quantities of milk – great calabashes full of the steaming, frothing liquid, so much richer than the fare from the Maasai's own modest cows. The scrappy, dry grass of the season did not seem to bother the camels. Indeed, they rejected it as inferior food, much as an elder might push aside maize meal in favour of meat. They stripped leaves from thorny bushes that even goats would baulk at, and chomped upon cacti whose prickles provided protection from virtually all the grazers who were natural to this place. For the camels, of course, were not natural. They were aliens from the far north, farther even than the Samburu themselves, who claimed to have bought the creatures from light-skinned nomads from a land where no trees grew and sand ate all save the hardiest plants.

That milk was the price of the Samburus' ticket through Maasai country, and of their admission to the protection of the *boma*. For the Maasai loved milk, and the villagers gorged upon it. It would be a different story when the rains returned, and their own cows' milk flowed freely once more. But for now, the newcomers were tolerated with a mixture of wary amusement and contempt.

No one held the Samburu in greater contempt than Mollel. At that time, he was on the verge of becoming a *moran* himself, and these itinerants offended his very sense of what it meant to be Maasai. They spoke Maa, albeit with a strange accent, and claimed to be related. To Mollel, however, the Samburu bore the same relation to Maasai as their mangy, ill-tempered stock did to the noble cow (as with most of his tribe, Mollel held an idealised notion of cattle which was at times far removed from the real state of their beasts).

The Samburu worshipped *Enkai*, but they thought, ludicrously, that he lived in the sky, instead of atop *Ol Doinyo Lenkai*. They wore *shukas*, but they wrapped them around both shoulders instead of crossing them over the chest and knotting them at the right shoulder. The colours of their shawls bore no rhyme or reason, seemingly being picked at random. Women wore red and men wore blue, which scandalised the teenage Mollel. Their beadwork was similarly confused, and – as though it were a mere whim of fashion rather than an intrinsic mark of identity – half the men didn't even have their earlobes pierced and stretched into loops.

In short, they were unkempt, undisciplined, undignified, ignorant, unsophisticated, cut-price Maasai. Mollel loathed them, and longed for the time when they would move on to inflict their presence on someone else.

Perhaps, though, the real reason for his contempt lay in the fact that Lendeva idolised them.

—Did you know, the young boy told Mollel breathlessly, after spending all day among his Samburu counterparts, that the reason their bows are so tiny is because their arrows are poison-tipped? Imagine that, Mollel. They don't need to aim for the neck, or hope that an arrow will somehow have enough force to pierce through an antelope's ribs. In fact, forget antelopes! That can take down a zebra, a giraffe. Even an elephant, Mollel! All they need to do is make the tiniest scratch in the hide, and . . .

Lendeva began to shake. His eyes popped and his body convulsed and he collapsed into the dust, kicking and writhing before a silent stillness descended upon him.

—The only thing you need to remember, he continued, springing once more to his feet and beating the dust out of his shawl, is to cut the infected muscle out of the animal straight away. Even if it's the rump, the best bit, you have to burn it or bury it deep, so your dogs don't get it. Otherwise it's certain death for them, too.

It struck Mollel as a cowardly, un-Maasai way of doing things. Where was the glory in bringing down an animal with a poison arrow? You might as well be a white man and use a gun.

This was the type of thing he was picking up from his new Samburu friends. Why, their *morans* spoke to him almost like an equal, when no Maasai *moran* would deign to engage with a boy in the lower age-caste, other than to deliver him a kick up the backside or a clip around the ear.

So it was with relief that Mollel saw the first clouds gather, far to the west, and watched them creep closer every day. When they burst, and the parched earth broke into life, and the first fresh grass appeared like a fuzz of hair on a bare, shaved scalp, the Samburu began to take apart their homes and lash them to the sides of their camels. Mollel witnessed the younger boy's sadness as he bade farewell to the awkwardly dressed, strange-talking youths, and it irked him: he inspired no such affection in his brother. The tears that flowed down Lendeva's cheeks were a sign of weakness, he told himself. An infection from the new-comers. The sooner they were gone, the better. Then everything would go back to normal.

Mollel tries to pull himself back to now. His thoughts are slippery and fugitive these days. Is it a recurrence of his old troubles, this inability to remain anchored? He thinks of the small plastic bottle of pills he carries in his pocket. They are supposed to help keep the dark thoughts away. Nothing is to be gained by dwelling on the distant or the disappeared. It is dangerous.

The roses, which have been steadily darkening, suddenly give way to a square of fleshy pink. Mollel's eyes protest at the colour clash, but he is grateful for it. It focuses him like a slap in the face. The Maasai – who love colour – also recognise its power. Their *shukas* – red for a man, blue on a woman – allow them to be seen for miles in a dusty brown landscape. A distant point of colour becomes a neighbour. A speck of humanity in the vast-ness of nature.

But here, these blocks of colour overwhelm. There is neither humanity nor nature in this space.

And then, a sound which, while faint, pierces the surreal at-mosphere. The sound of a woman's sobs.

Having walked the length of the polytunnel, the warrior and the two policemen draw up at an office: nothing more than an open-topped box delineated by a frame of planed timber and fibreboard panels with a door, which is shut. A white man stands in front of it, wide forearms crossed over his chest.

—You took your goddamn time, he says.

In the reflected pink light, his face resembles sunset on the sandstone cliffs that hang above the town, marking the entrance to Hell's Gate. Craggy. Weather-worn. Unforgiving. There is a certain type of *mzungu* – white person – who looks like they've been left out in the sun to dry.

This guy is biltong.

—Mike De Wit, he continues, putting out a massive red hand for Mollel to shake. He seems to know Shadrack already. I'm the manager here.

—British? asks Mollel.

The mighty brows gather. —Fuck, no! he spits. De Wit? African! I'm as African as you, *bwana*.

Mollel knows that just as any Kenyan can immediately identify a stranger's tribe from the way they speak, the way they look or dress, the gestures they use – so similar nuances also exist among the nation of white people. This is a fact he is perfectly prepared to accept: indeed, now it is pointed out to him, he can detect the clipped, plosive quality of this man's speech that characterises an Afrikaner. But he has had too little interaction with *wazungu* to intuit accurately where they come from. British was usually a safe bet. Failing that, American.

—What seems to be the problem, Mr De Wit?

The Afrikaner jerks a thumb at the cubicle door. From within, the sound of sobbing continues unabated.

—We have a simple policy here, he says. We pay a fair wage for a fair day's work. Steal, and you're out. Most people seem to accept that. But not this one. She's refusing to go. I put her in there, thinking she'd cry herself out sooner or later. Fat chance. She's not going to leave without causing a scene.

Shadrack looks sceptically at De Wit and the warrior.

—You're both big boys, he says. Why didn't you just pick the bitch up and throw her out onto the street?

—And have accusations of cruelty flying around? That sort of thing may not bother the Police Department, Officer. In fact, I get the feeling you positively encourage it. But we're a business. You know who we sell to? Big companies. Big names. Supermarkets, in Britain and Holland and Germany. They don't want their brand tarnished by some blogger with a bone to pick in Maili Ishirini. These girls all have cellphones. Some have video. How's that going to look to the PR department of a blue-chip company, when footage of a supplier beating up their workers gets posted on YouTube?

And yet, thinks Mollel, an entire village can be wiped out and no one cares, because no one was there to film it. Having found himself at the centre of a journalistic frenzy at one time in his life, the priorities and whims of the mass media confound him. Still, he understands De Wit's general point. If the woman needs to be removed, much better to hand the responsibility over to the police.

—You did right to call us, says Mollel. Are you intending to press charges?

This causes De Wit and the warrior to break out into hearty laughter.

—And spend all day in Naivasha courthouse waiting for Judge Singh to take his finger out of his ass? No thanks. Maybe if she'd made off with the payroll. But for what she took, it's not worth it.

—And what, asks Mollel, did she take?

De Wit's grey eyes crinkle under his brows. —What do you suppose she took?

Mollel looks around him. He knows that impoverished people will steal anything. Hell, the rich will steal anything too, for that matter, and more brazenly. Even so, there is little obvious temptation here. The overalls, perhaps, might have some value; the cutting knives. Even the baskets that the women wear on their backs. Is any of this worth the risk of losing a job?

This time, Shadrack joins in with the laughter of the other two at Mollel's blank response.

—Flowers, you idiot! he cackles. What else is there to steal here?

Flowers. Of course. Just as Mollel could not understand why anyone would buy them, he has been blind to the idea that someone would want to steal them.

A wail comes up from within the cubicle, killing the laughter. So much for crying herself out.

Shadrack, meanwhile, has produced a notebook and pencil. He asks: —What is the value of the flowers she stole?

De Wit screws his face into a grimace. —That depends.

—Depends on what?

—On your definition of monetary value.

—Oh, Christ, says Shadrack. This is getting a bit beyond me. I only need a figure for the report.

For once, Mollel has a twinge of sympathy for the younger man.

—Surely, he says to De Wit, a hint of annoyance creeping into his voice, surely the whole point of monetary value is that something is either worth so many shillings and cents, or it's not?

—Not really, says De Wit.

Mollel rubs his eyes.

—Go on then, he says. Explain it to me.

—So, yesterday, I'm coming back from a weekend in the city, De Wit starts. Traffic's slow heading the other way, back into Nairobi. It always is, Sunday evening. All the city workers returning from the country. The real jam starts on the road up the escarpment – you know how those heavy lorries struggle on the incline. I'm coasting down, passing all this traffic, looking out for hawkers. God knows where they come from, but the minute there's a traffic jam, they're out like ants at a picnic. Then I see her. She's walking through the lines of traffic. Arms full of roses.

—How many roses, roughly?

—Three hundred and twelve, De Wit snaps back. There's no *roughly* in this game. I could tell, even from that distance. Twenty-six bunches, twelve stems a bunch, three hundred and twelve stems.

—So did you stop? Did you challenge her?

—Pfft! says De Wit. I was off duty. It could wait until this morning.

—So you were in a moving vehicle. You saw your employee

selling roses on the roadside. Just a question, Mr De Wit. How do you know they were your roses?

De Wit gives him a scornful look. —Thirty years in this business. That's how I know they were my roses.

—And what would she have got for them?

De Wit shrugs. —I suppose she would have been selling them for maybe a hundred bob a bunch.

Mollel smiles. —So my colleague's question about value wasn't so very difficult. The roses are worth twenty-six hundred shillings.

—To her, agrees De Wit. But look.

He walks over to a shelf and returns with a gun-like device, which he brandishes at Mollel. In one swift movement, he presses it against Mollel's chest and the device clicks.

Mollel looks down. A small adhesive label is sitting on his jacket pocket. He peels it off and reads it.

The label is branded with a logo and a name unfamiliar to him. Underneath is a price: £4.99, it reads.

—Four pounds ninety-nine, says De Wit. That's five hundred and fifty-three shillings at today's rate. Twenty-six bunches at five fifty-three makes fourteen thousand, three hundred and seventy-eight shillings. That's a month's wages for her, right there. Or, to put it another way, one month's wages less for someone else.

—Sorry, says Shadrack, licking his pencil. What was that figure again?

—Fourteen thousand, three hundred . . .

Mollel interrupts him. —Don't put that down.

—It's only for the report, Mollel. She's not being charged, remember.

—Even so. Just put: between two thousand and fourteen thousand shillings.

—Not so clear-cut after all, eh, Officer?

De Wit can hardly keep the contempt from his voice. Mollel sighs. He feels a pang of nostalgia for his old life back at Central Police Post in Nairobi. Otieno might have treated him with the same contempt as this farmer, but at least Otieno had his stripes. And now he had to deal with the woman whose pitiful snivels could still be heard leaking from the cubicle behind them. He'd rather be facing down a *panga*-wielding mob.

But when he was sent away from Nairobi, Otieno's instructions were clear: *Keep a lid on that temper of yours. Keep your head down. Try to stay out of trouble for a while.*

3

—*Cheesy kama ndizi*, says Shadrack.

Mollel lets out a sigh and gazes through the cracked windscreen. It is shaping up to be another typical Monday in Hell.

They had escorted the woman from the flower farm and left her, still crying, standing next to her meagre belongings at the side of the road. She had lost not only her job, but her accommodation, as all the workers lived in dormitories on site. But she had ignored any attempt by Mollel to assist her with her bags, and refused the offer of a lift in their wheezing old Toyota saloon.

By the time they reach their second assignment of the day, they have already forgotten about her.

—This is proper detective work, says Shadrack, holding a compact pair of binoculars to his eyes. Cobra Squad.

Cobra Squad: Shadrack's favourite police show. When Mollel first arrived from Nairobi, Shadrack had asked him eagerly if he'd been in a unit like Cobra Squad.

—You know, with the sharp suits, the bulletproof vests, the fast cars and the guns . . .

Mollel had stopped him there. No, he hadn't been in a unit like that. Shadrack had immediately ceased to show any interest in Mollel's previous career.

Round the back of Maili Ishirini Police Post was a strip of three lock-up rooms, each with a window and a door and just enough space inside for a bed and some personal effects. At one end of the strip was a latrine and bucket shower. One of the rooms was occupied by Shadrack, one by Mollel and the third was a kind of lounge, containing a few old plastic chairs, a flower crate as a table and a fuzzy, squawking television set.

It was on this television set that Shadrack watched *Cobra Squad*. And he watched it religiously. Kenya's most wanted *mungiki* gangster could have turned up at Maili Ishirini Police Post to turn himself in, but if he'd done it between nine and ten o'clock on a Tuesday evening, he'd have had to wait.

From what Mollel had seen – and even he had to admit it had a strangely compelling quality which had started to see him linger around the TV room on Tuesday nights – *Cobra Squad* was a Kenyan attempt at making the kind of Nigerian melodramas that filled the airwaves. But unlike the *Naija* blockbusters, this was entirely home-grown. It owed a great deal of its popularity to the extended gunfights and a lot of rolling around in the dirt, although Mollel suspected that the main attraction for Shadrack was the female lead's ample bottom, which the cameras followed at every opportunity.

Five weeks since he moved to Maili Ishirini, and to date, Mollel's greatest achievement is to have learned the dialogue of whole episodes of *Cobra Squad* by heart. All from sitting in this car with Shadrack.

A donkey ambles into view. A few seconds later, a boy follows behind, swishing a stick. At his heels lumbers a dog. They make their way slowly past the tall metal gate and disappear from view. On the gate is a patch of fresh paint, distinguishable in its glossiness from the older area around it. Just visible, through the paint, are some tall, dark letters: WHORES GO HOME.

—We should have a name like Cobra Squad, says Shadrack.

—Donkey Team? suggests Mollel.

—I was thinking of Rhino Force, says Shadrack. Has a certain ring to it, don't you think? And you know, there are the rhinos.

Shadrack nods in the direction of the National Park, Hell's Gate, where there is a rhino sanctuary.

Mollel sighs.

Three days they have been on this stake-out. Three days Mollel has seen the same donkey, the same boy and the same tired, skinny yellow dog pass by.

—I don't suppose you ever did stake-out in Nairobi, Mollel?

He thinks of the times he used to ride the *matatu* mini-buses incognito, looking for pickpockets. Long hours in the shadowy alleyways of a slum, on a tip-off or on a hunch. One cold, wet night spent shivering in a doorway opposite a brothel waiting for a certain client to emerge. Boredom, tempered by fear, was the emotion that united these memories: the know-ledge that, sooner or later, an attempt at arrest would involve a few seconds of struggle, during which the flash of a blade or the stubby muzzle of a pistol could bring everything to an end.

—Once or twice, replies Mollel.

—Cool, isn't it, says Shadrack. Being paid to sit around and do nothing. *Cheesy kama ndizi.*

If he says that one more time, thinks Mollel – and then he recalls Otieno's injunction. *Try to stay out of trouble.*

—But it would be even cooler, says Shadrack, to be in Cobra Squad.

He makes his fingers into a gun and murmurs *Poa kichizi. Cheesy kama ndizi.*

It's not even proper Swahili. The closest translation would be *Crazy cool, like a banana.* The repetition of the phrase seems to comfort Shadrack. It appears to be some kind of mantra; a verbal tic, to the point where the rhyme trips off his tongue without him apparently even noticing it.

Mollel, though, notices it. Every single time. It makes his skin crawl, like ants creeping up his trouser leg.

To distract himself, he looks around the vehicle. This car, he reckons, must be older than Shadrack. And has twice the personality.

He knows every detail of the vehicle, from the windscreen, crazed with cobwebby cracks, to the glassless rear window patched with plastic and duct tape. The surviving windows are tinted for discretion, and the warm, dark interior smells of petrol. It reminds Mollel of the smoke-scented Maasai hut of his childhood, and he feels an overwhelming urge to allow his eyelids to slide and to seek solace from this boredom in sleep. Surely if he just closed his eyes for a moment . . .

—Look!

Mollel blinks and sits up with a jerk. A youth is shuffling along the high wall of the compound they're watching, trying to look casual. It is this affected nonchalance which, to Mollel's trained eye, immediately singles the boy out as a suspect. His head held stiffly, apparently looking at the ground, but in fact stealing sidelong glances all around – though he has not, as yet, clocked the unmarked car parked up the hill.

Mollel longs to pluck the binoculars from Shadrack to see if he can glean any sign of a weapon – a *rungu* hanging from the belt, or the hilt of a blade emerging from a sock. It's good to know what you're up against.

But his pride revolts against asking anything that may be seen as a favour from the younger man, so instead he goes with a more neutral question: —Do you think it's him?

Shadrack lowers the binoculars and glances at his notebook. —Witness said the spray-painter was small built, with short hair. Could be him.

Under his breath, Shadrack mutters: —Now, come on, my friend. Just make your move. You know you want to.

The youth pauses beside the gate and takes a quick look around.

—*Cheesy kama ndizi*, says Shadrack.

They watch as he turns to the gatepost with a swift purpose quite at odds with his previous demeanour.

—Go! Go! Go! yells Shadrack – in imitation of Cobra Squad – and he reaches down to release the handbrake.

Slowly, inexorably, the car starts to roll forward. Shadrack grasps the wheel tightly and aims squarely for the figure standing at the gate.

—We'd get there a lot quicker if you started the engine, says Mollel.

—The element of surprise, replies Shadrack.

The tyres crackle beneath them as they pick up speed. Too late: the suspect senses their approach and spins around, his hands at his crotch, a stream of piss spilling onto his leg.

Shadrack slams on the brakes and he and Mollel leap out. The youth, still exposed, seems to hesitate a moment between fight and flight – and then chooses dignity over both. He just has time to tuck himself in before the two policemen descend upon him, blocking his escape.

—Well, well. What's up, friend? You had some kind of accident?

The skinny youngster looks down at his wet trouser leg. —You guys scared me, he says.

—We *ought* to scare you, says Shadrack, grabbing his collar. You know who we are?

A nod. —*Polisi*.

—That's right, *polisi*. Now, give it up. Where's your spray can?

Shadrack grabs his wrist and raises the boy's hand. Mollel looks at it. There is no paint on his fingers or palm. He shakes his head, clearly scared.

—So how about you tell us what you're doing here? continues Shadrack.

—Nothing, Officers.

—Nothing? I suppose that's nothing on the gatepost, there. And all down your leg?

—It's just *kojozi*. Everyone has to *kojoa* sometimes, right?

Shadrack slaps the boy with the flat of his hand. The boy sinks to his knees in the wet dust. Shadrack leans down to his ear.

—Not on this fucking gate, they don't, he hisses.

Another flick of his knuckles against the boy's skull is the youngster's signal to leave: he gets groggily to his feet and stumbles away, protesting weakly: —I didn't know.

—What's wrong, Mollel? asks Shadrack, once the hapless figure has disappeared from sight. You look shocked. Don't like the way we do things in Hell, huh?

—It's fine, shrugs Mollel.

—You don't look fine. I saw you flinch when I hit that little *mavwi*.

—He wasn't our painter, says Mollel coolly.

—No, agrees Shadrack. But he still deserved it. The thing is, Mollel, there are those who deserve a lot worse. Are you going to be the one who dishes it out to them? Or are you going to – he snaps his fingers in the Maasai's face – flinch?

Mollel turns away and Shadrack laughs. At that moment, there is the sound of a bolt scraping and the gate creaks open wide enough for a woman's face to peer through.

—Did you get him? she drawls through lips daubed sparkling pink. Her eyelids hang heavy with booze and mascara and a copper-coloured weave sits slightly askew on top of her head.

—Not this time, replies Shadrack. A different kind of spray-painter.

The woman's nose wrinkles as she smells the urine. —Never mind, she says. We still appreciate your protection, Officer. That sort of thing's bad for business. You free for your thank-you?

—Now's as good a time as any, says Shadrack.

—What about your friend? the woman asks. She casts Mollel a well-lubricated, lopsided smile.

—I'll wait in the car, replies Mollel.

—Don't go taking it for a joyride, leers Shadrack. Oh, I forgot. You can't drive, can you? Well, I guess you can listen to the radio.

He throws Mollel the keys and disappears behind the gate with a wink and a *Cheesy kama ndizi*.

For ten minutes or so, Mollel sits on the car bonnet, kicking around the gravel under his police boot. Then he walks around the car. He notices the gleam of a nail head sticking out of the tread of one of the front tyres: the tyre doesn't seem any the worse for its presence, so he decides not to pull it out. At the back of the car, he sees that the boot is secured with a piece of fencing wire twisted through the hole where the lock should be. That's presumably why the spare wheel rides on the rear seat. With an effort, he untwists the wire and the boot springs open.

Inside, the boot has no lining: just a rough gunny sack placed directly onto the grooved metal. Mollel lifts the sack. It has the bitter, greasy smell of hemp, but otherwise seems quite new. Beneath the sack, the floor of the boot seems similarly clean, which is at odds with the rust-holes through which he can see the gravel on the ground below. He runs his finger along the surface of the metal. It's barely even dusty. This space has been cleaned in the past few days, even hours – while the rest of the car looks like it has not seen a brush or sponge inside a decade.

With the nail of his index finger, he scrapes around the corners of the boot, along the ridges of the welds, into the cracks and crevices. When he holds it up to the light, it is shining with black dirt and grease. He sniffs it. He takes a piece of cloth from his pocket, wipes the finger on the cloth, folds it and puts it away again.

He is just refastening the wire when he becomes aware of a figure approaching behind him. He straightens up self-consciously, his hand automatically reaching to cover his pocket. But bent nearly double under her load, the woman has not seen him. She moves like she is not of this world, each slow foot-step placed barely a few inches in front of the other. A fabric strap runs across her forehead and around to her back, where her burden hangs. As she draws level with him, he gets a look at her face, side on, and Mollel realises she is the woman from the flower farm: the one who had been sacked that very morning.

—Hey!

Her body stiffens, but she does not look up, as though failing to acknowledge him will make him go away. She knows the tone of authority when she hears it – and she knows it means trouble. Her pace quickens.

—No, wait. It's me. Sergeant – he corrects himself – *Constable* Mollel. From this morning.

Her head remains stubbornly bent, but she stops. She speaks: her voice is like wind in the grass.

—What? Mollel steps closer. I can't hear you.

—I said, don't arrest me. Please.

She looks up and her eyes meet his. They are wary eyes, weary eyes: weary from far more than just the hot, heavy walk.

They are the eyes of someone who doubts her ability to sustain more than the most basic task, lest the world collapse around her. Mollel knows those eyes, and remembers a time when they were his. A time when the only thing he could focus on was the task, and the more repetitive and unpleasant the task, the better he liked it. For while he was doing it, he wasn't thinking—

He has a vision, there, in that hot, empty road, of another place. A place where the sun was blotted out by smoke and dust. Of rubble all around. Every figure a skin of ashes. His own fingers stubbed and bleeding from lifting, sifting, scrambling through that heap, looking, looking – until he forgot what he was looking for and only remembered the looking.

He snaps his attention back to the woman standing in front of him. She is still avoiding his gaze. She lost her job this morning. That would be a blow for anyone.

When they left her this morning, she had told them she was going to leave town on the upcountry bus. At this rate, she won't make it to the stage before dark. She'll end up sleeping under a bush somewhere, waiting for the morning departure. And that is no way for any woman to spend a night, least of all one in this state.

He feels an urge to lift her burden from her, put it in the car. When Shadrack returns, the pair of them could drive her to the bus stage and Mollel could press some money into her hand. She would be grateful. Perhaps she'd even smile.

And yet, he does not offer.

He knows that even the offer would pain her. He knows that all she wants is to be left alone with her pain, and it is from pity – and empathy – that he spares her from any kindness.

She is shuffling hopelessly away as Shadrack emerges from behind the high gate. He walks toward the car and Mollel. The young man uses his lips to point at the retreating figure – as though it would be too much effort for him to use his hand. It's another habit that Mollel finds less than endearing.

—Isn't that . . .?

—The woman from this morning, yes, replies Mollel.

—What did she want?

—She didn't want anything, says Mollel.

—That'd be a first. They always want something, in my experience. You want to know my advice, Mollel?

Mollel does not answer.

—Don't get involved, says Shadrack, answering his own question. It's not worth it. Other people's problems just drag you down.

Mollel wonders whether he should tell his colleague that his trouser zip is down, but decides it is someone else's problem.

—Come on, says Shadrack. We've got to go into town. I got a call. There's some kind of problem at the courthouse.

Mollel gives Shadrack back his keys, and they set off. Leaning forward in the passenger seat, Mollel can see the woman in the cracked side mirror as they pass her. A speck, and she is gone.

Naivasha. The town, compared to Hell, feels like a teeming metropolis. In fact, it has only a few tens of thousands of inhabitants. Its status derives more from being the only sizeable settlement on the hundred-mile stretch between Nairobi and Nakuru, meaning it has a police headquarters, a prison and a courthouse, on whose steps a crowd has gathered.

Shadrack grinds the car to a halt and the two of them get out. They walk slowly across the road toward the courthouse, appraising the situation. About fifteen protesters, waving placards and chanting. All women, by the look of things. Two policemen from the Naivasha station stand between the protesters and the courthouse door.

The protesters part before them and Mollel and Shadrack join their town counterparts, with whom they exchange nods of greeting.

—Is this it? says Shadrack, doing his lip-point with disgust. I've seen prayer groups get more out of hand.

—It's not them we're worried about, says one of the policemen. It's who's inside.

From here, Mollel can see what's written on the placards. Many of them say WAR. Others, in smaller letters: *Women Against Rape*. One reads: *End impunity now*. Another, in heartfelt but cramped lettering: *Crimes against women and girls will no longer be tolerated*.

—Why? asks Mollel. Who's inside?

—Like you need to ask! cries a voice from among the protesters. Mollel sees a woman break forward and mount the first few steps toward the policemen.

—Now, Kibet, cautions Shadrack. Remember who you are.

—I'm off duty! Kibet snarls. Her hair is cropped short, like a schoolboy's, and her baggy T-shirt – emblazoned with WAR – cannot disguise her strong, wiry physique. The two Naivasha policemen shrink back. They have no intention of messing with her. She glares at them furiously.

—It's thanks to you guys that people like *him* walk free.

—That's hardly fair, says Shadrack, palms out in a conciliatory gesture.

—Not you, Shadrack, she says. You're alright.

—Yeah, he grins. I'm *cheesy kama ndizi*.

—But this lot . . . she glares at Mollel and the two others.

—I don't even know who you're talking about, says Mollel.

—Ask your friends here. In a minute, Raphael Gachui is going to walk out of this courthouse because someone mislaid the evidence in his rape case. Isn't that right, Officers?

One of the two Naivasha policemen lunges forward. —That's a serious allegation, he hisses. His colleague grabs his arm and pulls him back, shaking his head to say, *Leave it*.

As though on cue, a chorus of hoots and whistles rises up

from the bottom of the steps and Mollel turns. From within the dark interior of the courthouse, a stocky figure in a red leather jacket emerges. His eyes are hidden behind a large pair of sunglasses, and when he opens his mouth in a wide, face-splitting grin, his teeth dazzle gold in the sunlight.

He is accompanied by an entourage of five or six other young men, all wearing similarly lurid garb, and as he pauses at the top of the steps, Raphael Gachui grabs the hands of two of his companions and raises his arms in a triumphant V.

The cheering of his group and jeering of the women combine in a tumult that brings passers-by to a standstill. Shadrack casts Mollel a nervous glance. The gathering has gone from dozens to a few hundred in less than a minute. Apart from at the nucleus, the mood is merely curious – for now. But they both know that that can change in a heartbeat.

Gachui is now signalling for quiet.

—He can't be intending to speak! Mollel yells to Shadrack in amazement.

But he is. His cronies fall silent, and while the noise continues from the protesters, they aren't able to drown out his words entirely.

—I'd like to thank my supporters for never doubting me, shouts Gachui. And I'd like to assure the good people of Naivasha that nobody – he casts a smile down at the women below him, a floodlight beam of gold – *nobody* takes rape more seriously than I do.

His words drive them to greater fury. Kibet thrusts forward and seems about to break through to Gachui, but Mollel throws his arms around her. The impact nearly topples his gaunt frame, but he holds her tight against him, and he feels her spittle on his ear and her breath on his cheek as she screams:

—You'll get justice one day, Gachui. Some day when Mdosi's not there to pay off the police and the judges for you. You'll get yours.

—Shut your hole, *kalezi*, shouts one of Gachui's friends, and this time it is Shadrack who lunges. He grabs the youth by the neck.

—What did you call her? *Kalezi*? You'd better watch your tongue, boy, before someone cuts it out!

Kalezi is a Sheng word unfamiliar to Mollel, but Shadrack's reaction leaves him in no doubt of its offensiveness.

Gachui's cronies pack around Mollel and Shadrack, screaming at them and Kibet, who is screaming back. The situation is teetering out of control, but it is Gachui who ends it. With an almost imperceptible nod, he gathers his men around him and they stride down the courthouse steps, the crowd opening with mixed respect and fear to let them pass. A large blacked-out car has pulled up at the kerbside and the men get in. With a final flash of his gold teeth, Gachui looks back up at Mollel and Kibet and raises a finger to his brow in salute. Then he is gone.

Mollel releases his bear hug on Kibet and she scowls at him.
—I suppose you enjoyed that, she says.

—You should thank me! Mollel protests. I stopped you getting into trouble.

—I don't need protection from people like that!

—I wasn't protecting you, replies Mollel. I was protecting *them*.

—*That*, says Kibet, anger blazing in her eyes, is the *problem*.

For a moment, Mollel can't look away from the intensity of her glare. Then Shadrack places a pacifying hand on her arm and says: —Mollel was doing you a favour. You can't afford to get involved in anything like this. Our car's over there. I reckon it's near enough to end of shift for a drink.

The crowd has melted away. Kibet shrugs and says: —Just a quick one. Your shift might be ending, boys, but mine is just about to begin.

She walks toward the car.

Mollel is struck by the apparent trust this young woman places in Shadrack. Up to this point, his colleague has only ever appeared to him to be boorish and glib: one of the last people he'd suspect of taking an interest in women's rights. Yet this Kibet, who knows him, evidently thinks otherwise.

Perhaps there is more to Shadrack than there seems.

—Who's this Mdosi she was talking about? asks Mollel.

—Mdosi? The big man. He runs this whole district. Raphael Gachui does his dirty work for him.

—Why can't he do his own dirty work?

Shadrack snorts. —Don't you ever read the newspapers in Nairobi, Mollel? Come on. Let's grab a beer.

—Wait.

Mollel looks down at the car, where Kibet is waiting for them, drumming on the roof and scowling. He points with his lips. —The way she talks. Is she one of us? Is she *polisi*?

Shadrack laughs again. —She thinks she is. Come on, Mollel.

He leads the way down the steps, shaking his head. With a burst of annoyance and shame, Mollel realises he just pointed with his lips. He'll be saying *Cheesy kama ndizi* next. Not for the first time, he wonders what he did to deserve this assignment.

4

The manager is evidently not overjoyed at the prospect of playing host to the entire law-enforcement community of Hell.

—We try to keep a respectable establishment, he is saying, wringing his hands nervously as he walks before them. Need I remind you that the last time you were here . . .

—How's your alcohol licence? interrupts Shadrack.

—Per...perfectly in order, stammers the manager. Look, I'm not trying to turn you away. We're very happy to have your cu...custom. But, you know, the tourist trade is only just beginning to recover from the post-election violence and with so few guests, your group is more – how can I put this – more . . .

—More noticeable? asks Mollel.

They have walked the entire length of the lobby, dining room, lounge and bar and passed plenty of uniformed concierges, lounging bellboys and bored-looking, black-clad waiting staff – but not one single guest. Now, a guffaw echoes through the cavernous hall of the high-beamed hotel bar, with its mahogany panels and brass lamp fittings, sabre-horned antelope skulls and antique animal heads mounted on the walls.

At the far end, by a window inky-black but which, Mollel divines, must face the lake, three men sit around a small table covered with bottles. They are rocking backward and forward with mirth. The smallest of the three, wearing a dishevelled sergeant's uniform, is talking animatedly.

—And she said, I told you, fifty bob for a blow job. I never said anything about putting your *uume* in my mouth!

This announcement is greeted with much knee-slapping and a renewed chorus of raucous guffaws.

With the satisfaction of a speaker who has delighted his audience, the small sergeant raises his empty beer bottle in the air and waves it in the direction of a hovering waiter. As he does so, he looks up and sees Mollel, Shadrack and Kibet approach, in the solicitous company of the manager.

—Ah, Shadrack, he says. You're just in time. It's your round. Kibet, good to see you. You'll forgive a little banter among colleagues, I hope? All harmless stuff.

—I just want a drink, says Kibet. Shadrack nods, and waves at the waiter to take an order.

—And our new recruit, too! insists the sergeant.

—Mollel doesn't drink, replies Shadrack.

One of the other seated men – as huge as his sergeant is small – leans forward groggily and slurs: —I never trust a man who doesn't drink.

—That should make you the most trustworthy man on earth, eh, Munene? says Shadrack.

I mean it, continues Munene. He sits hunched, shoulders high, chewing like a buffalo. His alcohol-soaked voice rumbles, quiet and deep, from a place far within him.

—A man who doesn't drink is a man who hears your secrets but hides his own. If he's sticking around, I'm leaving.

Mungai, the sergeant, throws his hands up in protest. In his white uniform shirt, he reminds Mollel of the tiny oxpecker which flutters around the buffalo.

—At least stick around while Mollel has a soda, he says, soothingly. No one's giving away any secrets tonight.

—Don't worry, Munene, chips in Shadrack. If you start shooting your mouth off, the rest of us will shut you up. Won't we, boys?

Munene glowers, looking around as though deciding which fly to swat first. Shadrack, skinny as a *jembe*? Sergeant Mungai, who seems to be shrinking even further under his colleague's glare? Old, silent Choma – the fourth man present, though scarcely so – nursing a bottle of beer as his rheumy eyes gaze into the middle distance? Or feisty Kibet, apparently one of the boys, in Shadrack's parlance? Which of them could shut him up?

The very thought is so preposterous that his face breaks into a wide smile and a laugh gurgles forth from his lips.

Sergeant Mungai slaps him on the back. —That's the spirit!

He, too, is laughing. Shadrack and Kibet as well. Even old Choma, as though remembering something from the distant past, joins in with a wheezy chuckle.

Mollel glances around the group.

They look like any group of workmates enjoying a post-shift drink. They are relaxed in each other's company, and despite the differences between them – in temperament as well as physique – they seem to share an unspoken bond of trust.

Which is one of the reasons, Mollel reminds himself, that they are so dangerous.

—I'll take that drink, he says.

Shadrack looks at him with surprise.

—I never said I don't drink, Mollel replies. I just save it for special occasions.

—So today's special, bellows Munene. It's Thursday!

The waiter arrives with a tray of beers and hands one each to Kibet, Shadrack and Mollel.

Munene lifts a glass of whisky in his massive hand and leers: —To the incorruptible Mollel!

—*The incorruptible Mollel!*

Kibet lifts the beer bottle to her lips greedily, drinking it down from the neck. After several long gulps, she pulls the bottle away, gasps with satisfaction and wipes her mouth with the back of her hand.

—I needed that.

Sensing eyes beginning to return to him once more, Mollel raises his own bottle to his mouth.

At various stages in his life, Mollel has become aware of the effects of alcohol upon others – and upon himself. It is many years since he has tasted beer, and this cold, fizzy, European-style beer, he is relieved to note, is no harder to gulp down than soda. Perhaps even easier than soda.

He swallows his first mouthful and is hit by a familiar dual sensation: that of bitterness in his throat and warmth in his veins. As he tries to suppress a grimace, he hears the others laughing at some new joke – and then realises they are all laughing at him.

—We can ask them to slaughter a cow if you'd prefer fresh, hot blood, says Munene.

Mollel remembers the days when, as young boys, he and his brother used to drink the blood straight from the cow. It didn't have to be slaughtered, though – Munene was wrong about that. Their mother would apply a tourniquet around the cow's neck, tight enough to raise its pounding arteries underneath its pelt, but gentle enough that it did not have difficulty breathing. Selecting a vein that was fat and blue, it was the eldest son's job to raise the special bow – no longer than his forearm – and pull it back so that the short, stubby arrow with its rounded stone tip would twang the inch or two onto the beast's neck. If he did it right, the cow, held tenderly at the nape by his brother, Lendeva, would not even murmur.

Then it was quick with the calabash, the hollowed-out gourd, held up into the arc of bright red blood that spurted forth, collecting it within, careful not to spill a drop. If the tourniquet was released at just the right time, the change in pressure within the punctured vein would stop the flow immediately, and Lendeva would rush to press a poultice of leaves against the damaged spot.

And then – the drinking. Never, not once, had Mollel ever dared flinch at this, for it was a sign of weakness. Even the first few times, when he had hesitated and felt the blood start to congeal into slippery strings as it drained down his throat, he had resisted the urge to gag and had continued to swallow.

Remembering this, and holding Munene's gaze, Mollel raises the beer bottle once more and takes a deep, hearty chug.

When he lowers the bottle, it is old Choma whose eyes his meet. Choma, the only person present who, so far, has not spoken. Grizzled and lined, and looking lost in his constable's uniform, he raises an eyebrow at Mollel and nods. Without knowing what the gesture means – indeed, whether Choma means anything by it at all – Mollel raises an eyebrow and nods back.

—It's dead in here, says Shadrack. Remind me again, guys, why we come here?

—Because of the *pussy*, replies Munene with a broad smile.

Kibet puts her bottle down among the empties. —I got to go *kojoa*, she says, and walks off.

—She doesn't need to act so offended, says Munene. She loves it as much as we do.

—I don't know why people keep saying that, says Shadrack, glaring at Munene. She's not a *kalezi*. She's straight up.

—You believe what you want to believe, says Munene smugly. You're not going to get any of *that*, either way.

Suddenly Mollel understands the Sheng word the gangsters hurled at Kibet on the courthouse steps. The prefix *ka* is a diminutive, implying contempt. And *lezi* is obviously from the English. Lesbian.

As though to change the subject, Shadrack says: —There's no pussy here, anyway. This place is dead.

—Just you wait, says Munene. The tour groups are still on their way back from the National Park. Even with the numbers down, there's always some talent here later in the evening. And you know how excited these white women get at the thought of a little African adventure . . .

It would have to be a pretty desperate white woman – or any woman – who found Munene attractive, thinks Mollel. The only thing that saves him from being grossly obese is his great height, which means he is merely obese. He is as likely to crush a lover as satisfy her. And judging from the way he is slurring his words and waving his beer bottle around, he doesn't seem likely to satisfy himself in that regard, either.

—When do you think the tourists are likely to come back? asks Mollel, to change the subject.

—It's, what, seven o'clock, says Sergeant Mungai. So any time now.

—No, I mean, when will they start coming back to Kenya? It's been nearly a year now since the election. And I haven't seen anything like the numbers of tourists we had before. Half the hotels around here have shut down. This place looks like it's hardly breaking even. Hell, they're probably only surviving on what you lot spend on beer.

—You think we pay them? laughs Shadrack, but the sergeant casts him a warning glance.

—Tell me what it was like here, says Mollel. Tell me about what happened after the election.

A sombre silence suddenly descends over the group. No one seems to want to answer Mollel. They don't seem to want to look at each other, either.

Then, slowly, softly, Choma begins to speak.

—It was terrible, he says. Terrible.

—Choma's been in Hell thirty years, whispers Shadrack. He took it hard.

When violence erupted after the disputed election in December 2007, sleepy Naivasha thought it had escaped the horrors that were engulfing cities such as Nairobi and Eldoret. But then, in January, the attacks started. They were systematic and well planned. Groups of young men, organised by shadowy backers. They were Kikuyu; their targets, any Luo workers they could find. The Luo, to them, were foreigners, opportunists, in-comers with no links to the area. For their part, many of the flower farms had developed a policy, over the years, of recruiting Luos for just that reason: away from the diversions of family and friends, their workers were much more biddable.

At night the young men came, spilling over fences and over-powering guards. Destruction of property was not their aim, nor theft. They were disciplined. They went straight for the dormitories.

—By the time I got there it was all over, intones Choma. It was a question of helping the injured and . . .

He raises his beer bottle and Mollel notices that the old man's hand is shaking.

—I'm not a doctor, he croaks. It was all too much for me. They wanted my help, but I didn't know what to do. I just . . . I just . . .

—That's OK, Choma, says Munene, patting his back. Choma blinks, brings his bottle to his lips.

—You must have seen some pretty nasty shit in Nairobi, too, says Shadrack to Mollel.

Mollel thinks back to bullets whistling around his head in Kibera slum on election day. To the smoke and the tear gas swirling around him, searing his lungs. To the blackness enveloping him as he searched frantically through the burning labyrinth. And then, nothing.

—Yes, says Mollel. Some pretty nasty shit.

His head is whirling with memories, not just of that day but of others. Days of fire and blood. Some just a few months previously and one, one day ten years before. A day so distant it seems to have been part of him for ever, so recent that the thought of it never truly leaves his mind.

—Who died?

Kibet has returned from the washrooms and crashes down onto a seat next to Mollel. She looks at the sombre faces around the table. Oh, Christ, we're comparing war stories, are we?

—Well, you've got the T-shirt, says the sergeant.

She glances down at the letters on her chest. —That's a different kind of war, she replies. But if it's stories you want, I've got one for you. Happened just last night.

—What is it? asks Shadrack. I knew there was something bothering you.

With everyone's attention on her, Kibet pauses for a drink.
—Better make this my last one, she says. I'm on duty in half an hour.

She drinks, and then shivers. Shadrack slips off his jacket and offers it to her. She puts it around her shoulders. Once more, Mollel is struck by the change in the young man's demeanour. When Kibet is around, flashes of sensitivity emerge, standing in sharp contrast to his usual oafishness. Mollel wonders: which one is the facade?

—It gets cold up in Hell's Gate at night, she says, and draws the lapels of Shadrack's jacket across her chest. It was bitter last night. One of those nights when the stars are the warmest things out there. Usually, on nights like that, you can hear a lion huffing five miles away. But we had the heater on in the patrol vehicle, the engine running to keep the battery charged. That's why we never heard the screams.

Mollel does not like the way this story is going.

He exhales slowly.

He's had a bottle of beer. Just a bottle. His head should not be spinning like this.

—You alright, Mollel? sniggers Shadrack. Kibet, maybe you'd better go easy on the city boy.

—I want to hear, says Mollel.

—Yeah, shut up, Shadrack, says the sergeant.

—So, we're on one of the dust tracks, and I see footprints. Human footprints. That's not so common, up there. The odd hiker, perhaps. But there were trails, too. Thick, wide grooves in the dirt. And small splashes here or there. Just a few drops. In the headlights, it looked like oil on the ground, but when you got closer, you could see it was blood.

Kibet's words reverberate in the huge, empty room. Mollel has the feeling that everyone is listening: the manager, the barman wiping glasses behind the bar, the waiter waiting for the order for the next round – even the stuffed heads on the walls – everyone is hanging on what the woman will say next.

—We had a choice: follow the footsteps, in the hope of catching whoever did it, or track back to the source, in the hope of finding survivors. We chose to look for survivors. The trail led up to the edge of the forest, so we got out and continued on foot. It was slippery. There hadn't been rain for weeks, and yet the mud was heavy under our feet. Heavy, and red.

Kibet's voice is thick now. Mollel can see her eyes glisten in the subdued light of the bar. Looking around the other faces, he sees her emotion reflected in theirs. Mungai, the officious, pugnacious sergeant, is full of sympathy; Munene's great, slab-like countenance is etched with concern; old Choma nods encouragingly. And Shadrack – Shadrack has put a comforting hand on Kibet's arm, a gesture which Mollel is sure she would shrug off from anyone else.

For a moment, he is envious. Envious of this group, who are bonded tightly enough to air, and share, the dreadful things they have seen. The knowledge that each one implicitly understands. The camaraderie of soldiers.

Mollel has never had this. He's only ever had two friends in his life. One was his brother, and one was his wife. And now they are both gone.

If he'd ever had this, would he have ended up the way he has?

Who knows. Perhaps a beer or two, years ago, would have made Mollel a different man.

—When we got there, to the clearing, continues Kibet, we could see there were no survivors left. It had been brutal. Unsparing. Even the babies—

He's not sure he can take this.

He rises to his feet. The chair slides back noisily behind him, and he sways for a moment before steadying himself.

—There were five of them, continues Kibet. She's speaking quietly enough, but with the damned acoustics in this place, Mollel can still hear her as he heads toward the washrooms. —At first, we just saw their backs. Some were lying on the ground. Some were kneeling. It wasn't until we got closer that we saw what they'd done to them.

—What had they done? asks Shadrack, breathlessly.

—They'd taken off their faces, says Kibet. Every single one.

Mollel rinses his face in the sink, grateful for the feeling of cold water on his skin. He raises his eyes to look at himself in the mirror.

Perhaps it's the harsh lighting. Perhaps it's the fact that he seldom bothers to look at his reflection these days. Mollel is only in his early forties, but he sees an old man looking back at him. More than that, he sees his own father – a man he never saw again after the age of ten, but whose features remain etched on his own head, inside and out. The same high cheekbones and forehead. The same narrow nostrils and lips. The same looped earlobes, stretched in childhood, hanging down against his neck. The only difference: the long, thin scar rising up from his right eyebrow almost to his hairline. Mollel runs a thoughtful finger along it. If that's the only thing that differentiates him from his father, he loves that scar.

He hears the door open and swing shut behind him. He quickly grabs a handful of paper towels and vigorously dries his face. When he glances up again, he sees Kibet beside him, looking at him in the mirror.

—This is the men's room, he croaks.

—So what? If those guys saw me in here, it would only confirm what they think of me anyway.

Mollel screws up the towels and throws them into the wastepaper basket.

—I never heard about any massacre last night, he says.

—You wouldn't have. It's a KWS matter.

—KWS?

Mollel racks his brain to work out why the killings would be the concern of the Kenya Wildlife Service.

—Sure. Five elephants killed by poachers. Of course it's a KWS matter.

Mollel gives a short bark of laughter.

—What the fuck is wrong with you, Mollel? It's not funny.

They shot them all, even the babies. Then they used a chainsaw on the mothers to take the tusks.

Mollel shakes his head. —I didn't know you were a KWS ranger. For some reason, I thought you were police.

This was the wrong thing to say.

—I know you *polisi* look down on us, she says. But those creatures can't protect themselves. Not against thugs with pickup trucks and AK-47s.

—I don't look down on you, says Mollel.

—Come off it. You look down on everyone here, don't you, Mollel? You can hardly disguise your contempt for those guys. Well, let me tell you something. They may look like country bumpkins, but those four out there are finer policemen than you'll ever be.

—I'm not here through choice, protests Mollel.

—No, she replies. You were demoted, weren't you? At least, that's the story.

—What story? asks Mollel. But Kibet ignores the question. She casts him a disgusted look and leaves.

When Mollel returns to the group, Kibet is not there. She must have left for her shift.

—You're just in time, says Shadrack. Look over there. The main attraction has begun.

He points toward the bar with his lips.

Mollel looks over to the bar. A woman is there, checking her cellphone. She is a white woman, with dark, curly hair spilling down her back. She is wearing a businesslike jacket and skirt and expensive-looking high-heeled shoes; hardly safari gear, Mollel thinks.

—She's all alone, says Shadrack in whispered tones. I wonder if she'd like a little company.

—Nothing little about the company I'd give her, chortles Munene.

—She's gorgeous, groans the sergeant.

—She is totally checking us out, whispers Shadrack, excitedly. *Cheesy kama ndizi.*

46

Even old Choma can't drag his eyes away from her. Mollel is amused; from what he can see at this distance, the woman seems to have a pleasant enough face – albeit a little plump by Maasai standards – but she shows no sign of even having noticed the policemen, let alone flirting with them.

—What's up, Mollel? goads Shadrack. White chicks not your thing?

—Maybe *chicks* aren't his thing, says Munene. Maybe he's another one like Kibet.

Shadrack casts his colleague a warning glance.

But inwardly Mollel has to concede that Munene has a point. Chicks aren't his thing. Since his wife died in the bombing of the American embassy in Nairobi, eleven years before, he's hardly looked at another woman. Then he corrects himself. There had been one, but she was a mistake.

—So, says Shadrack. Who's going to go over and give her a try?

—It should be me, says the sergeant. I'm the ranking officer.

—Yes, replies Shadrack. But you're also married. We single lads have to live in those disgusting barracks. It's only fair we should have a go. Mollel?

Mollel waves his hand to show Shadrack that he won't face any competition from him.

Munene adds: —The only person I'm afraid of is my wife, so I'll sit this out. And as for you, Sarge, no offence, but you wouldn't stand a chance.

Shadrack cackles with glee.

—And I suppose you're a movie star! retorts the sergeant.

—I get no complaints, says Shadrack.

—Except when you underpay them!

—I resent that, says Shadrack. I never pay for anything.

—We've noticed!

Old Choma, who has been following the conversation with silent laughter, wipes a tear from his eye.

—Looks like you've lost your chance, anyway, he wheezes.

The others turn to gawp at the bar, where the figure of a man has just joined the white woman. Conscious of not wanting to draw attention to their ogling, Mollel turns his face from the scene.

—That's the sort of guy I hate, says Shadrack.

—What, good-looking? asks Sergeant Mungai.

—He's not *that* good-looking. I'm just as good-looking as he is.

Choma shakes with mirth.

—Look at him, says Shadrack with disgust. What's he got that I haven't?

—*Her*, by the look of things, says Munene.

The sergeant lets out a *shh*! —He's coming over.

Mungai, Shadrack, Munene and Choma suddenly take a studied interest in the ceiling, their beer bottles, their fingernails – anything but the approaching man. Mollel, who is already looking the other way, does not need to fake it.

—Mollel!

He turns. Facing him, arms outstretched, a wide, genuine smile on his face, is Kiunga.

—I thought it was you! What the hell are you doing here?

—You know each other? asks the sergeant, suspiciously.

—Sure, grins Kiunga. We used to be partners, back at Nairobi Central.

He leans down to shake the sergeant's hand and repeats the act with Munene, Choma and Shadrack, who accepts the gesture as though he's being asked to hold a dead rat.

—Collins Kiunga, says Kiunga. On attachment with the Diplomatic Police.

—I hear you're a Sergeant now, says Mollel. Congratulations.

Kiunga's smile fades. —Yes, he says. And I heard about . . . what happened to you. I'm sorry, Mollel.

Mollel shrugs. —It had nothing to do with you.

—Yes, but . . . they did ask me about you. I told them what I thought. I told them you were a damn fine policeman.

Shadrack laughs. —If he's such a fine policeman, how come he's been dumped on us?

48

Kiunga shakes his head. —Mollel's a stubborn Maasai, he explains. His methods didn't exactly go down well with the bosses. He's less interested in doing what they want, than in doing what's right.

—Yeah, drawls Munene. I heard that he thinks *doing what's right* means squealing on his colleagues for corruption.

—Good job there isn't any corruption here for him to find, adds Mungai hastily.

Kiunga laughs. —It's true. He's strange like that. But you know, those were only cases where officers were screwing over the system. When it comes to catching bad guys, Mollel throws the rule book out of the window.

—Kiunga . . . warns Mollel. He's aware of the others scrutinising him.

Well, it's true, isn't it? Kiunga's face becomes serious. Let me tell you gents something. If I was ever up against some serious shit, whether it was with the bosses or on the streets, there isn't another officer in the world I'd want to have beside me. This guy – he slaps Mollel on the back – he's a *noma*.

The slang word means someone trustworthy, reliable. Mollel is strangely flattered by Kiunga's praise, but also irritated by the attention.

—Don't leave your date waiting at the bar, Kiunga, he says. He reaches over to the table, picks up a fresh beer which someone has ordered for him and takes a slug.

Kiunga raises an eyebrow. —You're drinking now, Mollel? Then he glances back over to the white woman, who is looking pointedly at her watch.

—You're right, he adds. Look, I'm in the area for a couple of days. We'll catch up, Mollel, yeah?

—Sure, says Mollel, unenthusiastically.

—Nice meeting you guys, says Kiunga to the others, who reply with similarly non-committal grunts.

Kiunga goes back to the bar and exchanges a few words with the woman, then they leave.

—You've got a fan there, Mollel, says Shadrack.

—But somehow, you don't seem so keen on him, adds the sergeant.

—We worked together for a while, that's all, says Mollel.

He is saved from commenting further by the arrival of the manager.

—What is it now? barks the sergeant. You're not going to try to give us a bill again, are you? I thought we had talked about that.

—No, no, says the manager, wringing his hands nervously. It's just that ... well ... we have a little problem outside in the grounds. And we could do with a little police assistance. *Discreet* assistance. If you wouldn't mind.

—What sort of problem? asks the sergeant.

—A body, replies the manager.

5

The neatly clipped lawns are illuminated by white globes that stand at waist height along the footpath which leads to each cabin, every one a parody of a Maasai hut, with round walls, pointed thatched roof and French windows. A small, square sign with a number is planted outside. With the exception of one or two, the windows are all darkened and curtains drawn. Mollel wonders whether Kiunga is within any of these – with or without his white woman.

The air is heavy with the scent of roses, ever present in this town, sickly sweet and ever so slightly reminiscent of piss. The repetitive, high-pitched click of a nightjar drifts across the lawns, for all the world like the squeal of some piece of mal-functioning electronic equipment.

—This way, please, intones the manager. His voice is little more than a whisper. No flashlights, please, he adds, as they step into the darkness. At least, until we reach the water's edge.

The water's edge is considerably further than it used to be, judging by the hard, dried mud they have to cross when the lawn ends beneath their feet. Mollel can just make out the cracks which craze the ground here. The lake is in retreat.

The silhouette of a group is just visible as a deeper patch of blackness against the black horizon over the lake. As the police-men approach, the beam of a torch ignites and flashes across them.

—Cut that out! shouts Sergeant Mungai. What have we got here?

The beam tips down to the ground, reflected in the water, just a few inches deep, where it is visible between the thick, rubbery leaves of the water hyacinth. One of the blooms stands proud and purple, its petals fussily curled along the length of its stem. Beside it is a hand.

The light lingers there. This hand has not been in the water long. The fingertips have barely swollen; certainly not enough to disguise the chafes and scratches which run across them. The palm, too, bears deep lines.

Mollel is ankle-deep in the water now, standing right up against the body. A shocked-looking security guard runs the beam, shaking, along the length of the arm.

—The weed blows in from the lake this time of night, he says, in a surprisingly soft voice. She must have been brought along with it.

Mollel reaches down and plucks a clump of weed from where it lies across the back of the neck. He sees the braided scalp, recognises the T-shirt that clings to the limp shoulders. He knows who this is. But to confirm his suspicions, he takes one shoulder and, with a tug, turns her over. The action is accompanied by a noise – the slithering of the weed as it slips away, the trickling of the water as it runs under her, the sucking of the mud in which she has become stuck – a noise quiet but unbearable in the silence of this night. Even the shriek of the nightjar has faded to a respectful pause.

—Who is it? calls Sergeant Mungai, from where he stands on dry land.

Mollel can't answer. Not because he does not know who it is. He knows exactly who it is.

It is the woman from the flower farm.

She lies in the mud beneath him, so physically present and so dead, and Mollel is faced with the realisation that he has no idea of her name.

—It's someone we interviewed this morning, he eventually

manages to say. Shadrack, your notebook. You must have made a note.

—That woman from the flower farm?

—Yes.

The young man lets out a low whistle. —She didn't get very far, then.

—What do you mean?

—Well, it's just next door. Didn't you realise, Mollel? We're right by where we were this morning.

Mollel is taken aback. His sense of direction, usually so good, completely fails him around this lake. It must have something to do with the way its receding shoreline snakes back and forth.

—Jemimah Okallo, says Shadrack, reading the name from his notebook by the light of his cellphone. Sacked for stealing, he continues, for the benefit of the sergeant. Guess she couldn't live with the prospect of losing her job.

—It makes no sense, mutters Mollel.

—What's that? asks the sergeant.

—We saw her on her way into town. She was going to catch a bus home. Why would she come all the way back here?

—Her idea of revenge? suggests Mungai. Wants to make the flower farm feel bad about sacking her? Who knows? You can't get into the mind of someone like that, Mollel. It's not even worth trying.

Mungai insists on having an ambulance come right to the water's edge to take away the body, much to the manager's dismay. The look he gives the policemen as they re-enter the hotel implies that if they hadn't been here, he would be spared all this grief. It's almost as though they brought the corpse with them.

There are a few more tourists now, including a group of a dozen or so Chinese. Mollel remembers the days when a Chinese face was a rare sight in Kenya, when the person would be accompanied down the street by curious children, pulling their eyelids tight and shouting *Chinee, Chinee*! But now they are rapidly catching up with the *wazungu* and *wahindi*, the whites and the Indians, who make up most of the clientele in places like this.

The fuzzy-headedness which had been brought about by the beer has long since disappeared. The others seemed to have sobered up, too. Munene and the sergeant are questioning the guard who discovered the body. Choma is waiting in silent vigil beside the body for the arrival of the ambulance.

—Come on, says Shadrack. We need to question the manager.

They follow his retreating figure to an office behind the reception desk in the main lobby. The manager sinks into his leather office chair, which swivels and swings beneath him, and raises his hands to his face.

—This is all we need, he groans. Why couldn't she have washed up a few hundred metres down the shore? Then it would have been someone else's problem.

It strikes Mollel that in death, as well as in life, Jemimah Okallo was always destined to be someone else's problem.

Shadrack takes a seat at the desk opposite the manager. Mollel does the same.

—I want your guest registration records, says Shadrack.

—What for? You know she wasn't a guest.

—Just do it! the young man orders.

The manager sighs. —All of them? It will take a while.

—Just for the last few days.

—That's easier, the manager replies, relief evident in his voice. As you know, we haven't had many visitors.

He pulls a large leather-bound ledger toward him and opens it. He turns to the correct page and glances quickly at the entries.

—This is it, he says. Though what you hope to find out from this, I can't possibly imagine.

He'd never admit it, but Mollel, too, is intrigued about what Shadrack hopes to find. He's already seen a different side to the young man today, in his interactions with Kibet. Could he be about to display a burst of diligence and imagination in his investigation into the death of this unfortunate woman?

Shadrack runs his finger along the entries in the ledger. His lips, Mollel notices, move as he is reading.

Suddenly, he jabs his finger repeatedly against one of the entries and cries: —Ah-ha!

Trying not to betray his curiosity, which is now intense, Mollel leans forward to look at what Shadrack has discovered.

There is a room number, a name and a contact address. The name reads *Justine Oberkampf*. The contact address is a jumble of letters with that clumsy spiral symbol in the middle: an email address.

—You see, Mollel? asks Shadrack triumphantly. That's *proper* detective work for you.

Mollel and the manager exchange a dumbfounded look.

—It's the woman at the bar, says Shadrack, as though explaining to a child. The *mzungu* your friend was with. Now we know who she is.

—Excuse us for a moment, says Mollel to the manager.

He grabs Shadrack firmly by the arm and drags him out of the office.

—You're hurting me!

Mollel has thrust Shadrack up against the wall, in an alcove just off the hotel's lobby.

—Good, he says.

—What the hell is wrong with you, Mollel?

—People keep asking me that. I don't think there's anything wrong with me at all.

—Then why are you . . . he winces as Mollel tightens his grip. Why are you doing this?

—I'm trying to work out why, when we've got a dead body still lying out there, a woman we interviewed this morning, you're wasting time trying to get information on a woman who wouldn't give you a second glance if you were the last man on earth.

Despite his pain, Shadrack twists his mouth into a smile.

—Is it because she's with your friend, Mollel? Is that it?

He whines with pain as Mollel twists his wrist once more.

—You just don't get it, do you, Shadrack? There are more important things in this world than your cock. That's a human being out there.

Shadrack looks Mollel in the eye.

—Pity you only realise that now, Mollel.

He gives a sigh of relief as Mollel releases his grip, and sinks down the wall. He turns his neck and flexes his shoulders.

—What do you mean by that? asks Mollel, coldly.

—Well, you were the one who had the chance to talk to her earlier. When you spotted her on the road. I mean, she might not be dead right now, if you'd just bothered to stop and ask her what was on her mind.

If he wasn't so speechless at the sheer hypocrisy of it – after all, Shadrack had told him *don't get involved* – he'd punch the guy on his pointy lips.

But that's not what's bothering him, Mollel realises. He's bothered because Shadrack is right. After all, if anyone should have realised that this was a woman on the edge, it was him. He'd been close to that edge himself, many times before.

He'd mistaken her apathy for pride. If only he'd thought about it, just a word might have saved her. Just a kindness. A kindness he had considered offering, but had rejected.

He balls his fist and rams it into the wall.

—Jesus Christ, Mollel!

Pain washes over him, but he is grateful for it. For pain is the least he deserves.

He finds himself at the bar, standing where Kiunga's friend had stood. What was it people ordered?

—A whisky, he says.

—Certainly, sir. Which type?

—Just give me a whisky.

He nurses the small glass in his pounding fist. Then he raises it to his lips and knocks it back.

It's good, with a heat reminiscent of the spirit made from honey and fermented dung the elders used to drink back at the village. For a moment, a blissful, fleeting moment, the pain in his fist is deadened. And then it returns, along with the memory of the woman.

The woman. She had a name. Her name was Jemimah Okallo.

Sergeant Mungai approaches, the top of his head barely Mollel's shoulder height.

—I'm going to need a full report on this in the morning, Mollel.

—Another whisky, sir? Mungai gives the barman a nod, and another glass appears before Mollel.

Mungai pats his back. —Just make sure you report for duty on time, he says, and leaves.

Through the window, Mollel can see the red tail lights of the ambulance creeping across the lawn to the lakefront. So much for discretion. He can imagine the manager, scurrying behind, worrying about tyre tracks.

—The hard stuff, eh?

Shadrack has appeared on the other side of him. The young man pulls up a high stool and sits, elbows on the bar. He catches the barman's eye and points with his lips at Mollel's glass. The barman obliges and pours one for him.

—Don't you want to know what I found out, Mollel?

Mollel shakes his head. He drinks.

—Look, Mollel. I reckon we got off to a bad start. Just hear me out, alright? I'm not a stalker or anything. I wanted to know about her for a reason. I was suspicious the moment that smooth bastard, Kiunga, said he was from the Diplomatic Police. I mean, those guys don't just turn up in Naivasha on a whim. He's got to be accompanying someone.

He produces his notebook and opens it on the surface of the bar. Mollel sees a pencil scrawl in childish letters – Shadrack's transcription of the computer address entered in the ledger.

—Do you know what this means, Mollel?

He does not know. He does not care. But Shadrack is

determined to get his attention. For the first time, the young man seems to be craving Mollel's approval.

—This is her email address, right? You know what email is, don't you, Mollel?

—Don't patronise me.

—OK. So look. Look at it, Mollel.

Mollel looks down at the notebook. The clumsy pencil letters swim before his eyes. Shadrack gives up waiting for Mollel to decipher it and reads it aloud.

—Justine-Oberkampf-at-ICC-dot-org. Don't you see what that means, Mollel? She's from the International Criminal Court. And whatever she's here for, she, and your good buddy Kiunga, are trying to keep it secret.

6

His hand hurts. And his pride hurts, too. Kiunga had lied to him. Shadrack had proved to be a detective, after all – of sorts. Mollel still suspects that his intention had been to prove that the woman wasn't Kiunga's girlfriend, but what he had found out was something even more interesting. What it signifies, though, Mollel is still not sure.

The warrior Tonkei leads him once more through the tunnel of flowers. The same sickly, sour smell. The same intensity of colour. The same women plucking, their hands whirring away. Or at least, they look like the same women. He wouldn't know.

—I heard about the picker, says Tonkei.

—Jemimah. Her name was Jemimah Okallo.

—Sure. Well, I heard about her. It's a shame. She could have got a job somewhere else.

—Your boss would've given her a reference, would he?

Tonkei shrugs.

They have reached the end of the tunnel. Tonkei says: —So tell me, what is it you want to see, precisely?

—The lakefront. I want to see where she entered the water.

Tonkei shakes his head. —I can show you the lakefront, he says. But that's not where she got into the water. She must have jumped in at the hotel.

—Impossible, replies Mollel. The hotel security keeps a log of everyone who goes in and out of the front gate.

Tonkei snorts derisively. —Mollel, the flower farms were fighting off gangs coming over the walls less than a year ago. They killed dozens of people. You think we're going to let any ex-employee just walk in here, now, unchallenged? Whatever the hotel security is saying, she didn't come through here.

—I'd like to see the lakefront anyway.

They have stopped at the edge of a wide green field, which stretches as far as the eye can see.

—You're at it, says Tonkei.

Mollel looks down at the plants at his feet. He recognises the same fleshy, round leaves and bulbous stems that covered Jemimah's body last night. He tentatively puts out his foot and pushes.

The plants wobble up and down at his touch, widening in a ripple which spreads away from the spot where he stands.

—Water hyacinth, says Tonkei. It's choking the whole lake.

—Can't you ... I don't know, says Mollel. Can't you poison it?

—And poison the water we use for the farm? Not to mention the drinking water for the whole district. No, Mollel. That's not an option. All we can do is keep pushing out our water intake pipes further and further into the lake, in the hope they don't get clogged. That's ours, right out there, look.

He points to the centre of the lake, where a wooden structure on stilts is just visible. A metal pipe snakes its way toward the structure.

—If that gets jammed, we have to get out the macerator.

—The macerator? asks Mollel. What's that?

Tonkei points to a flat-bottomed fibreglass boat with an outboard motor on its stern, and a cruel-looking drum covered in spiked blades attached to another motor on its front.

—That'll cut a channel through the stuff, at least. But otherwise it's like a can of bug spray against an invasion of locusts.

Mollel bends down and picks up a handful of the weed. At the top is the upright stem, bristling with delicate purple petals, which he recognises from the night before. Underneath, the round, coin-like leaves and the tuberous stems. At the very bottom, trains of dripping, trailing slime.

—It's an invader, says Tonkei. The British brought it over from South America. The ladies wanted it to make their ornamental ponds look pretty. Flowers have a lot to answer for, don't you think?

Mollel rips at the mass of plant tissue in his hands. The stems break easily between his fingers. Inside, it's evident why the plant floats so well: its tissue is a honeycomb of air-filled cells, like foam. It is a triumph of adaptation. And it disgusts him. He lets it fall with a splash back to his feet.

—Can you walk on it? he asks.

—Do you want to try? asks Tonkei. No, I didn't think so. It supports its own weight. Birds, frogs. Out in the centre of the lake, there are little islands of the stuff where it's matted, and other plants have grown on top. Even saplings. But no, it won't take the weight of a man. Or a woman.

—So she must have had to wade through it?

Again, Tonkei shakes his head. —Not unless she has ten-metre legs. The water's shallow for a short while, then it falls away steeply. This is a volcanic crater. She couldn't have swum through it, either. No one could. But you're wasting your time, Mollel. She wouldn't have had to do either.

—What do you mean?

Tonkei motions with his hand, out to the horizon and back in again.

—It comes and goes. Like the tide.

—But there's no tide on lakes.

—That's why I said *like* the tide, Mollel. One thing we can always rely on here is the wind. Mornings, the sun heats up the slopes of the mountain behind us. Mount Longonot. Pushes the air down here and blows the weed away, toward the centre of the lake. Look, you can see it happening even now.

He is right. Barely perceptibly – but inexorably, nonetheless – the farthest fringes of the mass are dissolving and small patches of black water are becoming visible between the weed.

—Then in the afternoon, the wind comes in from the Gilgil plain. Brings it all back again. That's what would have washed her up at the hotel.

—Except I saw her alive in the afternoon, says Mollel.

—So it's like I said. She entered the water at the hotel. She never went any further than the spot where she drowned.

But that was in four inches of water, thinks Mollel. Was it possible, even for someone determined to kill themselves, to drown in four inches of water?

He scans the water's edge, determined to find something, unable to shake the sense that there is something important here that he is missing. But it eludes him. Finally, he gives up.

—Show me where she lived, he says.

The dormitory blocks are not bad, as dormitory blocks go. Certainly better than the grim accommodation Mollel and Shadrack share at the back of the police post. There is row upon row of low, whitewashed, tin-roofed buildings. Every few metres there is a door, painted faded blue, with a number on it. The scene reminds Mollel, bizarrely, of the luxury hotel next door.

Laundry dries on wires between the blocks; here and there a child plays. The whitewashed walls are stained to knee height with the splashback of year upon year of the rainy season; the door jambs are dully burnished by the hundreds of fingertips and hips which have brushed against them as the workers pass.

Tonkei leads Mollel down the central passage between two of the blocks; then stops. A door numbered 103 stands open.

—This is it, he says. But you won't find anything. She took it all with her yesterday, remember?

—Do me a favour, says Mollel. Stop telling me what I will and won't find.

He pushes the door open and steps within. A string hangs from a switch attached to a rafter supporting the iron roof, Mollel pulls it. A lightbulb attached to another rafter comes to dim life.

There are two bunk beds and a cupboard. The upper bunk of one of the beds is stripped, revealing the bare mattress.

There is nothing unusual or unexpected about the way the room looks. But there is a smell which singes Mollel's nostrils. An elusive, slightly acrid smell. One which he finds hard, at first, to define.

It is the smell of burned hair.

—Four women per room, says Tonkei. It's a safeguard against them bringing men back. Not that they don't try.

The smell, perhaps, comes from one of the women's styling regime. Even now it is beginning to fade, and as his eyes become accustomed to the gloom, Mollel is able to make out more details of the environment.

Attempts have been made to personalise this space. On the walls and cupboard door are pasted a number of well-worn photographs.

—Are any of these her pictures?

—Don't think so. If she had any, she took them with her.

Whatever she took with her, thinks Mollel, it would have fitted into the basket that she was carrying on her back when he saw her. That basket hasn't been found yet.

His eyes linger on some of the photographs. Most of the workers here are Luo, he has been told. So the families would be hundreds of kilometres away, on the banks of another lake altogether: Lake Victoria. A hotter, steamier place. Not suitable for flower farms, but far more hospitable to members of this tribe.

The photos show gangly children in their Sunday best. Aged parents, in dappled shade, shawls across their laps. The people back home, that these migrant workers have left behind. He wonders how many people were dependent upon Jemimah Okallo's salary, which she would have sent home diligently every month.

Another question occurs to him.

—How do they send their money home?

Tonkei laughs, and unclips his cellphone from his belt. He waves it at Mollel. —The same way as everyone else.

63

Everyone else, apart from the technically challenged Mollel. He's been aware of the ability to send and receive money through the phone network for some time, but he's never used it himself. He knows how to use his own phone for calls and messages, but that's it. His mother-in-law was complaining about it the last time he spoke to her. Since he was posted to Hell, she has been looking after Adam. Before he left, he gave her a set of post-dated cheques and instructions for her to make a monthly trip to the bank to draw upon his salary. The whole thing was, she insisted, a ridiculous waste of time.

Having spoken to the women who shared Jemimah's room – all of whom professed shock and sadness, but were unable to shed much light upon someone who, it seemed, was a very solitary room-mate – Mollel collects her personnel file and prepares to leave the flower farm.

On the way out, Tonkei leads him along the side of the poly-tunnel instead of directly down the middle of it.

—You're taking a lot of interest in this case, Mollel, he says.

—It's my job.

—Yes, but ...

Tonkei pauses. They're standing beside a wide, square pit. The smell of rotting plant matter and decaying petals is overwhelm-ing, and flies buzz around them. It seems an unlikely place for a chat.

—Yesterday, when we met, I assumed you were like the rest of them. The other *polisi*. I know all of them. Idlers, out for what they can get. But the way you're dealing with this. You're differ-ent. You care.

Too late, thinks Mollel. If I'd cared more yesterday, I wouldn't be here now.

—Why did you turn you back on your culture, Mollel?

The question takes him by surprise.

—Who says I have?

Tonkei laughs. —Your trousers, for one thing. When did you

last wear a *shuka*? Don't you know that Western garb is bad for the circulation?

Mollel can't help smiling. His mother always told him the same thing.

—Look, says Tonkei, dropping his voice. You can take the Maasai away from the village, but you can't take the village out of your heart. You're a man of honour, Mollel. I can tell. Why don't you come back to your roots? Become an elder? Buy a few cows, find yourself a nice Maasai bride or two and leave this shallow, foreign world behind?

For a moment, the idea seems almost tempting – and then Mollel remembers Adam. Everything he does, he does for Adam. It had been that way even before he had been born. Mollel's wife, Chiku, had spelled it out very clearly: *Village life is not for our son. He won't grow up barefoot, herding goats instead of going to school. He's going to make something of himself. Just like you have, Mollel.*

Still Mollel says nothing. Tonkei continues: —There's a lot of us who feel this way, Mollel. A lot of us who feel the modern world has encroached too far, for too long. This land used to be ours, remember?

Now Mollel understands. He's getting a political speech: the same political speech he'd heard at the fireside ever since, as a teenager, he became a warrior. Puffed up with pride at their new-found status, the boys would swap stories of the great Maasai heroes, those who had killed lions and leopards, who had defeated the Kikuyu and the British. And the unfairness of the Maasai lot, relegated to a tourist attraction in their own land, stung them bitterly.

Wanting to change the subject, Mollel says: —I've been away too long.

—You never left, says Tonkei. We could use someone like you, Mollel. Think about it.

Before he has time to wonder who *we* are, Tonkei points down at the pit. A fresh layer of plucked roses is scattered on top of the stinking mass of thorns and foliage below.

—I wanted to show you this, says Tonkei. See the flowers on top? They've been thrown away, because they're imperfect.

Mollel squints to get a better look. From this distance, he can't see anything wrong with them.

Tonkei kneels and reaches in to retrieve one of the stems. He holds it up for Mollel to examine. The petals are bright and curl uniformly round the bud. The stems are long and straight.

—Look closer, says Tonkei.

There, near the tip of one of the petals, Mollel sees a scattering of tiny dots: freckles on the face of the flower.

—Is that it? he asks. Is this what they call imperfect?

—That's what the Europeans want. Every flower has to be identical, every flower has to be perfect. Those that aren't end up here. It could be up to half of them.

—Couldn't they be sold locally? Or at a lower rate?

Tonkei shakes his head. —It would destroy the market. To keep prices at a premium, they have to restrict the product.

—What a waste, says Mollel.

—That's what Jemimah thought, too.

—Jemimah?

Mollel is surprised.

—Sure. She saw the flowers being thrown away every day. She must have come down here, just as we have, and taken some of them. And when she had two dozen, she sneaked out and tried to sell them on the roadside. Unfortunately for her, the farm manager happened to see her doing it.

—So you mean, says Mollel, barely able to contain the outrage welling up inside him, you mean, she wasn't even stealing? She lost her job for helping herself to something that was going to be destroyed?

Tonkei taps Mollel's chest.

—Now you're talking like a Maasai, he says.

7

Leaving the flower farm brings a relief which is not merely related to the heavy, hothouse atmosphere. There is something about the place that evokes a sensation of oppression in Mollel. a constriction in the chest, a burden upon the mind.

They have taken the sky and bound it.

He takes a deep breath of the air of Maili Ishirini. He closes his eyes and for a moment, he could be in Nairobi. A passing truck has belched out exhaust fumes which blend with the smell of maize cooking on a charcoal *jiko* nearby. The sounds of women's chatter, of chickens, of music drifting from a nearby bar. This is an unrestricted, informal world. A community which has emerged through the individuals who are from it, rather than some construct of nature.

He misses Nairobi. He misses home.

Had he opened his eyes to see his far-off son, or his long-dead wife, Mollel would hardly have been surprised. When he does open them, he sees a figure almost as familiar. But he knows this one has not been conjured up by his imagination.

Kiunga is walking toward him. Beyond, at the gate of the Lakefront Hotel, a car is pulled over, its driver's door open and engine running and the woman, Justine Oberkampf, sitting in the passenger seat. She does not look happy.

—Hello again, Mollel, says Kiunga. They shake hands. I guess we're crossing each other's paths a lot these days.

—I guess so, says Mollel. You didn't introduce me to your friend last night.

He nods toward the woman.

—Oh, sure, says Kiunga. He is evidently embarrassed. Her name is Justine Oberkampf, from the United States.

—Who is she? asks Mollel.

—Oh, some diplomat, replies Kiunga, affecting breeziness. Doing some kind of fact-finding after the election. Not really sure what it is. I just get to drive her around, hold her hand, you know.

He lowers his voice confidentially.

—Between you and me, she's a right bitch. But she won't be around for long. I can't complain. It gets me out of Nairobi; I drive a nice air-conditioned car. There are worse jobs.

—I'm sure, says Mollel. So, what are you doing here?

—Oh, nothing important, says Kiunga. I could ask you the same question.

—And I could give you the same answer, says Mollel.

He looks over at the smart SUV. Oberkampf is applying lipstick while looking in the mirror on the sun visor.

With a whirl of dust and a rusty clank, Shadrack's battered old Toyota pulls up. The passenger-side window judders open. Shadrack is leaning across from the driver's seat, cranking the window down.

—You done at the flower farm, Mollel? he asks. He is talking to Mollel, but glaring suspiciously at Kiunga.

—Yes. No leads.

—I don't want to interrupt your little reunion. . .

—You're not interrupting anything, says Mollel. I guess you'll be leaving town soon, Kiunga. Been nice seeing you.

He offers a cool, formal handshake.

—Yeah, won't be around much longer, replies Kiunga.

There is a blast on a horn. Oberkampf has grown tired of waiting and is summoning her driver back to their vehicle.

*

Shadrack says nothing about seeing Mollel with Kiunga, but Mollel can tell it's playing on the young policeman's mind. There is no *cheesy kama ndizi* or talk of *Cobra Squad*. Mollel steals glances at Shadrack's profile as they drive around the town on their usual patrol.

Is that a frown of anger on his face, or fear? Or is he just squinting into the late afternoon sun?

The patrol takes them along dusty tracks and through dismal, apathy-drenched villages, little more than a collection of huts clustered around the shade of a convenient tree. They stop frequently along the way, ostensibly to check in with the local chief or elder, to get reports of any crime or nuisance. But in reality, this is a much more important and time-honoured task: the collection of dues. Each roadside vegetable stallholder, each owner of a small kiosk, every chief and even a pastor or two emerge to greet Shadrack, shake his hand and slip a little something into it, while Mollel waits in the car and pretends not to notice.

Usually this is Shadrack's favourite part of the job. To him, it's something of a vocation, and he takes to the role with relish. He pats backs and exchanges jokes, as though he is the one dishing out benevolence. But today, Mollel notices, the young man's heart does not seem to be in it; he barely speaks as he takes his dues. And Mollel is not the only one to have noticed. The hate-filled, scornful glances people usually cast at Shadrack when he turns to leave are replaced with puzzled stares.

The day has dragged into the long, hot stretch of afternoon by the time Mollel and Shadrack arrive back in Hell. To Mollel's surprise, they drive straight past the police post and start climbing the murram road toward Hell's Gate National Park.

—Bit late for a safari, isn't it? asks Mollel.

—Relax, Maasai, says Shadrack. You've taken me on your mystery tour today. It's time for me to take you on one of my own.

They crackle and fishtail up the gravel road, the Toyota making slow but steady progress, raising so much dust that

Mollel has to wind up his window, depriving him of his only relief from the heat.

After much grinding of gears and a final, wheezing dash up the steepest part of the slope, they arrive at a set of metal huts and a counterweighted steel pole barrier set across the road.

This is the side entrance to Hell's Gate. Not the fancy tourist entrance, further back toward Naivasha town, where the ticket office and gift shop is sited. This entrance exists only for the KWS rangers, so they have easy access to the far side of the lake when they need it.

Each of the huts shares the characteristics of a Maasai homestead and the chalets at the luxury hotel: they are round, with pointed roofs. In fact, they are not exactly round, but octagonal, made from rectangular panels bolted together in a rusty pastiche of the archetypal African home. On several of the huts, rickety television aerials extend, strapped to sticks to gain a bit of height and get better reception.

Staff quarters. Just like the police post, or the flower farm, in these parts people tend to live where they work.

Shadrack beeps the horn and a tired-looking KWS ranger, vest hanging out of his trousers and feet flapping in unlaced boots, comes to the barrier. He nods at the policemen and swings up the metal pole.

—Where are we going? asks Mollel.

—You'll see.

Progress along the rocky tracks inside the park is slow, because Shadrack has to bring the car almost to a complete halt at every rut and slope they encounter. He throws the car into first gear, causing the engine to squeal and a foul smell of burning grease to rise from the bowels of the machine.

Around them, candelabra trees like giant thumbtacks punctuate the landscape, their shadows lengthening and their rippling, leafless limbs turning blood red in the evening sunlight.

The track continues to ascend and at times, Mollel gets a

glimpse of the lake unfolding below him. It glitters tantalisingly. Even the weed which clogs the edges lends an attractive, feathery delicateness to the outline of the water.

With a final, lurching effort, Shadrack forces the car up and over the final incline and, with apparent relief, the engine purrs as they roll across flat land for the first time since they left the highway an hour ago.

A wooden sign reads: *Special Campsite. Overnight camping with KWS permit only.* The only structure is a wooden hut which sits over a pit latrine. There are no campers here to enjoy the spectacular view. The sun is now descending over the lake, which mirrors the sky painted in red and gold. In the distance, the long squares of the flower farm's plastic roofs glow in response to the low sun, as though reaching out to soak up the very last rays of warmth.

In the distance, the town of Naivasha twinkles seductively, and below them – almost directly below – the community of Maili Ishirini seems to defy its epithet of hell. Mollel can just make out figures moving around. It looks like a haven of peace and tranquillity.

Probably because the town's policemen are here.

The police post's other vehicle – a pickup truck with a high chassis and chunky tyres which would have made easy work of the sloping track on the way up here – sits parked at an angle near the cliff edge. Someone is sitting within the cab, sideways, their legs hanging out of the door, which stands open. Another figure is sitting on the bonnet, and one more – the instantly recognisable, massive form of Munene – stands sentry-like beside them.

Shadrack cuts the engine and pulls on the handbrake. Mollel says nothing. But his sense of unease, which has been growing all day, has now been replaced by all-out fear.

Why have they brought him here?

Shadrack gets out of the car.

—You coming?

Mollel casts a last look at the sun, which is already halfway below the horizon. As he watches, it elongates, slides and shrinks.

Then it is gone.

He gets out of the car. A flinty greyness has come over the scene with the disappearance of the sun. In a few minutes it will be completely dark – and in anticipation, the first few stars are already starting to emerge overhead. Below, flickering on one by one, like cells springing into life, the greenhouses transform into incandescent strips and squares.

The light from below makes him realise for the first time the precariousness of this edge. No more than a few metres ahead of him, the ground severs and drops away. This is the top of the red, rocky cliffs which are visible from the town, and so dominate the landscape. An eagle screams somewhere, and following the sound, Mollel sees it wheel, a black speck against the grey-blue sky, high over the rolling ground below.

—Glad you could join us, Maasai, says Sergeant Mungai.

He hops down from the bonnet of the pickup. Choma, who is sitting within, nods at him.

—What's this all about? asks Mollel, trying to sound casual. But he's aware that his voice sounds stretched with tension. His heart pounds in his chest, and though he feels his cellphone sitting against his leg in his trouser pocket, he can't imagine what help it would be.

—Relax, Mollel, says Shadrack at his elbow. Just friends, having a little chat. Beer?

Mollel feels anything but relaxed, and the atmosphere is anything but friendly. But he accepts the beer which Shadrack offers him from a cool box in the back of the pickup. The sound of the popping cap, and the metallic rattle as it falls onto the stony ground, only serve to heighten the tension.

Munene takes a swig from a bottle of his own.

—We've been waiting a while, he says.

—This old car hardly made it, says Shadrack.

—I don't mean that, says Munene. We've been waiting a while for this little chat, with our Maasai friend here.

—Over a month, adds Sergeant Mungai.

—Five weeks, six days, chips in Shadrack. That's how long I've had to watch this creep.

Anger takes its place alongside fear inside Mollel. —You've been watching me? I would have thought you might have learned something.

—Oh, I've learned plenty, says Shadrack. Like, you're a spy.

In the gloom, Mollel looks from face to face, but he cannot read them. They barely register as more than silhouettes – except for Choma, who is still sitting inside the lighted cabin of the pickup truck. He winks at Mollel, and for the first time, Mollel realises this is not a friendly gesture but a facial tic.

He takes a swig of his beer. He wants to have an empty bottle in his hand when he eventually faces whatever he's going to face.

—You've been watching too many episodes of *Cobra Squad*, he says, playing for time.

—Oh yeah? Sergeant Mungai swaggers around to where Mollel is standing. He is drunk. Mollel suspects the others are, too. Even Shadrack is now chugging from a bottle as though desperate to catch up. We had you for a spy the minute I got your movement order from Nairobi. It just didn't ring true. Detective Sergeant busted down to Constable? I mean, if you'd offended Vigilance House that badly, you'd be off the force altogether.

Vigilance House: the police headquarters.

Mollel shakes his head and tries to give a rueful smile.

—They'd have sacked me long ago, if they could. But they can't.

Shadrack scoffs. —Thinks he's Superman!

—They can't sack me, says Mollel, because I've already said too much. You know about my history. I blew the lid on a big procurement scam. They stuck me out on traffic patrol as a reward.

—And yet your buddy Kiunga was talking about you being at Nairobi Central.

—For about a month, insists Mollel. I was on secondment. And I ended up putting more noses out of joint. Tried to arrest the Superintendent's golfing pal. As soon as they could, they picked the most godforsaken place they could find and posted me here.

—Yes, here, says Mungai. Funny, isn't it, Mollel, that you should end up here.

—Is it? asks Mollel. You tell me.

Mungai has now drawn level with him and they stand face to face. He juts his chin up.

—Why here, Mollel? Why us? It's not about Shadrack's little pocket-money collection. The *chai* ladies in Vigilance House have more lucrative operations than that going on. So somebody there must think that somebody *here* is into something big. And we want you to tell us, Mollel, what they think it is.

—Maybe they just decided it was time you had a proper policeman around the place.

The pain knocks him back. Mungai has dealt him a jabbing blow under the ribs. For a small guy he packs a powerful punch, and Mollel is sent reeling. As the initial shock abates, and the stars stop swirling around him, he sees the tiny, round outline of Mungai and considers that if he rushed him, he'd be able to pick the man up and pitch him over the cliff while barely breaking a sweat. And then he sees the massive figure of Munene looming nearby and considers that if he did so, his own flailing body would be next.

If that wasn't what they already had in mind for him.

—I don't know why they chose to send me here, he groans. I'm no spy. Seriously. You have nothing to fear from me.

Now Munene lurches toward him.

—We might have believed that before last night, Mollel. Before your buddy turned up with an international investigator in tow. You must think we're stupid.

Right now, it is not their stupidity Mollel is cursing, but Kiunga's.

He feels the massive hands grab his shirt, and he is whirled toward the precipice. For a moment, he prays to a God he doesn't believe in that his buttons will hold out. He hears the faint tinkling of glass – the bottle, which must have flown from his hand as he was thrust toward the edge, has only just landed. Pure darkness lies beneath him, but he can feel the heat rising from the ground a hundred metres below; he can smell the grass and the earth and hopes that, in a matter of seconds, he won't be rushing to meet it.

—Whatever it is, says Mollel, his voice reedy with panic, I don't care. So you take a bit of *chai* money here and there. Who doesn't? You're welcome to it. I've seen you guys at work. You're not bad guys. You're just trying to make a living. I'm not going to take that away from you.

For a while, they seem to be having a silent debate among themselves. Mollel can almost feel the conflicting emotions within the group. On the one hand, they suspect that Mollel knows more than he is letting on. Yet it's hard for them to find out what that is without revealing their hand. He isn't about to encourage them to do that: then they'd have nothing to lose. Ignorance is his best defence, right now.

—What about Kiunga? demands Mungai.

—Yeah, says Shadrack. And his *mzungu* bitch. You were talking to him again today.

—We ran into each other, protests Mollel. It's a small town.

Munene thrusts him forward and Mollel feels his stomach leap. He is still being held – just.

—Look, Mollel, says Munene. There's your wife.

The others laugh.

His wife?

Chiku?

Mollel's head spins. Is this some kind of sick joke?

Then his eyes fall upon the tall pillar of rock which rises in parallel to the cliffs. At some point it must have been conjoined, but time and weather have cleaved it away and there it stands, alone, isolated, aloof.

The *wazungu*, with that habit they have of christening geographical features after one of their own, call it Fischer's Tower. But everyone else calls it the Maasai Bride.

—How'd you like to fall at *her* feet, Mollel? growls Munene. If the rangers find your body down there in the morning, no one's going to ask any questions.

It is with an empty, sick feeling that Mollel realises Munene is right. Should his shattered corpse be discovered at the foot of Hell's Gate, Otieno would deny all knowledge of any operation he'd been sent on. No one wants to be associated with failure. And once his medical file was pulled, why then, it would be the simplest thing in the world to portray his death as suicide.

He had been troubled for a long time, people would say. *Ever since the death of his wife.*

Perhaps Kiunga would know. Perhaps he'd tell Adam, some day, that his father didn't kill himself. Kiunga would just know. Just like Mollel knows about Jemimah Okallo.

Even as he dangles over the cliff edge, Mollel is amazed at the capacity of his mind to wander. Perhaps, he thinks, he needs to up his tablets.

And that gives him an idea.

—My pocket, he gasps.

—What? demands Munene. The big man's brain may be slow, but he possesses enough cunning of his own to suspect a trick from others.

—Let me show you what's in my pocket. It explains everything.

There must have been some kind of signal to Munene to acquiesce, because Mollel feels himself being hauled back from the edge. Even though he knows it may only be a temporary reprieve, the relief washes over him like a wave.

His arms are released, and Mollel reaches into his pocket.

—Slowly now, says Munene.

—What am I going to do, pull a knife on the three of you?

He takes out his hand and holds it, palm up, toward them. There, sitting innocuously, is a plastic bottle of pills.

Mollel chucks them underarm to Mungai, who catches the bottle. He squints at the label, then moves over to stand in the light of the pickup's cab.

—Duloxetine, he reads, stumbling over the unfamiliar word.

—I've seen him guzzling them down, says Shadrack. Does it when he thinks I'm not looking.

—I'm not exactly proud of it, says Mollel.

—What are they for? asks Mungai. HIV?

Mollel shakes his head.

—It's something else, he says.

He senses a shift in the attitude of those around him. A fear – slight but palpable.

—I'm not ill, he continues. At least, not physically. But according to the police medical service, I need these pills to keep me stable. I've had . . . problems in the past. You can look up the drug and check.

Mungai gives a nervous giggle.

—So you're mental, he sneers. Nuts. *Wavuvu. Kichizi.*

Munene backs away from him slightly, as though fearing contagion.

—*Kichizi kama ndizi*, mutters Shadrack, automatically.

They all look at him, as though searching for outward signs of his malaise. And he sees, even in this darkness, a shift in their attitude toward him. A reappraisal.

—Now do you see? asks Mollel. I'm no spy. Who'd trust a crazy guy with keeping a secret like that? They didn't send me here to spy on you. They sent me here so that I could do no harm.

A hoarse, dry voice, like the rustling of leaves, weaves through the night air.

—Bring him over, says Choma.

Munene shoves Mollel, who stumbles over toward the pickup truck. Inside, Choma's grizzled head is illuminated by the cabin light. Mollel can just make out the old man's face. Mollel understands, now, that whatever Mungai's seniority in rank, it is Choma who calls the shots round here.

The old man appears to be studying him. —I get the feeling that we have that in common, Maasai, he says. You've just taken a big gamble, you know that?

Mollel knows that. He also knows he had no choice.

—What was the gamble? asks Mungai.

—Letting us know he's sick, replies Choma. Think about it. With that information on file, if he ends up at the bottom of the cliff, no one will ask any questions. It's as good as giving us permission to do it. And you knew that, didn't you, Mollel?

—So he really is crazy, says Shadrack.

—Perhaps not so crazy, replies Choma.

A few minutes ago, he was being held over a cliff edge. Now he's patiently waiting as Choma, Shadrack, Sergeant Mungai and Munene talk in hushed tones near the pickup.

He's not supposed to be able to hear what they're saying, but every now and then a snatch of their conversation drifts over to him. Munene seems the most violently opposed to his presence, gesticulating in his direction, raising his voice at times.

—He's screwed over his colleagues before; who's to say he won't do it again?

This time, Mollel also hears Choma's answer.

—We can use him.

—Use him? Munene scoffs.

They look over in his direction and Mollel drops his eyes. Once again, they lower their voices. After a few more hissed dissents, some kind of agreement seems to be reached.

Sergeant Mungai calls Mollel over.

—We have a job for you, he says.

Interesting, thinks Mollel, that Choma still allows the sergeant to give the orders. Even when it's perfectly evident where those orders originate from.

—Your friend, Kiunga. He said you were a *noma*, says Mungai.

—He's not my friend, mutters Mollel.

—He says you do what's right. Even if it means bending the rules.

Mollel shrugs. —I never considered *the rules* to be the same thing as *what's right*.

—So it looks like we might be able to work together after all, says Mungai. But first, we've got a test for you, Maasai.

He points over at the hut housing the latrine. The door is shut, and Mollel wonders what he can mean.

—Go on. Take a look.

Mollel walks over to the hut. He feels the eyes of the others on him as he crosses the patch of grass to the latrine. The door has a catch on the outside to stop baboons or monkeys from entering. He slides the catch over and opens the door.

There is a figure within.

Behind Mollel, a torch beam flashes into life and picks out the interior of the hut. Slumped on the floor at the back, the hole of the pit latrine in front of him, is a man. His eyes roll wildly and he is shaking with fear. His wrists and ankles are bound. His mouth is gagged, too, but Mollel knows what lies underneath: a set of bright, gold teeth. It is Raphael Gachui, and the last time Mollel saw him he was standing on the courthouse steps, having just been released from a rape charge.

Munene pushes Mollel aside and reaches into the hut. He pulls Gachui to his feet and rips off the gag covering his mouth. Gold teeth flash as he coughs and spits. Gachui tries to flex his stiff muscles, but with wrists and ankles bound, he simply stumbles. Munene pulls him up again. Once more, Mollel is struck by the power of this giant.

—Remember Raphael Gachui, Mollel? asks Shadrack. The rapist?

—I was acquitted! shouts Gachui.

—Charges were dismissed, says Choma. We've yet to decide whether you're acquitted.

He looks over at Mollel.

—Well, Maasai? he asks. You say you don't think that the law and justice are the same thing. How about meting out a little justice of your own?

Mollel looks at the snivelling figure before him. He seems a million miles away from the sneering, jeering figure who had taunted the crowd on the courthouse steps just the day before.

And yet he still has a flash of spirit within him, as Mollel sees when Gachui catches his eye. He is, as yet, unbroken.

—I don't know what he's done, says Mollel.

—We told you, says Shadrack. He's a rapist.

—He was acquitted by a court of law.

—He was acquitted by Judge Singh! splutters Munene.

That makes even Gachui laugh. Mollel has been at Maili Ishirini long enough to know just how much faith the local populace has in Judge Singh's convictions.

Munene kicks Gachui to the ground. —Shut up! he cries. The accused will not speak unless spoken to!

Mollel looks at the circle that has formed around the prone figure of Gachui. Choma, still up in the car, is watching, aloof.

—Oh, he did it alright, says Shadrack.

Apparently he is to be the prosecutor; Mollel, the judge.

—Go on, says Mollel.

—It was February. Just after the violence. We had a lot of new arrivals from Rift Valley, from Nakuru. The IDP camp had just been set up outside Naivasha.

IDP. Internally Displaced Persons. What a store of human tragedy hid behind those three letters.

—You've not been out there yet, Mollel. Well, I guess you've seen some pretty bad living conditions in Nairobi. But three families to a tent? Twenty people, or more, in a space the size of your barrack room. No running water. Latrines? Forget about it. Two weeks before, the whole place had just been a field. They barely had time to knock down the termite mounds before they had to start pitching the tents.

Shadrack kicks a stone at Gachui.

—These were Kikuyu people, Mollel. My people. *His* people.

Gachui shakes his head, as if to disavow any shared blood between him and the policeman.

—Not that he has loyalty to anyone, continues Shadrack, other than Mdosi and his fellow stooges. These people were kicked out of their homes with no warning. The Kalenjin came for them, and they came with fire.

—*Cut the grass*, they said, *that grows under our feet. Kill the jackal that preys on our chickens.*

These were people who had lived alongside one another for decades. Generations. And yet, the trouble spread. When word got out of what happened in Eldoret ...

Eldoret. When the incumbent President, Mwai Kibaki, had been declared winner in the polls, the Kalenjin majority in Rift Valley had turned on his Kikuyu tribespeople. Two hundred had sought sanctuary in a church; they had been burned along with the building, those fleeing the flames brought down by youths with *pangas*. Men, women, children, babies.

All of this Mollel knows from the news reports that filtered through in the days after it happened. In the months since, there has been no shortage of ghastly details emerging. But no justice.

—The saddest thing, continues Shadrack, was what the families brought with them. These people were leaving their homes, their lives. I remember them turning up here, in town. All they knew was, they'd be safe if they headed east. To Kikuyu land.

Maasailand, thinks Mollel for a moment, the words of Tonkei echoing in his mind. Almost as soon as he thinks it, he dismisses the thought as tribalist. And yet, the casual appropriation of this place as *Kikuyu land* rankles with him still.

Is this what we've become? he thinks. *Is this what it means to be Kenyan today? To constantly squabble over language and tribe and land?*

Shadrack is continuing to speak. The case for the prosecution: he has obviously thought long and hard about this. Perhaps this was even the cause of his frown, earlier, as he drove Mollel to this place. For he must have known that someone would be found guilty tonight – and right now, it seems like it is not going to be Mollel.

—Back in Eldoret, their wealth was their land. A quarter-acre. Some maize. A goat. Some chickens. They didn't have time to bring anything useful, so they turned up in Naivasha with what? TVs. There must have been a hundred TVs piled up near the gate of that IDP camp. All useless. No electricity to run them. No room for them in the tents. But in most cases, after cash, it was their most valuable possession. What were they going to do, leave it behind?

Shadrack's voice cracks with pity, or anger.

—Once they're in the camp, that's it. No one comes or goes. They register as IDPs, which means they get shelter and food, but if they leave, they lose their status. They're trapped.

Gachui is rolling his eyes. He evidently has as much respect for this impromptu court as he does for the more formal version. Mollel can't help feeling, though, that any overt display of contempt would be most unwise.

—So, continues Shadrack, you have a concentration of five thousand people, uprooted, scared, traumatised. And what does Mdosi and his goon here see? An opportunity.

Gachui shrugs and gives a weak smile. —If it wasn't us, he says, it would be someone else.

Shadrack walks over, raises his boot and kicks Gachui to the ground.

—But it *was* you, wasn't it? he spits. First on the scene. When other people smell fear, you guys smell money.

—What was the racket? asks Mollel.

—What wasn't it? Anything these guys needed. Most of them had brought their savings, raided their mattresses. But they hadn't brought the mattresses. Or for that matter, washing powder, basic foodstuffs, babies' nappies. Toys, books, pencils. Underpants. Soap. Razors. Tampons. You name it, the IDPs needed it. And Mdosi and his men were there to supply the goods. At a price.

—A big markup?

—Better than that. No markup at all. They just bought the goods in Naivasha and sold them in the camp for the same price.

—So what's the problem?

—No problem. Until people's cash started running out. Then, Mdosi was all too pleased to extend credit to his captive audience – at interest of a hundred per cent a week.

Mollel looks at the kneeling figure before him. Gachui seems resigned to his fate, but completely devoid of contrition.

—The people running the camp were in on it too, continues Shadrack. They got their cut. Especially when they were slow in delivering the aid supplies.

—What does this have to do with rape? asks Mollel, resenting his adoption of the judicial role, even as his curiosity forces him into it.

—Because what's loan-sharking without enforcement? says Shadrack. It would only take one customer to default, and then they would all have followed – and Mdosi's nice little sideline would have gone bust. So one guy – he was a teacher, back in Eldoret – was expecting his salary cheque to come through. Problem was, the school administration were all Kalenjin. They claimed he'd abandoned his post. The cheque never came. And when Gachui here came collecting, he liked the look of the guy's wife, and decided to claim payment in kind.

To Mollel's amazement, Gachui starts to laugh. He laughs deep, and he laughs heartily.

—What are you laughing at, you pig? demands Munene.

Gachui raises his head. —At you. This. You dare judge me, you *polisi*, when you're behind every protection racket in town? You, who take a percentage from every brothel, a cut from every bar and a commission on every *matatu* route?

—Shut up, warns Munene, with a glance at Mollel. But Gachui continues to chuckle.

—You just do what you need to, he says. Just fucking do it, already.

—Do what? asks Mollel.

Gachui raises his eyes to meet Mollel's. The humour drains from his face.

—Do what you did to the others, he says. Kill me.

—Shut up! shouts Munene, and aims a kick at Gachui's skull, sending him crashing into the dirt.

Mollel rushes forward and grabs Gachui's shirt, hauling him up. The gold-toothed grin shines black with blood in the moonlight.

—What do you mean? demands Mollel. What do you mean, *the others?*

Gachui's eyes roll in his head. He mutters something, too low for Mollel to hear.

—What? What are you saying?

Mollel lowers his face to Gachui's. He can feel the heat emanating from the man's skin, feel the moisture of his breath, smell the reek of his fear.

Gachui croaks something like, *Spare me.*

—Spare you? Is that what you're saying? Spare you?

—Spare me, says Gachui. His eyes focus once more on Mollel. *Spare me your bullshit.*

Mollel releases his grip and Gachui nearly drops to the dirt once more, but he has enough strength left to haul himself up at the last moment.

—I know what all this is about, he continues. This is about giving yourselves the justification to do it. So you accuse me of rape. Fine. Say what you like. Give yourselves the outrage you need to kill me. But don't kid yourselves. Deep down, you know why you're doing it. Really. Because rape has nothing to do with it. You're just eliminating the opposition.

Mollel looks up at the others. They are avoiding his gaze. It may be because what Gachui is saying is true. And it may also be the fact that no one wants to look another person in the eye just before they commit murder.

Munene raises the rifle in his hand.

Mollel steps forward and smashes his fist into Gachui's head.

Blow upon blow he rains down, each one meeting less resistance. Gachui is on the ground. His fists pounding, Mollel straightens up and delivers a boot to the prone man's abdomen.

The white moonlight picks out blood upon the ground. Still Mollel's boot keeps driving into the figure.

The moonlight wheels and swivels around him, the lengthening shadows whirl before him.

Then he feels hands upon his arms, arms around his waist. Pulling him away from the body at his feet, which does not stir.

And with the action, a sound. The sound of gravel under car tyres. An engine cutting out. Doors opening.

—*Mollel!*

The voice is Kibet's.

Mollel looks away from the prone figure below him for the first time. For the first time he becomes aware of lights shining at him: the headlights of a car. Flashlight beams aimed at him. And behind the beams, KWS rangers and the pinpoint muzzles of guns.

—We're police officers! shouts Munene.

—Lower your guns, barks Mungai.

—We saw the lights, says Kibet, her voice full of horror. What's going on here? Mollel? What is going on?

8

She was the daughter of Ole Samante, so the myth goes. He was a simple elder from a small village beneath the blood-red cliffs beside the glittering lake. He did not have wealth – barely a dozen cattle – and he claimed no prowess as a warrior. But he had a daughter, and he loved her with all his heart.

Her name is not remembered, but her beauty is; such beauty that suitors came from every clan to ask for her hand. Among the Maasai people, tradition demands that the bride bring the dowry, but the young girl's beauty turned tradition on its head. One after another, the men, young and old, came with greater and greater bounties.

—Oh, Father, she sighed. I do not love these men. Do not make me leave you.

And Samante, loyal father, promised that the girl would not have to take as her husband any man she did not love.

One day, there arrived a warrior fine and proud. He wore a lion skin, and his spear was tipped with bronze. His father was one of the wealthiest and most powerful Maasai elders between the white-capped mountain and the glittering lake, and he brought with him a dowry beyond compare: a herd so large its approach was heralded by a dust cloud that blotted out the sun.

His name was Yandani, and the girl began to wonder whether taking a husband might not be so bad. He wooed her with the finest skins and amulets of beaten gold; with bolts of woven cloth and with an Arab chest full of medicinal herbs.

Finally, Yandani told her of their sons, tall and proud princes, who would come to unite the Maasai and conquer their enemies, and daughters, princesses who, just like their mother, would dazzle all with their beauty.

So the day of the wedding was set. As everyone knows, a Maasai bride must be led, by her husband's female kinsfolk, to the marriage place outside her home village.

She dressed in her finest blue shuka – a gift from her betrothed – and a collar of gleaming white shell beads. Her head was freshly shaved and her scalp glistened with oil. The ceremonial scars on her cheeks burned as her face flushed with pride and pleasure. All agreed she was the most splendid bride they had ever seen.

The mother of her betrothed bade her welcome, and his sisters kissed her and giggled. —You will be a fine addition to the family, they told her.

But she noticed two women who did not share their joy. Their faces were hard as stone and their eyes flashed with anger and jealousy.

—Do not mind them, the mother told the girl. Your sister-wives will come to love you, too.

Sister-wives. The girl had not thought to ask; and yet now she saw it so clearly. One held an infant on her hip, one carried a child within her. Her would-be husband's children. How many more children might there be? And how many more sister-wives might come after her, when she, like they, lost the bloom of maidenhood?

She could not help it: the girl did what no bride must ever do in those last moments, as she is being led to be wed. She thought of her home. She thought of her father, her loyal, doting father, and the protection of his hearth. She looked back.

And she was turned into a tower of stone.

Mollel reflects on the tale of the Maasai Bride as he passes it, sitting in the back of the KWS pickup truck beside Kibet.

Chiku, his wife, had been a good Catholic. —It's the story of Lot's wife, she told him. From the Bible.

Mollel let her believe it, but he felt, instinctively, that the

Maasai myth predated her book. He had been raised on stories of snakes and apples, floods and monsters, nights in the wilderness and bodies brought back to life. When Chiku started taking him to her church all those uncomfortable, trouser-clad Sundays, he heard the same tales again, only with different names. The lesson he drew was not, as she suggested, that the Maasai had purloined the stories. He felt that the stories existed within men, just like love, and blood, and hatred, and passion. Inevitably, they would come out. The details might change, but the stories would remain.

The story of the Maasai Bride, he felt sure, arose from a man looking at that lonely shard of rock and summoning a tale of loneliness and betrayal.

Tonight, that man is him.

Kibet will not meet his eyes, and he does not have the words to say to her. The look of horror on her face when she interrupted him laying into Gachui remains burned on his memory.

It had only been the day before that he had held her back on the court steps. Wouldn't she, too, have assaulted Gachui then, if she had had the chance?

But he knows it is not the same. That was in the heat of the moment. Her anger had as much to do with the failure of justice as with the man himself. Mollel's attack had been in cold blood.

More than she knew, and more than he could ever tell her, he longs to reveal the truth. *Kibet*, he longs to say, *I did it to save his life. He was about to be shot.*

But he can't tell her that, for two reasons.

First, he still does not know whether she is a part of this gang or not.

And the second reason he hardly dares admit to himself.

Underneath it all – the need to be accepted by the gang, the need to pass their test, the need to save Gachui's life – there was something else. Something in every punch, every kick.

He enjoyed it.

*

The soft, grey-backed dawn yields to the needles of sun slanting through the trees, picking out webs as yet unbroken, gleaming and heavy with dew, spiders fat and pendent upon them.

The sun glints on the burnished, gold-barked boughs of the acacia trees, its warmth infusing the skin even while the air chills the lungs and reappears in plumes of mist.

Beyond, the lake glitters clear. Only an inky-black line on the horizon hints at the malign, choking weed which drifts back and forth with such regularity.

—Enjoying the garden?

Mollel looks round. It is the hotel manager.

—It's very beautiful.

—Glad you like it, the manager says bitterly. Shame our paying guests won't be enjoying the view this morning.

—Why not? We've done everything we need to here.

—I asked you to be discreet, hisses the manager. Half a dozen policemen tramping around all night, lights everywhere. Guests tend to notice that sort of thing. Who wants to spend time in a garden where a body was found? We've had four checkouts already, and breakfast hasn't even finished yet.

—I'm sorry for your loss of trade, replies Mollel, between gritted teeth. But this was a woman's life we're talking about.

—And what about the lives of the sixty people who work here? We've already stood down half our staff since the electoral violence. If we go under, what are those people going to do? The dead are gone, Officer. There's nothing you can do to help them. You need to look to the living.

It's a refrain Mollel has heard before, and he sympathises – to a point. If he had had more concern for the living Jemimah Okallo, he might not be investigating her death now. But he has always found it easier to deal with the dead. The dead may be just as reluctant to yield their secrets as the living, but they always do so, eventually.

You just need to know how to ask.

—*Weh!* calls the manager across the lawn, and Mollel cringes.

Weh is about the most contemptuous way to address anyone in the Swahili tongue, and he would never use it. It suggests that the extra syllable in *wewe – you –* is too much effort to bestow on such a lowly person. He looks over to see the object of the manager's scorn. A gardener is hunched in the bushes some distance away, years of practice having taught him how to become almost invisible.

—Why aren't the sprinklers on? This grass will scorch in no time once the sun's up!

The gardener approaches, wringing his hands in a grubby cloth. —It's the pressure, sir, he stammers. The weed must have blocked the inlet pipe again.

—Well, sort it out! barks the manager, pointing at the lake. You've only got a few hours before the weed returns, and you won't be able to get the boat through it.

He shakes his head and turns to Mollel once more. —Look to the living, he says.

His gaze shifts to beyond Mollel, and a flicker of annoyance passes over his brow. —One of your colleagues, he remarks. At least this one's a paying guest.

The gardener melts away and the manager turns on his heel, wishing a brisk *good morning* to Kiunga, who approaches Mollel with a grin.

—Just like old times, eh, Mollel, he says, slapping the Maasai on the back.

—Except I'm the constable now, and you're a sergeant.

Kiunga laughs. Mollel continues to look out at the lake.

—You can drop the hostile act, Mollel. There's no one about.

—I wasn't expecting you to show up so soon, replies Mollel.

—Change of plan, replies Kiunga. Besides, it's a good job I did. Those guys hardly seem to be warming to you.

—I was doing fine. They'd begun to accept me. The last thing I needed was another Nairobi cop turning up, with an international investigator in tow.

Kiunga laughs. —Your detective skills are still as sharp as ever, I see. Do they know?

—They found out. And I nearly got killed last night because of it. Someone else, too. Raphael Gachui.

—Mdosi's man?

—The KWS turned up just in time. I came away with Kibet, but he was left with the police. I need you to find out what happened to him.

—Sure thing, boss. I can still call you boss, right? I mean, I outrank you now.

—Only on paper, replies Mollel. Only for this mission.

If it succeeds, he reflects. His demotion was all part of the cover story to allow him to infiltrate the police at Maili Ishirini. Too many disappearances of unsavoury characters had begun to attract attention. But if Mollel failed to discover who was behind it, there would be no way back.

—Tell me about this change of plan, says Mollel. You were supposed to keep your distance until I'd discovered more about how the gang operates.

—Our hand was forced, replies Kiunga. Since the post-electoral violence, we're supposed to be cooperating with the UN. So this investigator shows up. Says she's looking into extrajudicial killings. And names Maili Ishirini as a *location of interest*, I believe she called it.

—How did she know?

—That's what we want to know. That's why Otieno assigned me to babysit her.

Otieno. It made perfect sense that he'd be behind this. Ever since he'd been promoted from Nairobi Central to the national police HQ at Vigilance House, Otieno had wanted to establish his reputation as someone who'd clean up the force. That was why he'd turned to his old clean-up man, Mollel. He wasn't going to have some outsider steal his thunder. If cleaning up meant playing dirty, he'd be the first to do it.

—We were probably only put on to this because the investigator was on her way, says Mollel, with a sigh of resignation. I never thought it was likely that Otieno cared much about the disappearance of a few scumbags.

—He would have been tipped off by the Interior Ministry as soon as her visa application was filed, agrees Kiunga. But the question is, who tipped *her* off? How did she know to come to Maili Ishirini?

—Mdosi himself? ventures Mollel.

—If he's her source, they're being very subtle about it, mutters Kiunga. She's not been anywhere near the prison in all the time we've been here.

—Could she be going behind your back?

Mollel sees a flicker of irritation – and something more than that – cross Kiunga's face. Kiunga hesitates, then shakes his head.

—No third party? continues Mollel. No go-between delivering messages from the prison?

—No, Kiunga says, forcefully.

Mollel reflects on the web of espionage that has enveloped this small, insignificant town. Mollel on the police. Kiunga on Oberkampf. Mollel, supposedly, on Kiunga. Or is it the other way round? And the police gang will only be willing to keep Mollel alive if they think he can find out what they need to know.

Who is Oberkampf's informant?

Kiunga's phone beeps. —It's her, he says, checking his message. She's looking for me. Best she doesn't see us together.

He pats Mollel on the shoulder and leaves. Mollel is relieved to find himself alone again. He watches a flight of white pelicans, far off, against the escarpment. As they spiral on a rising column of early-morning heat, their spread wings catch the sun when in profile, disappear when head-on. Flashing in and out of existence.

He hears a rustle nearby and frowns with annoyance. Is he not to be left alone for a minute? He turns, expecting to see a person, and immediately finds himself looking up at a looming figure at least twice his height.

The giraffe nods its massive head at him and looks around for something else to browse. It is the type known as a Maasai giraffe, Mollel notes, with dun starburst spots against brown, rather than the geometric netting of its larger, reticulated cousin. This one is elderly, too; its hide is patched with grey-blue moult and its large, soulful eyes are cloudy. It is an entirely artificial being, for no creature of this seniority would survive in the wild – it would have been pulled apart by lions or dogs long since, or even bullied to the point of snapping one of those delicate legs by one of its own kind.

Mollel no longer minds the interruption. He feels a kind of connection with this ageing captive, employed to entertain the tourists. Indeed, it is the best sort of companion, asking nothing but lending by its presence a certain companionable solicitude.

His eyes return once again to the lake. A solitary pelican has crash-landed beside the water inlet pipe and is flapping noisily against the floating cage at its end, no doubt having spotted a fish or frog inside.

Mollel recalls the gardener complaining that the pipe was blocked, and he walks toward the lake edge to try to get a closer look. Ponderously, as though mere whim happened to be leading him the same way, the giraffe follows.

From here, Mollel can make out the metal pipe, about eighteen inches in diameter, which runs from a small brick-built cube in the gardens – housing a pump, he assumes – out to the cage floating in the lake, buoyed by a couple of blue plastic oil drums. Similar oil drums are lashed at intervals to the pipe. It must be thirty metres out to the cage. Presumably the intention had been to keep the mouth of the pipe out beyond the clogging grasp of the weed when it blew in to shore. But that was in the days before the level of the water had dropped, its precious resource gulped so voraciously to feed gardens like this one and the insatiable thirst of the flower farms.

Reminded of the flower farm, Mollel looks across to the gleaming polytunnels next door. Invisible behind a high hedge from the hotel, at the shore it is clear that the two operations inhabit much the same space—including, it seems, some of the same facilities. A pipe, apparently identical to the one running from the hotel, leads from the outbuildings of the flower farm to the same cage which the pelican is still worrying so determinedly.

The flower farm and the hotel. Where Jemimah Okallo worked, and where her body was found. The two places so discrete – until the retreat of the water left them exposed.

At the intake, the pelican is still wrestling intently with something caught in the grille. Mollel shades his eyes against the glare from the sunlight on the water.

Mollel gives a sudden *ha!* of revelation. The giraffe casts him a glance full of reproach for breaking the silence, and lopes away.

Eager to test his theory, Mollel approaches the pipe. The heat of the sun means that the mud at the water's edge is dry and hard, right up to within a few inches of the tiny waves lapping the shore. He places a hand upon the metal; it is cool, but he can feel the tension between the sun's rays on it and the cold water beneath.

Mollel thinks he knows, now, how Jemimah Okallo's corpse came to be on the hotel shore, on the wrong side of the weed, when no one had seen her come through the gate. It had nothing to do with the timing of the weed's daily migration across the lake. It had everything to do with this pipe.

Emboldened, Mollel steps up onto the pipe. He is not quite as sure-footed as he was as a child, dancing on the rocky slopes and thorny goat tracks in bare feet. But he feels confident enough in the ability of the pipe to bear his weight that he ventures forth, despite the knowledge that the ground will shelve away suddenly ahead of him. And despite the fact that he, in common with every Maasai he has ever known, has never learned how to swim.

He feels the rust of the pipe, velvety against the soles of his feet, and is grateful that it is not slippery smooth. He places one foot gingerly in front of the other and begins to tread along it, stealthily, like a tightrope walker.

The first section is easy. He makes it to the floating oil drum with ease, pauses a moment and then moves forward to the next.

This, he is sure, is how Jemimah Okallo must have made her way out onto the lake. Now he is following in her footsteps.

Ahead of him, on the pipe, a water spider scuttles away and springs nimbly onto a lily pad. Even though he knows it presents no danger to him, Mollel can't help but shudder. He checks himself: far better to worry about the hippos, whose grunting call he can hear distantly. One of them could bite him in half, and would, too, if it felt threatened or had a calf nearby. But even so, it is the spider that fills him with a near-visceral sense of revulsion. He has always hated spiders. Ever since his youth.

It had been one of the infrequent days when Mollel had chosen to graze his cattle close to where Lendeva was tending the family goats. There was some good pasture in under the ridge of a kopje, and Mollel lay on his side listening to the peaceful clunking of his cattle's wooden bells mingling with the higher-pitched tinkle of the goats' metal bells and their bleats and calls above him. He was glad that he no longer had to tend the goats; they were troublesome beasts, and it was a job for little boys. Now he had graduated to the cows, it would only be a few years before he became a *moran*, and beyond that, the day when he would have his own sons to go out and do the herding for him.

He closed his eyes and dreamed of a thousand-head herd of cattle. He would be the richest man in Kajiado district. Why, with a fortune like that, he would be able to afford a wife or two . . .

A stone landed near him and sent up a shower of dirt. He jumped to his feet and shielded his eyes against the sun. Atop a rock above him, crouched like an agama lizard, was Lendeva.

Mollel launched a stream of abuse, but Lendeva merely grinned and disappeared from the rock. He re-emerged, scrambling through the scrub which grew around its base, and walked toward the spot where the stone had landed.

Mollel was about to aim a swipe at his younger brother's ear, but, as usual, the boy walked with a purposeful air which caused his anger to dissipate and be replaced by a sense of intrigue. Mollel watched as Lendeva stooped to pick up the rock. He glanced at the ground beneath it, then tipped up the rock and examined its underside, which he turned and presented to Mollel with a smile.

Stuck to the bottom of the rock, flattened and smeared with black juice, was a baboon spider.

—I saw it walking straight toward you, said Lendeva. Didn't want it mistaking your gawping mouth for a nice nest-hole.

Certainly, that would have been an unpleasant awakening. The creature was nearly as large as his own hand, and was capable of delivering a debilitating bite. Mollel looked in awe and not a little revulsion at the round body and thick legs, covered in the olive baboon-like hair which gave the spider its name.

—You don't like them, do you? asked Lendeva, with that insolent air which so infuriated Mollel.

—They don't bother me, Mollel lied.

—Oh yeah? Well then, come take a look at what I found.

It hung as though levitating, just above head height. When there was a breath of breeze, it swung and shook, but returned to its spot between the two thorn bushes. Lendeva approached and stood right underneath it, and for the first time Mollel was able to make out the anchor arc of slightly thicker silk which bound the lowest part of the web to the earth while its upper portion sailed in the sky. A shiver of light passed across the entire structure at that moment, and Mollel saw its filaments stretch and spiral their way up to reach the very top of the bushes above them.

This was *ol kedi*, the golden spider. Slimmer and spindlier than its grounded cousin, but with an even wider span, it crouched with the tip of each of its angled legs upon one of the trigger lines from which the rest of the web spread.

Mollel tried not to let any emotion flicker across his face, but every instinct in his being cried out for him to run away. He knew that these spiders, sensing threat, could spring onto anyone nearby and render them an immediate bite. He'd heard tell of children who had unwittingly blundered into one of these webs and been found dead, their flock loose and untended, a weal on their head where *ol kedi* had struck.

He affected an air of nonchalance and studied the spider. It seemed to be composed of geometric shapes and right angles, like sharply bent wire. The abdomen dominated the body, a rectangular lozenge the length and thickness of Mollel's thumb. It was black, with a series of golden spots. Beneath it, a shield-shaped head ending in a row of gleaming spheres, each orb a vigilant eye. And there, the jaws. Two cruel mandibles that left little doubt over their power to devour prey or inflict agony.

Lendeva pulled his drinking calabash out of his belt and shook it. Rather than sloshing, it gave a rattle. He looked up at his older brother slyly. —Time for supper, he said.

He pulled the softwood stopper out of the neck of the calabash and tipped it over his hand. Something shot out and fell into his open palm. It was a field cricket. The insect stretched its rear legs and waved its antennae cautiously.

It did not have much time to adjust to its new-found freedom, however. Lendeva tenderly closed his fingers around it, then lifted his arm and flung the creature skyward.

Joyously, it whirred into the sky, wings a buzzing blur, legs trailing. Its flight lasted approximately one second, before the cricket found its progress arrested by the web.

For a while, Mollel thought it must surely tear itself free. The cricket seemed so much more powerful than the ethereal structure in which it was enmeshed. It kicked its powerful legs, but all it succeeded in achieving was to wind the filaments more closely around its thrashing limbs.

Ol kedi, meanwhile, sat immobile, apparently unimpressed by the catch. Its only movement was caused by the vibration of the web itself. Mollel wondered whether it was perhaps dead. How could one tell, he wondered, when it was almost impossible to consider such a thing alive in the first place?

And then, suddenly, it moved. Any doubt of its life was immediately dispelled by the purposeful, swift movement of its legs across the surface of the web. Just as a crocodile waits for its prey to exhaust itself, the spider had been biding its time until the point at which the cricket had become so tightly bound that its attempts at escape would no longer be able to damage its attacker.

The spider raised its head high from its body and sank its two sharp mandibles straight into the thorax of the prone cricket, driving them mercilessly through its shell. The cricket's struggles and the spider's advance both immediately ceased in that moment, and a sort of serenity descended upon them, as though the two creatures were sharing some kind of communion.

—Beautiful, isn't it, grinned Lendeva.

He did not wait for Mollel's answer, but picked up a twig from the ground and used it to point at the very tip of the spider's golden-blotched abdomen.

For the first time, Mollel saw a tiny brown spider, no bigger than a seed, its legs finer than hairs, scuttling back and forth excitedly on the back of the larger creature.

—A baby? Mollel asked with surprise. He had seen scorpion babies, little glistening replicas, riding on their mother's back. But there were hundreds of them, not just one.

Mollel looked more closely at the frantic little mite running in circles on its gigantic mate. His repulsion had abated now that the spider seemed occupied with its food.

—Her husband, scoffed Lendeva. She's the powerful one. She does all the work. All he has to do is have sex with her.

—He reminds me of Uncle, Mollel joked.

Lendeva laughed heartily and slapped Mollel's arm in appreciation. Before long there were even tears of hilarity running down his cheeks.

Mollel, too, felt the pricking of tears. It had been a long time since the two had felt like brothers.

Eventually, Lendeva stopped laughing and wiped his eyes. When he turned to look up at Mollel once more, his face was serious.

—I forgot about Uncle, he said.

And so had Mollel. Amid their absorption with the spider, they had failed to notice darkness creeping upon the landscape around them. Uncle would be waiting for them to bring the herd home before the branches were drawn across the entrance to the communal *boma*. If he had to go out there to reopen it himself, his anger would not be a pretty sight. And though he was small, like the male spider, he was capable of delivering a bite as fierce as any of the species.

Progess along the water pipe is slow, but steady. Mollel edges out, body angled sideways, soles of his feet wrapped around the curve of the pipe, arms outstretched, occasionally waving to restore a little lost equilibrium.

Soon the water hyacinth all around begins to thin out. A black and white kingfisher plunges into the dark water and Mollel sees its sparkling trail cut deep below him. The water is so clear, and apparently bottomless, that he feels a sudden sense of vertigo. He wobbles, crouches, and only just manages to retrieve his poise. He sighs with relief.

The kingfisher is gone now, but there is something else moving down there. Or is it just his imagination? He thought he saw a shape, but maybe it was just the shadow of a cloud.

No. There it is. Unmistakably, a hippopotamus is swimming, far beneath the pipe. Its movements are simultaneously graceful and comical, as it kicks its legs as though walking in slow motion. Then it spins and turns onto its back, its massive pink belly facing upward. A small stream of bubbles escapes from its mouth and sparkles its way up to the surface.

And then the beast is gone, far beyond the pipe. Mollel is awestruck. He has seen the animals moving on the surface of the water before, as well as on land, and he knows that their ponderous figure belies their ability to put on a devastating turn of speed, should they put their mind to it. But he had never thought of a hippopotamus as graceful before.

He continues his progress along the pipe. Out here, it is dipping far more with his weight and he is unable to stand up again. Inching out on his hands and knees, he gets closer to the cage where the pelican is still fussing at something inside.

A snort makes him start. The hippo has resurfaced on the other side of the pipe and sits with its ears, eyes and nostrils lined up in his direction only a few metres away. There is little doubting its hostility, but it seems content for now simply to observe the intruder in its territory. That suits Mollel fine – as long as it does not come any closer.

As he reaches the end of the pipe, he sees that his supposition was correct: the inlet from the flower farm joins inside the same cage. The pelican, disturbed by his approach, gives a reproachful cry and takes to the sky.

Mollel looks inside the pipe at what the bird was trying to get to. There is a knot of yellow grass, or reeds. No – it is something else. He sees the pattern of weaving. It is a basket.

He reaches in. The basket is just beyond his grasp. He tries again, twisting and turning his arm between the protective bars. Every time, he comes tantalisingly close. His fingers even brush across it. He has the feeling that with just one more effort . . .

And then he slips.

He is plunged deep into the water. Green light absorbs him. Coldness surrounds him.

He feels himself sinking, sinking. He thrashes his arms and legs, but not knowing how to swim, is unaware if this does any good at all. The sensation of being pulled downward is sickening and unstoppable.

His lungs feel as though they are about to burst. And then, just as he thinks he is destined to sink for ever, he feels air on his face.

He gulps a huge, relieved gasp of air before his face falls under once more. He could not make out the cage or the pipe in that frantic moment, but he did see something which gave him hope: a clump of weed.

When he comes up next time, he arches his back and thrusts his hands toward the weed. Even as the blessed air rushes into his lungs, he feels dismay and terror fill him: the weed is simply sinking beneath him.

Another attempt. He kicks more violently than ever, and manages to grab more handfuls of the thick, rubbery leaves. This time he thinks he can feel some resistance. As his head goes beneath the water another time, he seems to not sink quite as deep.

Once more he resurfaces. Once more he stretches for the weed. Once more his fall is lessened: this time he has the stuff all around him and under his body. One more effort allows him to haul himself into a position where the weed is, if not entirely supporting his weight, at least preventing him from slipping under once more. He has a chance to catch his breath.

A snort brings him back to reality. The hippo is close now. And there is more than one. He turns his head frantically. Where is the pipe?

One of the hippos spins and presents its wide grey backside to Mollel. With a flick of its tail, it disappears. The others follow suit.

The noise of an engine is what has driven them away. With a sort of ecstasy, Mollel looks up and sees the black shape of a boat coming toward him.

He closes his eyes in relief.

When he opens them, the boat is closer. But Mollel's relief rapidly drains. What he had taken for the splash of a bow wave is actually a thrashing, frothing turmoil of water. It is the macerator on the front of the boat, heading straight for him.

—Hey! he manages to call. Hey! Hey! I'm here!

But there is no pilot visible, and the spinning, bladed wheel continues to advance. At the cost of slipping from his precarious perch on the thin raft of weed, Mollel raises his arms in the air. He manages to wave a couple of times, still shouting out, before he slides into the water.

And still it comes.

The momentary height he gained above the surface while waving has allowed Mollel to orient himself. The metal cage is not far from him, barely more than a few metres – but it might as well be a mile away to a non-swimmer. He has only seconds before the machine is upon him, tearing him to shreds.

Then he recalls the hippo that had swum beneath him. He fills his lungs with a huge gulp of air, takes a quick look at the thrashing blades and allows himself to sink.

He stays down as long as he dares. It is an unusual feeling, he reflects – even at that unlikely moment – that a few minutes before he had been desperate to return to the surface, whereas now, he wants to prolong the time he can spend down here as much as possible. The last thing he wants to do is bob up like a cork right in front of the jaws of the macerator.

A shadow passes over him, just as fuzziness begins to cloud his eyes. He can't help it any more. He has to resurface, whether it means being cut to shreds or not.

His head clunks against something, and he slides along it. His hand makes out the side of the boat, and he clings to it gratefully.

—Hold on! cries a voice. As though Mollel had any intention of doing anything else.

He feels the boat wobble and tip, and sees the shape of a man appear above him. A hand is extended, which Mollel grasps, and in the next moment he is hauled aboard.

Mollel is aware of a screaming, searing noise. The macerator is grinding into the cage, sending sparks into the air. Shadrack, streaming with water, is panting furiously. He reaches around Mollel to a switch which he flicks, and the macerator stops its attack.

The cage is cut open. While Shadrack sets about trying to restart the outboard motor, Mollel takes his opportunity. He reaches over and pulls the sodden basket out of the mouth of the inlet pipe.

9

The instant the boat hits the shore, Shadrack leaps out. His soaked clothes clinging to his skin, he looks slighter than ever, but he immediately flies at Tonkei and grabs the Maasai by his *shuka*. Tonkei, though considerably larger, puts up no resistance.

—Who set that thing off? screams Shadrack. You could've killed him!

—Easy, easy! yells Tonkei. It wasn't me. I was on the other side of the greenhouses.

—I can vouch for that, booms a voice. It is De Wit. Now get your hands off my guard. You come here looking for a fight, I'll have your ass in gaol, policeman or no policeman. Judge Singh is my golfing partner, and I happen to know his opinion of flatfoots who throw their weight around.

Shadrack releases Tonkei with disgust. A crowd has gathered – another couple of Maasai guards, a dozen or so flower pickers. Kiunga is there, too. He is puffing hard, presumably from having run around from his car. Without venturing into the water, the only way to get here from the hotel is a long circuit through the hotel gardens, out onto the Maili Ishirini road, back in through the flower farm's security gates and along the length of the greenhouses. This last stretch he must have run: no wonder he's panting.

—Are you alright? he asks Mollel, helping him out of the boat.

—Fine, says Mollel. But he is aware of a tremble in his voice.

—You're cold, says Kiunga. Let's get you a change of clothes. Pass me that.

He is referring to the sodden basket which Mollel retrieved from the grille at the end of the intake pipe. But Mollel clutches it to his chest.

—I'll keep this, he says.

Meanwhile, Shadrack comes toward them, shaking his head.

—Useless, he says. They all claim no one was here. I suppose it was a ghost who set the machine running!

—Good job you were here, says Kiunga. You're a pretty nifty swimmer.

—Kiambu district under-sixteen silver medal, smiles Shadrack. Might have come first then, too, if there had been hippos in the pool.

Mollel is aware that it's normal to thank the person who's just saved your life. But normal be damned. Last night, Shadrack and the others had almost killed him, or threatened to do so. He still doesn't know if they believe his story about the pills, or think he might be useful in some way because of his link to Kiunga and, through him, the investigator.

Thankfully the awkward moment is interrupted by the arrival of someone from the greenhouses with a blanket each for Mollel and Shadrack, in which they wrap themselves gratefully. A steaming cup of *chai* is pressed into Mollel's hands by one of the pickers.

—Just what were you doing out here, anyway? Kiunga asks Shadrack.

—Following up on the drowning.

Mollel raises an eyebrow. —I thought you said it was a clear-cut case.

Shadrack shrugs.

—You must have been pretty close to the water's edge yourself, says Kiunga. You didn't see anyone start up the boat?

—I was just around the corner. It was the sound of the engine that brought me here. The first thing I saw was the machine moving off with no one aboard. Then I realised it was heading straight for someone in the water. I didn't stop to think.

—Back to work, you lot, barks Tonkei at the pickers.

—I've got to get back too, says Kiunga with a glance at Mollel – a glance Mollel sees Shadrack pick up. Do you two need a lift anywhere?

—No thanks, says Mollel, injecting a note of hostility into his voice. We'll walk.

After a quick stop by the barracks for a change of clothing, Mollel and Shadrack stand at the single desk of the main room in Maili Ishirini Police Post. Mollel tips the sodden basket over the desk and the contents spill out. A wet shawl slops out first, then, with a plastic clatter, a cellphone.

Mollel picks it up. The phone is a cheap one, well worn, to the extent that many of the numerals have been rubbed away and the edges have become smooth, like a pebble. Water is beaded behind its blank screen. Mollel presses and holds the power button.

Nothing.

He takes his own phone from his pocket and snaps off the back. He removes the battery and slides out his SIM card, which he places carefully on the desk. He then repeats the operation with Jemimah Okallo's phone, this time drying her SIM card on his sleeve before putting it into his own device.

He reassembles his phone, turns it on and is greeted by an annoying chime of music. Shadrack moves round to look over his shoulder.

Immediately he begins scrolling through the contacts. There are only a few names. One, he notices with a pang, is *Sweety*.

Now he turns to the text messages. A list of messages in the inbox. Nearly all from Sweety.

With a moment's hesitation and a slight twinge of conscience, he opens the first message.

—Do you speak JaLuo? he asks Shadrack.

Shadrack gives a contemptuous laugh. —Easy enough to get someone to translate, he says.

Luckily, there is enough Swahili in the messages for Mollel to get the gist. They are affectionate, slight: messages sent without thought but conveying constant thought. Messages of love.

Mollel had no cellphone back when he was married – the idea of possessing one in the late 1990s would have seemed as remote and preposterous as owning a yacht – but if he had had one, these are the sorts of messages he would no doubt have received from Chiku.

—I guess we've got to make contact with whoever this is, says Shadrack. I'll check the personnel file and see if there's a husband.

Mollel continues looking through the messages. He stops when he sees one from a number without any name associated to it. There's something sinister about this anonymous chain of digits, and he pauses a moment before opening it.

NAMBA 103. LIPA BEI ELFU ASHA KWA NAMBA HII AMA TUTAKU RAPE HELAFU TUTAKUOA.

It's barely Swahili, barely even Sheng. But the message is clear enough.

Number 103. Pay ten thousand shillings to this number or we will rape you and we will kill you.

Number 103 was the number of Jemimah's dorm room. *This number*, later in the message, must refer to this anonymous phone number. She'd be expected to send the money through the cellphone network.

—*Bastards*, hisses Shadrack.

No wonder she was desperate enough to steal discarded flowers to try to sell them by the roadside. How much did De Wit say she would have got for the roses he saw her selling? A couple of thousand? She'd have to sell a lot more to get to the figure she needed.

*

Mollel knew how fear could be used to control. He had been brought up observing the tactic first-hand. Uncle had been expert at it.

He and Lendeva called their uncle Uncle precisely because it was forbidden for them to do so. Since their father had disappeared, leaving nothing behind him but a stink of drink and sickness, four dry seasons had passed, and, according to customary law, he was now presumed dead. This meant that all he left behind now belonged to his younger brother.

Their father's cattle were now their uncle's cattle.

Their father's goats were their uncle's goats.

Their mother was now their uncle's wife.

He was now their father.

Which was why both Mollel and Lendeva steadfastly continued to call him Uncle, despite the frequent rages and beatings this act of defiance elicited.

Likewise, although the cows and goats assimilated themselves into their new herds, Mollel's mother refused to submit meekly to the traditional role ascribed to the widow of an elder brother.

—I was married to that drunkard when I was thirteen, she used to say. I may not have grown up to be the wife he wanted, but I was his only wife in all that time. And that's something to be proud of. So why should I take my place as junior wife to two girls barely old enough to be my daughters?

Certainly, Mollel's aunts had no desire for a new sister-wife. Especially such a feisty one. And such a beautiful one, for his mother was still young; she was plump, and in her aloof dignity, she had more than her fair share of admirers. Including, both wives knew well, their husband. For although Mollel's mother barred him from the home that she still shared with her boys – which was now, legally, his house too – there was no disguising the fact that Uncle, with his lascivious grin and his licking of lips, was taunted beyond reason by this woman whom he possessed and yet did not, who belonged to him and yet kept him so firmly at arm's – and sometimes spear's – length.

*

Instinctively knowing it will be a fruitless task, Mollel asks Shadrack to try to get some information out of the cellphone provider. Listening in as the younger man talks, using the office phone, he is able to follow the one-sided conversation. No, they can't tell him who sent the message – it was from an anonymous, prepaid number. No, they have no record of money being sent to that account. No, they can't tell him what other calls or transactions that account might have made, where the SIM card was purchased or which location the message was sent from – not without a warrant.

—Fine, says Shadrack. I'll get a warrant. He slams the phone down. Both policemen know that the gesture is about as useless as the threat. Getting a warrant would mean going up to Naivasha courthouse and begging Judge Singh to issue one – and the story was that Judge Singh did nothing unless he was motivated to do so. They could not afford that sort of motivation.

Mollel leaves Shadrack cursing in the darkness of the police post and steps out onto what passes for the main street of Maili Ishirini. Over the road, the main gate of the flower farm, with its high, white plastic roofs appearing over the top of neatly trimmed hedges. Slightly further up, the entrance to the Lakefront Hotel, with its guard post.

It is market day. The stalls of *mitumba*, second-hand clothing, are piled high with freshly laundered and neatly folded clothes of all colours. Sheets and towels hang from rope suspended between the stubby acacia trees planted against the roadside. Some of the stalls have been set up on trestles, but many more are simply spread on rugs on the ground.

At least the market imbues the town with a little more life than usual. Bargain-hunters drift from stall to stall, stopping to sift through the piles. Mothers drag their children along, holding up items against their bodies for size. The air is filled with the sound of vendors crying their wares; with laughter, gossip and haggling.

The only permanent stores in the village are set in a row of five, each one with a door and window. There is a *duka la dawa*, a medicine store, selling painkillers singly or by the dozen, dusty bottles of cough mixture, antacid and condoms. Next in the row is a general store, with plastic buckets and basins piled high in front, placards advertising washing powder and powdered milk, strips of razor blades, matches and packets of tea hanging from the window frame. The final two units are a hairdressing salon and a beer house – social hubs for the female and male population of Hell.

In the middle of this parade of shops is a cellphone outlet. It is emblazoned with multicoloured posters covering all of the networks. A hand-painted sign next to the door lists the services offered: *Phones for sale, Repairs, Calls for 2/-, International Calling Cards, Battery Charging, Internet, Word-processing, Photocopy, Printing, Money Transfer.*

Mollel enters the cool interior.

—No net, says a voice.

—What? asks Mollel.

—No net, if that's what you're here for. The server's down.

—That's not what I want, he says. Can you help me do a money transfer with a cellphone?

The woman behind the counter looks at him with amusement. —Sure. You've never done it before?

Mollel shakes his head.

—I'm surprised. Some of the people who use it most are Maasai. They're the ones whose villages are usually the most remote. I have a customer, a Maasai, who comes here every month to send some of his salary back home. His wife has to walk for two days just to get reception on her phone. But he only gets one week's leave a year, so that's the best way of doing it. I suppose you want to send some money to your wife?

—I don't have a wife, says Mollel.

—Oh really? The woman, a plump lady in her thirties with a buck-toothed, pleasant smile, looks him over. I'd have thought you'd have three or four by now. But I dare say you're a good

Christian gentleman, from the way you're dressed. I've seen you around town, haven't I? Why aren't you in uniform?

Mollel is beginning to resign himself to the fact that dealing with this woman is going to stretch his powers of endurance, as well as of conversation. He has no wish to discuss his morning dip in Lake Naivasha. So he explains that he is off duty, and wants to send some money to a friend to pay off an old debt.

The woman – she has already introduced herself as Beatrice – readily agrees to give him the help he needs.

—But let me come round next to you, she says. Then we can both see what we're doing.

It's a small shop and she is a big woman. She takes Mollel's phone, fitted with Jemimah's SIM card, and holds it up close to her ample chest. —Look at this, she says. Just tell me if I'm going too fast.

Mollel shuffles uneasily as she casts him a sideways glance and a toothy smile. She uses the movement to sidle closer.

—Alright, she says. We're ready to begin.

—What happens at their end, when I've sent the money?

—They get a text message, Beatrice says. It contains a code, which they can present at a shop like this one, and get their cash.

—As simple as that?

—As simple as that.

—Before they come to collect their cash, do they know how much I've sent?

—Not on this network. They won't know that until they come to the shop. I enter the code into my terminal, here, and then it comes up with the transaction details. As soon as the money is claimed, the sender gets a confirmation text.

—So I wouldn't have to send ten thousand shillings, says Mollel, as much to himself as to Beatrice. I could just send one hundred.

Beatrice raises her eyebrows. —I know what you're up to, she says.

—You do?

—Yes, you naughty boy. You're buying time. You want your friend to think you've repaid his loan in full, when you're only paying off a part of it. I suppose he lives a long way from a place where he can cash in the transaction?

—I suppose he does, says Mollel.

—You're sneaky ones, you Maasai, she says. Then she squeezes his arm. But I like the way you think.

Having established that there is no credit stored on Jemimah's account, Mollel takes a one-hundred-bob note from his wallet and Beatrice does the appropriate business with his phone. When it comes to identifying the recipient, Mollel takes the phone back from her – careful not to reveal the message – and gives it back with the number of the sender on display.

The whole thing is surprisingly quick and easy. Mollel wonders if his mother-in-law might not have a point after all.

—So now what?

—Now, you wait for a text saying your payment has been picked up, Beatrice tells him. I hope that means your friend will be off your back for a while. Is there anything else I can do for you while you're here? Anything at all?

—No, thanks, says Mollel. He glances toward the bright white space of the doorway – he is eager to leave, for more reasons than one.

Beatrice leans forward and slips Mollel's phone into his breast pocket. She gives it a pat.

—I've stored my own number in your contacts, she coos. Just in case you ever need any assistance. You can call me any time. Day or night.

And she gives him a slow, deliberate wink.

Mollel is so disconcerted as he slips out of the door that he replies: —*Cheesy kama ndizi.*

He strolls among the *mitumba* stalls for a while, pretending to look at the clothing on display. But in fact, he is anxiously watching the shop he has just left. Customers come and go, and each time he glances at his phone, hoping to get the text message that will tell him his payment has been picked up.

But no message comes. He wonders how much of a delay there is within the system. He needs to know the instant the cash is paid out.

That is, of course, if the money is picked up here. Beatrice had explained that the money could be picked up anywhere in Kenya. There must be thousands of these little shops, from Mombasa to Mandera, and whoever sent the threat to Jemimah might be entering any one of them right now. But he has a feeling it's going to be collected here. The fact that they used Jemimah's room number suggests that it was someone who knew her – or at least, had enough information on her to cross-check her phone number with the accommodation. That probably means someone from the flower farm itself. And this is the only place in Maili Ishirini where someone can collect a mobile money transfer. And if someone local thought that ten thousand shillings was waiting for them, would they bother making the long trip into Naivasha town just to receive it?

He glances again at the store. Beatrice appears at the door and offers him a gleaming smile and a coquettish ripple of her fingers. He nods and turns away, grateful for the distraction provided by the arrival of a buzzing moped, picking its way between the stalls. It clatters to a stop outside the parade of shops. The rider kicks down the stand and dismounts, heading straight for Beatrice's shop. Mollel tries to get a look at him, but he's still wearing his helmet: a yellow one. Below it he wears dark overalls and gumboots.

He's not inside for long. He leaves just as a big flowery bed-sheet hanging on one of the lines billows up in front of Mollel's view. Crossly, Mollel pushes it out of the way, but the man is already back on his moped and speeding off.

Then Mollel's phone beeps.

Your payment has been collected. Thank you for using this service.

He dashes to the store. Beatrice has come to the doorway.

—I thought you'd be back before long, she says with a smile. A girl has a feeling for these things ...

—Who was that? demands Mollel, abruptly.

—Just a customer. Are you jealous?

—Do you know him? Did he say who he was?

Her smile disappears. —I don't go interrogating everyone I meet. Apparently you do.

—Please, says Mollel. It's very important.

She looks at him with renewed scrutiny. —You told me you were off duty, she says.

—I'm never off duty.

A look of disappointment crosses her face. He can see her processing the information, reappraising their conversation. All the questions, the waiting outside, the meaningful glances – she can see, now, that they were not intended for her.

—Well then, she says. He's a colleague of yours.

—A colleague?

Certainly he was not one of the four from this police post – none of them rides a moped, and Mollel would have recognised them, even with a helmet on.

—A kind of colleague, she says. He looked pretty unhappy when he only got a hundred shillings from me. He insisted on seeing the transaction on the terminal screen. And while he put the money in his wallet, I saw his ID card. I didn't take any notice of the name, but I recognised the logo. He works for the prison service.

10

Coming out of the shop, Mollel is greeted by the sight of Shadrack lolling by the door, chewing on a stump of sugar cane.

—Anyone would think you were following me, says Mollel.

—Funny, that, replies Shadrack.

For the second time this day, though for very different reasons, Mollel is pleased to see his colleague, grateful for the opportunity to tap his local knowledge.

—Tell me, says Mollel. Do you know someone from this village who rides a moped, wears a yellow helmet?

Shadrack narrows his eyes and spits out a wad of sugar-cane fibre.

—Could do, he says, slowly.

Working alongside Shadrack these past few weeks has allowed Mollel a certain access to the workings of the young man's mind. It's not been the most edifying experience. Even now, Mollel can see his brain processing the information, rolling through potential matches to the description.

—He works at the prison, prompts Mollel.

And then he sees a small, sly smile twitch at the corners of Shadrack's mouth. Mollel almost winces in anticipation of the exclamation, *cheesy kama ndizi*, but it does not come.

—No, says Shadrack, shaking his head regretfully. Doesn't sound like anyone I know. Tell you what, let me make a call or two. Could be one of the others might have an idea.

He picks up his phone and turns his back on Mollel, walking nonchalantly away. Mollel can hear him muttering, hand cupped around the phone, but can't make out what he is saying.

A sense of foreboding begins to creep up on him. Shadrack, for all his low cunning, is usually relatively guileless in Mollel's presence. Why would a lead in the Jemimah Okallo case suddenly cause him to act so cagey? What has changed since last night?

Last night.

Suddenly Mollel feels his stomach lurch as violently as though he is being thrust over the edge of the cliff once more. They had let him go for a reason.

The young man has finished his call and is sauntering back toward Mollel.

—That was the Sarge, he says, a grin playing over his lips. Thinks he knows who your moped rider is. He's coming to pick us up.

—Wait, says Mollel, playing for time. Don't you want to know how he's linked to the death of Jemimah Okallo?

Shadrack's smile fades. He looks into Mollel's eyes as though appraising him.

—You can tell me about it in the car, he replies.

The answer dispels any remaining doubt Mollel may have had. Shadrack clearly believes that Mollel has let slip the identity of Oberkampf's informant – the go-between giving her information from Mdosi, in prison, on the disappearance of his men. And if they think they know that, Rhino Force will no longer have any use for Mollel. He remains what he was before. A suspected spy. And an inconvenience.

An engine's roar makes him look up: the police pickup draws to a halt just in front of where Mollel and Shadrack are standing. Sergeant Mungai is behind the wheel, Choma beside him. Munene stands in the back, hands spread wide on the roof of the cab.

—Well, Maasai, Munene calls. *Kuja*. Get in.

Shadrack places an arm on Mollel's sleeve.

It feels like a hood over his eyes.

Mollel is certain that getting into that car could be one of the last things he does.

—Wait, he says, trying to keep a rising note of fear out of his voice. He pats his clothing exaggeratedly. I've lost something.

—Whatever it is, says Mungai, it can wait, can't it?

—Not really, says Mollel, shaking his head emphatically. It's my pills.

The other policemen look at one another.

Mollel says: —I need my pills.

He senses the ploy is working. If there is one thing certain to inspire discomfort in others, he knows very well, it is the spectre of madness.

—Fine, says Mungai. We'll swing by the barracks, get your pills . . .

—The flower farm, says Mollel, hurriedly. I had them at the flower farm. Now I think about it, I seem to recall them falling into the boat as I got out of it. I was too shocked to pay any attention at the time.

—OK, says Mungai, with a tone of barely disguised exasperation. We'll go to the flower farm, see if anyone found your pills. And then will you come with us?

—Of course, says Mollel.

He knows that, if nothing else, he has bought himself a few minutes. He had been hoping that, somewhere between the row of shops where they picked him up and the flower farm, they might have run in to Kiunga. Or even Kibet – she had saved him once before. But she was nowhere to be seen, and no one seemed to raise a glance at the policemen as they crossed the main road and headed into the flower farm.

What could he do? Appeal to Tonkei or De Wit for assistance? He could just imagine their amused, quizzical response. Shadrack and the others would laugh, no doubt, and Mungai would point at his forehead: *He's crazy.* Then Munene's iron grip would close around his forearm and he would be led, inexorably, to the pickup. And to whatever came next.

—Nothing? asks Munene.

—I'm still looking, says Mollel, crouching to look under the seat. This boat is little more than a fibreglass shell. He can't keep up the pretence much longer. It is with a huge sensation of relief that he hears the booming, staccato voice of De Wit.

—Bloody hell. I can't keep you boys away, huh?

Mollel rises and steps out of the boat.

A plan is beginning to form. It's a long shot, he realises, but it may be his best chance at survival.

He steps up to De Wit.

The man watches him approach with amused grey eyes. He folds his wide, speckled forearms over the chequered expanse of his chest.

Mollel stops directly before him. Watching, Rhino Force shuffle uneasily. Tonkei, who has accompanied them to the water's edge, instinctively places his hand on the club that hangs at his waist.

—What did you say? asks Mollel, quietly.

—I said, I'd have thought you'd had enough of this place for one day.

—That's not what you said, says Mollel. I believe you referred to *boys*. I don't see any boys here.

—Leave it, Mollel, warns Mungai.

—It's just a figure of speech, *bwana*, chuckles De Wit.

—Maybe in your country, replies Mollel. But here, grown men don't take kindly to being called boys.

—OK, says De Wit, with a shrug. So I'm sorry.

—And what about Jemimah Okallo? Are you sorry about her, too?

De Wit looks at him blankly. Tonkei murmurs: —The dead girl.

—You don't even know her name, says Mollel with disgust.

Shadrack steps forward and puts a hand on Mollel's arm. —Come on, buddy, we've got a job to do.

Mollel shrugs the hand away. He's pointing a finger now,

directly into De Wit's face. —She'd be alive today if you hadn't sacked her.

—For stealing, snarls De Wit.

—For stealing what? asks Mollel. You told us those roses were worth hundreds of shillings. Then I found out they were worthless! Discarded. What else have you been lying to us about, Mr De Wit?

—OK, that's enough, says De Wit, stepping back from Mollel. I want you lot off my premises now. He takes his cellphone from his pocket and raises it in warning.

Mollel reaches out and knocks the phone from his hand. It clatters to the ground.

—You don't get to tell us what to do! he shouts.

—Mollel! barks Mungai.

Mollel does not heed him, nor the raised voices of the others. He swats away their attempts to restrain him as he lunges forward. His fist connects with De Wit's face. It's like punching a tree trunk. A wave of pain soars through his hand and arm. He doesn't get a chance at a second blow: they are all upon him, now. All except De Wit, who, blood pouring from his nose, has reeled away and is fumbling for his cellphone, then jabbing at it with meaty, trembling fingers.

—You've done it now, *bwana*, he says thickly. Judge Singh's going to put you away for this!

11

—Order! I will have order! Order in this court!

Judge Singh bangs his gavel but the clacking merely adds to the commotion in the crowded, sweaty room. The fans swirling overhead do nothing to relieve the soupy heat, but seem to revolve in sympathy with the turmoil below.

It is not every day that Naivasha courthouse sees a policeman being hauled before it.

—Mollel! Mollel!

Mollel looks up from his unfamiliar position in the defendants' dock. Kiunga is trying to reach him through the crush. Eventually he makes his way there and puts his hands around the iron bars that separate him from Mollel and the disparate cluster of other defendants who are crammed into the space.

—I came as soon as I heard, says Kiunga, leaning forward. I'll call Otieno. Get you out of here.

—No, whispers Mollel urgently. Not Otieno. Just do one thing for me, Kiunga.

—What is it? asks Kiunga. Anything!

—No conversing with the defendants! barks Judge Singh, hammering frantically. His voice is raised almost to a scream. Finally he seems to have broken through the chaos, and the babble of voices begins to diminish.

—Tell the truth, insists Mollel. Whatever you're asked, tell the truth.

—At last! gasps Judge Singh, in response to the hush that has descended upon the courtroom. He puts down his gavel and mops his brow with the cuff of his gown.

Kiunga looks quizzically at Mollel, then moves to take his place on the public benches.

—I should send the whole town away, mutters Judge Singh, shaking his head.

Bearded, bespectacled, turbaned, gowned. He is third-generation Kenyan – everyone knows the story of how his grandfather laid the first rails on the Lunatic line to Uganda – but Judge Singh retains his well-rounded subcontinental vowels.

—Who's up first? he sighs. His clerk approaches the bench and whispers something behind a cupped hand.

—Ah yes. He frowns. Mollel. Who is Mollel?

Mollel stands. Judge Singh makes a display of looking at him through, and then over, his glasses.

—Mollel, he says again, thoughtfully. He looks at his notes. Common assault. A most grievous crime. Do you have anything to say before I pass sentence?

The clerk coughs and scurries to the bench once more. Some words are exchanged.

—Well, why didn't you say so? snaps the judge. Then he turns to Mollel.

—This is an arraignment hearing, Constable Mollel, he says with a glare, as though Mollel had somehow attempted to mislead him.

—Yes, Your Honour.

—That was not a question, Constable. Kindly do not speak unless directly addressed. I hope that is understood.

Silence. The judge raises his eyebrows. Mollel shifts uncomfortably.

—Yes, Your Honour, he ventures.

The judge gives a *hmm-hmm* of satisfaction, and turns once more to his notes.

—You are accused of assaulting one Michael De Wit, a man

well known in this community as being of excellent character. How do you plead?

—Guilty, Your Honour.

—Indeed, replies the judge, in a bored tone.

Then: —What? What did you say?

—Guilty, Your Honour.

—Indeed? the judge asks, this time with surprise in his voice. You understand the charges, I take it?

—Yes, Your Honour.

Judge Singh blinks behind his thick glasses. Then he snaps his fingers for the clerk. There is more intense whispering between the two.

—The case is a serious one, says the judge, once his clerk has returned to his seat. Rendered all the more serious by your position as a police officer. However, taking into consideration your unblemished record . . .

Mollel looks around the court. In the public gallery sit Rhino Force: Shadrack, Mungai, Munene and Choma. In the row behind them is Kiunga, who gives him a thumbs-up.

—Not entirely unblemished, Mollel pipes up.

—What?

—Not unblemished, Mollel repeats, remembering to add: Your Honour. As I don't have counsel, may I call a witness?

The judge's clerk shoots him an empty-palmed shrug. Judge Singh slides his glasses down and pinches the bridge of his nose. —Why not? he sighs, resignedly.

—You are Sergeant Collins Kiunga, of Nairobi Police? Mollel asks.

—I am, says Kiunga, with a nod.

—And how long have you known the accused?

—The defendant? Kiunga looks lost for a moment. Then he realises Mollel means himself. Oh, yes, ah. I see. Well, I've known you . . . I mean, the accused, for nearly a year. Since just before the election.

—Thank you, says Mollel. And in that time, would you say

that the accused has always behaved in a professional and consistent manner?

—Oh yes, replies Kiunga, emphatically. You're ...

He gets fed up with referring to Mollel as the accused, and turns to address Judge Singh directly. —Mollel is one of the best policemen I know, Your Honour. I'd trust him with my life.

He turns back to Mollel with a broad grin, which immediately fades when he sees Mollel rolling his eyes in exasperation. *Whatever you're asked, tell the truth*, thinks Mollel, as though attempting to transfer the words telepathically to Kiunga.

—I've heard enough, says Judge Singh. Mollel, pending sentencing, I'm minded to release you to your colleagues.

Mollel sees Shadrack clench his fist victoriously.

—Wait, wait, he calls out. Your Honour, I have a few more questions.

—You've proved your point, Constable, snaps the judge. Even for a crime committed on a flower farm, there is such a thing as over-gilding the lily.

He smirks and looks around the court for approbation of his joke. None comes, save for an obsequious smile from the clerk.

—Sergeant Kiunga, continues Mollel, before the judge has a chance to stop him. Can you please tell the court whether, when you were working with the accused, he showed signs of erratic or violent behaviour? When questioning a suspect, for example?

Tell the truth. Whatever you're asked.

Kiunga looks at him. Conflict plays across his open, guileless face. His unease captivates the courtroom, already transfixed by the bizarre spectacle that is unfolding before them.

—Answer the question, if you please, Sergeant, insists the judge.

—Well, says Kiunga, quietly. It was a difficult time ...

—Did the accused, says Mollel, pointedly, ever threaten or intimidate witnesses?

—He did, mumbles Kiunga.

—Did he ever behave erratically?

—He might have done.

—He did, didn't he? He suffered blackouts. Fits of rage!

Kiunga looks at his former partner with incomprehension. Mollel is glaring at him, knuckles tight around the bars of the dock.

—Yes, Kiunga admits. All of those things.

Shadrack stands and faces Kiunga. —You traitor! He lunges toward him, only to be pulled back down into his seat by the mighty Munene. Judge Singh bangs his gavel furiously.

—Order in my court! he shouts. I may well send *two* policemen to prison today!

When the confusion has died down once more, the judge shakes his head.

—I've had quite enough of this case, he says. I'm well aware that the police service in this town seem to regard it as their private fiefdom. Well, they won't make a mockery of my court. You, Constable Mollel, you have succeeded in convincing me that you present a danger to the public, and shall be remanded in custody. Next case!

As Mollel is led from the dock, he glances at the faces in court. Smiling with satisfaction is a group he recognises as Mdosi's goons, the same ones who had welcomed Gachui upon his release from this very courtroom just two days before. In front of them is Kiunga, looking at Mollel with an expression of devastation. But old Choma winks at him as he passes, and Shadrack calls out: —Don't worry, Mollel! We'll take care of you yet!

There is another face, too. One he sees but does not entirely register until it is too late. A sad face, hidden among all the others at the back of the court.

Kibet.

12

Mollel gathered his cattle and then hurried to help Lendeva marshal his goats. Normally, this favour would have been far beneath his dignity, and Kep, his little white dog, looked at him with a certain sense of affront at being ordered to round up these plebeian animals. But as he thrashed his stick around, whistling and whipping the goats into order and driving them home, Mollel glanced over at Lendeva and the two of them shared a companionable smile.

Darkness had descended upon the *manyatta* by the time they reached it, and the *boma* was closed. There was no sign of their Uncle, whose absence was noted with both relief and anxiety by the latecomers. Relief, for he was not there to berate them with a stick or strap. Anxiety, for if he had waited so long that he had given up, he would be all the more furious when the time came for him to mete out punishment.

The two boys helped one another to lift the heavy, thorn-clustered branches of the *boma* gateway aside so that the animals could enter, then carefully replaced them, ensuring there were no gaps any wider than the thickness of an arm, and that no point was lower than Mollel could reach at full stretch. This was the minimum requirement for protection from lions, and although any leopard would make short work of such defences, even such a determined creature would find it impossible to drag out its kill once it had managed to get itself inside.

Still not knowing whether they had escaped a beating, or merely postponed it until morning, the two brothers headed back to their home.

This was the semi-permanent *enkaji*, not the nomadic construction of stakes, rope and skins which the family occupied whenever they trekked upcountry in search of dry-season pasture. The *enkaji* was made from lath daubed over with dung, with a thatched roof on top, a couple of narrow, hand-sized slit windows like vertical eyes – the same word was used in Maa for window and eye – and a low, arched doorway which was covered by a leather flap.

Except this time, it wasn't just covered by a leather flap. When Lendeva lifted it, he was confronted by a wall of timber planks.

Mollel heard his yell of surprise and indignation, and whoever was inside heard it too, for there was a sudden cry from within: their mother's cry.

Lendeva beat on the timber, and Mollel recognised even in that moment that it was the boys' own shared bed-shelf, upended. He pulled the smaller boy aside and gave it a flying kick, which sent the structure careening across the grounds.

The first thing to escape was a mass of smoke. There was no chimney in these *enkajis*, to keep pests out of a living area which was often shared by newborn or sick livestock.

Next out, spluttering, came Uncle. He was naked, and Mollel had to grab Lendeva to prevent the boy from flying at him.

—Well done, boys, he gasped. Thank *Enkai* you came. Your mother and I . . .

Mollel's mother appeared immediately afterwards at the doorway. She was semi-clad, clutching her *shuka* about her, her bent posture expressing shame and agony. Even in the light of the embers from the fireplace, they could see that her face was swollen and bruised.

Again, Lendeva strained forward, like Kep after a snake. Mollel nearly lost his balance trying to prevent the boy from knocking Uncle to the ground. Neither of them was in any doubt that he had come to claim his rights. But striking one's father – and whatever the reality of the situation, this man was legally their father – was among the most heinous of all crimes in the Maasai code.

Not long after Uncle tried to rape their mother, he was dead.

His own daughter, one of his real offspring, found him. The girl was collecting water at sunrise when she came across his corpse, twisted into an unnatural shape, mouth gaping and flecked with foam, eyes staring blankly.

Consensus in the *manyatta* was that he had been killed by Mollel's mother.

—You drove one of my sons to drink and death, screamed Grandmother, as the stiff, contorted figure was carried into the *boma*. Now you've murdered the other one! You're *laibon*! A witch!

They fell upon her house, pulling it apart. They overturned Mollel and Lendeva's bed, broke the cooking pot, dug holes in the earth floor. They found what they were looking for and came out clutching herbs, leaves, a knife, fragments of bone. Never mind that similar items could be found inside any home: this was the proof they needed to back up their assertion that witchcraft was the only explanation. Why else would he have left his home in the middle of the night, and be found with his body bearing the indisputable signs of magic?

A meeting of elders was convened, but no conclusions could be reached until Uncle's body had been taken up the mountain. Mollel immediately volunteered himself and Lendeva for the task.

—Are you insane? asked their mother. They'll never allow it.

—Why not? We're his eldest sons, insisted Mollel.

But the legal argument, so binding in life, was rapidly dismissed in death. No one from Mollel's family was allowed near the corpse, and in the end it was a group of *morans* who carried it away to the far, secret spot where the dead man's soul would be united with *Enkai*.

Pending the elders' decision, animals which had been their

own would pass over to the dead man's other wives and family, so Mollel and Lendeva were relieved of all herding duties lest they be tempted to strike away from the village with their former charges.

Perhaps it was fortunate that they were ostracised, because it gave Mollel the opportunity to take Lendeva aside and suggest his plan.

—We need to find Uncle's body.

One of the more garrulous *morans*, in exchange for the promise of a fine kid, should their flock be restored, let slip where the corpse had been taken.

—It's seated facing the setting sun, under a shelf in the rock where the old ones' paintings are. But if you want to see him, you'd better hurry. There won't be anything left by morning. The hyenas will make sure of that.

It made sense that the body had been deposited in the place that the old ones had found so sacred. The Maasai seldom dared go there, spooked by the strange scratches and daubs of pigment on the walls and ceiling of the wind-carved scoop in the side of the granite cliff. You could still see the blackening caused by the fires they lit, those old ones, so many generations before: long before the Maasai came to this land.

All Mollel knew of them was that they fell into neither of the categories that applied to most people. They had been neither herders nor farmers. They were a small people, so it was said, and scarcely knew metal. When the tall, disciplined Maasai descended upon them with their warriors and spears, they disappeared, leaving little behind but legend and these indecipherable inscriptions. Whatever they meant, the old ones obviously thought they conferred some kind of protection. And so it was here that Uncle's body had been placed, as though applying an antidote to the magic which had claimed his life.

It took a while to scramble there, up a path which was scarcely more than a *dik-dik* trail, and Mollel found himself reflecting that it was probably a good thing he had been banned from carrying the corpse himself. On the other hand, he'd never have bothered to treat it with such reverence, and would have been quite happy to leave it to fester where it was found, were it not for his burning desire to examine the remains himself.

Ahead of him, Lendeva bounced over the rocks like a klipspringer. Nearing the sacred site, Mollel heard him let out a loud *Ho! Tsh!*

He rounded a bush to see Lendeva walking away from him, his arms flapping wildly. As though in imitation of the boy, a big brown vulture had risen up on its scrawny feet, wings spread wide, and was flapping in similar fashion. As Lendeva drew closer, it finally conceded to the inevitable and took to the air, flying away from the cliffside with lazy, heavy beats. Something was hanging from its beak; a round something, which flew on the end of a piece of sincw.

An eye.

The body had been knocked over onto its back by the bird's ravages, but it remained in its sitting position, the legs cramped up and hands hovering above the knees. Lendeva stood above it.

—*Supai*, Uncle, he greeted the corpse with a grin.

Uncle grinned back.

His brown-toothed grin was more hideous than the gaping hole left by his plucked-out eye. The stretched lips were still flecked with traces of foam and his face left little doubt about the contortions which must have played across it in those final moments. Apart from rearranging the twisted body into a sitting position, little care had been taken over its presentation. There was also a strong smell, which indicated that the process of leakage had begun. Mollel was familiar enough with that from his livestock, but he'd never seen it in a human corpse before.

—Now, big brother, asked Lendeva. Are you going to explain why we're here?

—You start at his head, said Mollel. Look for a wound. A bruise.

Anything, in other words, that would ground his death in the physical world.

As Lendeva's hands traced the domed skull, Mollel turned his attention to the feet. They were easy to examine, thanks to the way the body had fallen: small, hard things, pockmarked with ring-shaped lesions which continued up the legs. But ringworm was nothing unusual. In fact, there was a disappointing lack of anything, as Mollel worked his way up, that could account for such a sudden demise.

—Have you found anything? he asked Lendeva, who had now made it down to the torso. A broken neck or caved-in skull, however mysterious its provenance, would at least rule out magic. But Lendeva shook his head.

There was no avoiding it; Mollel would have to remove the *shuka*. Gingerly, he untied the knot at the right shoulder and laid it open on one side. While Lendeva lifted the body up – in its stiffness, it pivoted on its backside – he continued unwinding the cloth. The final section, around the waist, came loose with a further waft of putrid stink.

The first thing Mollel saw was the tiny, shrivelled penis. It, and the area around it, was covered with small, round lumps; some of them almost the size of the pathetic organ itself. Whatever caused the complaint, and Mollel did not wish to speculate too much on that matter, it was unlikely to have been magic. But neither, unfortunately, was it a probable cause of death. This looked like something Uncle had lived with for a long time – in fact, now that he thought of it, Mollel realised the lumps accounted for the habit the little man had long displayed of scratching his crotch at every available opportunity.

Attempting to breathe as shallowly as possible, and through his mouth, Mollel turned his attention to the left buttock. There was evidence here, too, of both ringworm and the genital lumps. To examine the right buttock, he had to stand up, step over the body and kneel once more on the other side.

He gasped.

There. The right buttock was discoloured a deep purplish

black. The stain spread under the skin, making it puff out like rotting fruit.

Getting closer – even the gagging smell could not prevent him now – Mollel ran his fingertip over the flesh. It was cold and as hard as stone. Harder, even, than the undiscoloured section, which retained a little give under his touch.

His fingers found it before his eye saw it: a tiny hole. He squinted for a closer look. There it was, undoubtedly. A tiny, round hole. Nothing else.

Mollel called Lendeva over and the two of them looked at it.

—We should have known Uncle would get bitten on the ass some day, said Lendeva.

—That's what did this, isn't it? said Mollel, seeking confirmation of his suspicions. *Ol asurai?*

Lendeva agreed it was a puff adder. Nothing else could have caused such a wound.

—The only difficulty, mused Mollel, is that there is only one fang mark. There should be two. Of course, there could be any number of reasons. The snake might have been injured. Its other fang might have got caught in the folds of his *shuka*. But it's going to cause problems when explaining this to the others. Anything which looks unnatural is going to back up their claim it was magic.

While Mollel talked, Lendava had wandered over to a nearby thorn bush. He twisted a long, straight thorn from one of the branches and returned with it to the corpse, crouching down once more.

With sudden brutal force he rammed the thorn into the dead man's flesh just adjacent to the first wound. Pulling it out, he revealed a perfect hole, exactly the same size, the pair of wounds now clearly recognisable as a snake bite.

—There, said Lendeva, with satisfaction. Let's see them argue with that.

The elders came to the hillside just as the sun was setting: Lendeva had run swiftly to summon them while Mollel sat vigil with the corpse. His mission was to protect the evidence from hyenas, vultures, or any other scavenger that might be attracted to the rapidly putrefying form.

This vigil was what the *morans* were supposed to have done, but allegations of magic, the sacred location, or, more likely, laziness, had led them to shun their duty. Mollel found himself strangely glad to be doing it in their stead. He felt not the slightest hint of grief or regret over his uncle's death – indeed, insomuch as he felt any emotion, it pleased him – but the fourteen-year-old was a stickler for tradition, and tradition dictated that vigil be sat with a corpse.

He also felt a certain sense of satisfaction at having solved the mystery. Not only because it meant clearing his mother of having caused the death through witchcraft, but also because he had done his duty to the truth.

Yes, and to Uncle. For though few would mourn the little man – even his surviving wives and children were unlikely to lament him for long – he deserved to have the story of his death told accurately.

And although he had always felt that his future was planned out – boy, warrior, junior elder, senior elder, and eventually, perhaps, chief – for the first time Mollel was aware of another imperative. It was a sense of something besides destiny. It was *purpose*.

The verdict of the elders was unanimous: death from the bite of *ol asurai*, the puff adder. No one could understand why Uncle had walked out of his home in the dead of night. Perhaps he had gone to urinate and become disoriented. What mattered now was that Mollel and Lendeva's mother was no longer suspected of being a *laibon*, and their cattle and goats could be returned to them. Also, her missing husband had no more younger brothers, and so she was now free.

—You did well, said their mother to her sons. I've been thinking. The pair of you should join the police. You'd make great detectives.

Mollel laughed, but Lendeva did not.

—Really, Mother? asked the younger boy. You mean that? You want us to leave the *manyatta*? Wear *iloridaa enjekat* like the town people?

Mother giggled at the vulgar reference to trousers – the term meant *fart catcher* – but Mollel was cross.

—Of course she doesn't want that, scolded Mollel. We're to become warriors, Lendeva. Then we'll be able to look after you properly, won't we, Mother?

She looked at him with tears in her eyes, then clasped them both to her.

—Oh, my boys, my boys, she murmured. Go. Go away from here. Go as far away as you can. And don't stop.

13

—So, says Mdosi. You're the famous Mollel.

He's not what Mollel had expected. He is tall, yes, but not massive. The Big Man's name derives from his status, not his stature. His features are round, boyish; his eyes slope upward in a pleasant manner, as though amused.

His face, though, is not amused.

The door of the dispensary closes behind Mollel. He has no doubt that the guards who brought him here are waiting just beyond it, blocking his exit. Mdosi has lowered the shank of glass he pulled from the pot, and is carefully examining the Maasai.

—I heard about your little performance at the courthouse. There are four thousand men in this prison, Mollel, and we are the only two who are here by choice.

—I thought as much, says Mollel. A man like you doesn't end up in prison for a minor offence, unless he wants to.

—I figure it's the safest place for me right now, replies Mdosi. And as you can see, it's not too uncomfortable.

Mollel looks around the single room of the dispensary, that has been converted into Mdosi's private residence, with its curtains at the window, its rug, its calendar with scenes of snow-capped Mount Kenya, the small television flickering silently on a stool. And perhaps most enviable of all, there is a bed. The full-sized, proper bed.

Once again he is struck by the similarity in how people live.

Jemimah Okallo in her dormitory room at the flower farm. He and Shadrack, in their barrack rooms at the police post. And now Mdosi, Naivasha's richest man, and public enemy number one. All in their little rooms. All of them prisoners.

—So, Mollel. What brings you here?

—I wanted to see you. And I heard you're not taking visits from police officers.

Mdosi snorts. —Can you blame me? My men have been receiving visits from your colleagues. They suggest going out for a little walk, and they never come back. Gachui's just the latest. No one's heard from him in days.

Mollel recalls the prone and bloodied figure of Gachui lying at his feet. What had happened to him after Shadrack had dragged Mollel away?

Then he thinks about the others trying to get him into the car yesterday. Had he gone with them, he has no doubt he would have found out exactly what had happened to Gachui. Mollel suppresses a shudder.

—So they're after you, too, Maasai? says Mdosi, guessing at least half of what Mollel is thinking. I don't envy your choice. At least here I'm surrounded by my own people. You? You've got nothing.

—You want to stop these people smoking your boys, says Mollel. Believe it or not, so do I. The difference is, I've actually got a hope of doing it.

—Hah!

—I'm serious. I can't crack this gang until I know what they're doing with the bodies. And I can't discover that until they trust me.

—Well, you've blown that, haven't you, Mollel? They trust you so much they want to kill you!

—At the moment, yes, says Mollel. Which is why I'm here. I need to give them a reason to think they *can* trust me.

He puts his hand behind his back, lifts his tunic and removes an improvised shank from the waistband of his shorts. He holds it up.

Mdosi's eyes flash toward the door, but he's ready with the weapon of his own.

—Don't call out, warns Mollel. Not yet.

Mdosi shows a glint of teeth. —So you are the same as them after all, Mollel. I suppose you think I deserve it. Well, maybe I do. But I'll tell you one thing. You kill me, and you'll never get out of this prison alive.

The two of them stand facing each other in the flashing light of the TV. Bizarrely, Mollel can't help noticing that the programme being shown is an episode of *Cobra Squad*.

Mdosi makes a sudden dash toward him, but Mollel parries, knocking his hand away with his forearm. In the confined space, Mdosi crashes into the wall, sending the calendar fluttering to the floor.

—You alright in there? comes a voice from outside.

Mollel is holding the shank at Mdosi's throat.

—You're fine, Mollel hisses.

—I'm fine! shouts Mdosi.

—Now listen, says Mollel. This is what we're going to do.

Mdosi sits on the edge of the bed. Mollel kneels before him, blade in hand.

—Are you ready for this? he asks.

—Just do it, says Mdosi.

Mollel raises his left hand and runs the fingertips across Mdosi's temple. He is tender: as tender as his mother was when she shaved his head for the ceremony which marked the end of his days as a *moran*, and the commencement of his time as an elder.

Though he cannot know the intricacies of the ritual, Mdosi does not flinch. For a Maasai, flinching at this stage would mean a lifetime of shame. Mollel's fingers find what he is looking for: the vein that runs from the edge of the eyebrow to the scalp. He follows it to the hairline where, invisible to the eye, but not to the touch, it forms a tiny ripple in the skin over the hard, round skull beneath.

He presses and rubs the spot. Then with a swift, deft movement he swipes the blade horizontally across the vein. For a moment nothing happens. Then a few tiny beads of blood prick and glisten amid the short dark hair on Mdosi's brow.

—Is it done? asks Mdosi.

Mollel does not answer, but rises up to apply pressure to the cut. He puts down the shank, now, and starts to massage the scalp above the gash with both thumbs. For a moment he doubts his own expertise. He does not wish to do this again. And then it comes, quickly, suddenly. A pulsing stream.

Mdosi spits away the rivulet running into his mouth and raises his hand to greet the hot wetness pouring down his cheek.

—Let it flow, says Mollel. He wipes his own palm across Mdosi's cheek and smears the red print across the stripes of his tunic. He repeats the action a few times. Mdosi's own tunic is soaked deep red at the left shoulder. His ear, nose, chin, all shine with blood.

Mollel returns to the cut and presses his thumb into it. For the first time, Mdosi winces.

—I need to do this, Mollel whispers, solicitously. Now, come to the ground.

With his thumbs still pressed hard against the slippery cut, Mollel lowers Mdosi to the floor. —The flow has died down, he says. The vein wall there forms a seal quite quickly. It looks like a lot of blood, but you'll be fine.

—I'd better be, says Mdosi. I'll never be far from you, Mollel. We have a bond now.

—Trust me, says Mollel.

Mdosi closes his eyes. Then Mollel pounds on the door.

14

The noise swells and spreads. It fills every open space and passes through every closed door. It rattles the bars and shakes the walls. A noise you can feel in your feet and your chest. A noise both animal and mechanical, as the prisoners howl and hammer at the doors.

Fear flashes through the eyes of the guards. It flickers across the trophies and cups which wobble behind the glass doors of the cabinets. It rebounds from the plaque which bears the gilded name of every governor – switching suddenly in the 1960s from Andersons and Dickinsons to Okewmbas and Olouoches – and stirs the flags that hang from crossed spars on the wall: flags of Kenya, of Rift Valley province, of the prison service. Even the flat-screen monitor of the governor's computer trembles on his desk.

—We've got to call the army, sir, insists one of the officers.

The governor, roused from his bed, or someone's bed, holds up a finger that brooks no dissent. —Three months in this job, he says, wearily. Three months. I'm not going to be the governor who calls in the army to do a job his own guards are too scared to do.

—With respect, sir, says the officer, it's not that they're scared. We send our boys in there, now . . . they'll be ripped apart.

The governor closes his eyes and listens to the sound of the riot as though it is distant birdsong wafted in on a warm breeze.

—Why can't we just tell them this character, this Mdosi, is it? Why can't we just tell them that he's not dead?

—They wouldn't believe us, sir. His men saw him covered in blood, not moving. He stayed like that all the way to the ambulance.

The governor sighs. —And what are we supposed to do with *him*?

By *him*, he means Mollel, who is sitting between two of the innumerable guards packed into the governor's office, ostensibly for his protection, but in reality for their own.

—May I make a suggestion, sir? asks Mollel. He is not expected to speak, and his voice raises the hackles of the guards. —A quick call to Judge Singh could have me released into the custody of my colleagues in the local police. You might find that simply having me off the premises defuses the situation.

—Oh, you'd like that, wouldn't you, Mollel? replies the governor. Perhaps you'd like me to organise a flight to Cuba, while I'm at it? We don't have an extradition treaty with Cuba, do we, boys?

—I don't think so, sir, replies one of the officers, missing his sarcasm.

—No, Mollel, sighs the governor. I'm not going to have an escapee on my hands, in addition to a full-blown . . .

He stops himself before he says the word *riot*, and substitutes: *disobedience*.

Mollel shifts in agitation. He knows that one call to Otieno at Vigilance House – or wherever his boss might be at this time of night – would have him freed immediately. But the fact of the call would undoubtedly leak out. The same network of hearsay and gossip that he's relying on to spread word of his attack on Mdosi, thus restoring his trust with Rhino Force, would also paint him indelibly as a police spy.

He's going to have to bide his time.

Another officer makes an *Ah-hmm* noise.

—Well? What is it?

—The prisoner has a point, sir. Having him here is not helping matters. And we can hardly keep him in your office for ever, can we?

The governor concedes the point. —Get on to the Officer in Charge at Kamiti. Tell him we have an emergency transfer. But don't say anything about the disturbance. In the meantime, break out the hoses. A good soaking should calm them down. And if anyone asks, there's a small fire in the kitchen. Nothing anyone else needs to worry about.

Kamiti Prison. So it's back to Nairobi after all, for Mollel. Close to home – close to his son. But still behind bars. And far from this case.

He is led from the governor's office, cuffed and still damp with Mdosi's blood, through the small, thick wicket in the massive front gate of the prison's main building. The sounds of the riot still echo around him, and he sees a group of guards running to take command of a bowser with pump and hose. He does not envy those about to be on the receiving end of that washdown. But he realises his own situation is hardly more enviable.

For the first time, he wonders whether Otieno might not disown him. After all, this was supposed to be a secret operation. How would he explain one of his officers assaulting a civilian, and attacking another prisoner in gaol? Would he even bother? The same history of erratic behaviour that Mollel had called upon to ensure he was put away in the first place could now count against him. *It's just Mollel. He was always going to get locked up, one way or another.*

It all sounded so clear-cut and sensible when Otieno first assigned him to the case. *We'll avoid the paperwork on this one*, he'd said. *Keep it on a need-to-know basis.*

In other words, even back then, he was covering his own ass.

—Get in.

A shove on the back propels him into the prison bus. Mollel climbs the step and makes his way down the aisle. The first four rows of the bus – about one third of its length – are the same as any other bus: shabby bench seats and the stink of sweat. After the fourth row, though, there is a cage: thick iron bars form the doorway and mesh grids the opaque windows.

Prison officers, it seems, cannot see a doorway without pushing someone through it, no matter how cooperative their charge. Mollel is thrust through the final door into the bus's rear section, where he stumbles into one of the bench seats, his cuffed hands unable to reach out and prevent him from falling.

The inner door is locked behind him and he sees the guard exchanging duty with another, this one wearing a thick greatcoat and bearing a battered AK-47. The guard wearily takes a seat up front, sinks into his collar, crosses his rifle over his chest and gives every impression of being asleep. Before long a driver emerges, scowling and rubbing his stubble. He exchanges a few gruff words with the guard, takes his seat, and after a couple of rattling false starts, the engine splutters into life. The handbrake is released and the vehicle starts to move.

Wrists bound, Mollel finds it possible to maintain only the slightest grip on the back of the seat in front, so every corner sees him either sliding toward the aisle or crashing into the mesh over the window. Through the opaque glass he sees the lights of the town slipping past. It's a curious and nauseating sensation, looking down the length of the bus, unable to see out apart from through the distant windscreen, where odd flashes such as the backs of trucks or roadside hoardings are momentarily illuminated in the headlights. It's like being at the end of a moving version of the flower farm's polytunnel.

From the movement of the bus, Mollel is able to sense their progress. First, the long, straight road across the plain – few lights here – to the settlement of Mahi Mahiu, where the road branches to Narok and where a set of vicious speed bumps nearly sends Mollel crashing into the ceiling.

They head straight on, and a short distance beyond the town, the front of the bus begins to tip as the gradient increases. They are starting to mount the Kikuyu escarpment, a hair-raising climb of a kilometre in altitude in the space of fewer than ten kilometres by road. Mollel is glad, for once, that he can't see out to glimpse the broken or missing crash-barriers on each hairpin bend, the countless spots where hapless or impatient drivers have plunged to their doom into forested cliffside so steep even the plunderers of such wrecks are reluctant to descend to take their pickings.

The bus, ancient and ill-serviced, makes heavy going of the incline. The engine groans, each shift of the gears like a gasp for breath, a sickening split second in which the bus seems to be inexorably sliding backward before its hold on the road is regained.

Despite his best efforts, Mollel can't help but imagine the bus sliding off some misjudged corner, teetering on the precipice, then free-falling into the blackness below.

He'd be smashed like a tomato in a crate.

He becomes vaguely aware of a white flashing light, and it takes him a moment to realise that the source lies outside his own head.

The opaque rear window of the bus is illuminated in fitful, rapid bursts. Mollel can see two diffuse points of light: headlights. Some fool, eager to shave a few minutes off their journey back to the big city, has become frustrated with the fume-spewing, road-hogging prison bus and wants to force it deep into the overgrown rock face which abuts the inner lane, so that they can overtake. Better that, Mollel supposes, than the precipice.

He hears the leaves and branches, now, whipping the side of the vehicle as the bus driver tries to comply with his impatient tailgater. But still the lights flash, and now the honking of a horn accompanies the urgent semaphore.

Mollel can feel that they must be on a straighter section of the escarpment now. With a sudden growl, the car attempts to overtake, and he sees the white lights replaced by red in the side windows as it rushes past.

He expects the journey to regain its old rhythm but can tell that something is amiss. Above the huffing of the diesel engine, he can make out words being exchanged. He hauls himself up and mounts the sloping aisle. Reaching the door of the cage, he can see that the driver has his window open and is looking at the car alongside. The guard is there too, gun poised. Then there is a switch of gears and the bus swings to the right, onto level ground, the handbrake is slammed on and the engine shifts to an idling growl.

Now what? thinks Mollel.

The guard, slowly and cautiously, slips his rifle from his shoulder. He turns it around and bears it, butt first, before him. Then, as though approaching an unfamiliar dog, he inches his way toward the door.

The bus door opens with a scraping metallic sound, and a hand appears. The guard reluctantly passes his rifle forward and it is snatched away. Immediately he claps his hands to his head. The driver, too, eagerly copies this action, and the pair of them shuffle out of the vehicle.

Mollel shifts and strains to make out what is going on. He hears voices, and sees figures moving in the headlights of the bus.

He is sure of two things: first, that whoever pulled over the bus and disarmed the guard is sure to be the next person through that door.

And second, that they intend to kill him.

He is surprised to find himself contemplating which fate would be preferable: cowering under the back seats while the cage is raked by automatic fire, or bouncing off the ceiling once the handbrake has been slipped and the bus tumbles down the cliff to a fiery explosion below.

Most likely, it will be both.

As if on cue, a figure mounts the bus and leans over to the driver's seat. Instead of engaging the gear or slipping the handbrake, which Mollel has been expecting, he simply cuts the engine. After so long, the absence of sound makes Mollel's ears ring. The man starts to walk decisively down the aisle toward the cage. He carries an AK-47 and wears over his head a woollen balaclava with eyeholes.

So be it. At least let it be quick. Mollel grasps the bars of the cage door and closes his eyes.

He hears a metallic click and feels the bars fall away from him.

—Come on, says Shadrack. Let's get out of here.

They dismount the bus and Mollel is greeted by the sight of three more hooded figures, all bearing guns. There is no mistaking the giant form of Munene, the portly Mungai and the bandy-kneed Choma. On the ground, hands behind heads and faces in the dirt, are the prison guard and bus driver. Mollel is relieved to see that they appear to be unharmed – though not as relieved as he supposes they must be.

The bus has pulled over by a curio stall, one of the many perched on the edge of the precipice here, designed to lure in tourists in awe of the expansive view across the Great Rift. In daytime, the wooden trestles would be piled high with carvings, sheepskin hats and Maasai *shukas*. A hand-painted sign proclaims: WORLD'S END. BEST VIEW. PHOTOS NO CHARGE.

The car that Rhino Force had arrived in sits purring beside the bus. Mollel does not recognise it: it was presumably borrowed for the occasion. Shadrack puts a hand on Mollel's head as he guides him, still cuffed, into the rear seat.

15

A soon as they reach the long, straight road at the top of the escarpment, the policemen pull off their masks and begin to laugh loudly. Riotously. Mungai turns around in the front seat and pinches Mollel painfully on the cheek. Munene, driving, punches the steering wheel with exhilaration. Even old Choma's shoulders twitch with pleasure.

Mollel begins to feel nervous about the three AK-47s whose barrels are bouncing around in close proximity to his face. Having been so recently reprieved from a bullet, he does not relish the prospect of receiving one through carelessness.

They turn off the road and onto a wooded path. Waiting for them there is Shadrack's faithful old Toyota.

So this is to be the place. This narrow, rutted track, with tall, dark trees receding on either side, is to be the last place he sees on earth.

Here, dense forest forms the fringe of the plateau, eventually giving way to a patchwork of small farms, tea plantations and the occasional village, which merges into another, and then another, until there are no more villages, just the continual, scrappy sprawl which heralds the beginning of the outskirts of the great city of Nairobi.

Mollel feels a pang of homesickness. This is the closest he has been to his home – and his son – for weeks. Why, he could walk from here. Thirty miles is little more than a stroll for a Maasai.

He would arrive at Faith's funny little house in Kawangware in time to see Adam bounding in from school.

Even as he composes the image in his mind, he forces himself to expel it. Such thoughts can be nothing but torture, for there will be no homecoming. Not for Mollel.

—You see, Mollel? says Shadrack. Rhino Force look after their own. Not like that Kiunga pal of yours. Some friend he turned out to be.

—He was never my friend, replies Mollel. Just someone I used to work with.

Distantly, he can hear a cockerel greeting the first grey fingers of dawn.

—Tell me something, Mollel, says Shadrack quietly. Mollel turns to face him. In the creeping light, with dark rings under his eyes and a hint of stubble on his chin, the boy looks older than his years. You did it for a reason, right? I mean, he was threatening you, or something?

—Yeah, says Mollel. Something like that.

—I knew it, says Shadrack. I knew there had to be a reason. I mean, even in *Cobra Squad* they never shoot someone in cold blood. Not unless that someone's got a gun on them.

A surge of hope rises in Mollel's breast. There is a shadow of humanity in Shadrack's words which is at odds with his imminent execution.

And yet, why else would they spring him from prison, if not to put him in a place where he could never testify against them?

—That was a pretty brave thing you did in there, Mollel, says Mungai. Brave, or stupid. If we hadn't got you out, I wouldn't have given you twenty-four hours. Even if they'd transferred you to Kamiti. Mdosi's connections go deep.

The light begins to pick out details in this anonymous scene: first, individual trees. Then branches and leaves. And Mollel is starting to allow himself to believe that this dawn may not be his last.

He ventures conversation.

—What's the word on Mdosi? Last I saw, he wasn't looking too good.

—Still hanging on, replies Munene. But he'll know now that even inside, he's got no protection.

—You did well, Mollel, says Shadrack. You proved yourself.

Before Mollel can ponder this statement, Mungai thrusts a thick red and black chequered blanket into his hands. —Here, he says. Sorry it's not a Biashara Street three-piece suit. But I reckon, in the circumstances, it's your best option.

Shadrack produces the keys he took from the guard and un-cuffs Mollel. Then he opens the car door and steps out. Old Choma does likewise on the other side of Mollel, leaving him to slide along the seat and place his bare feet on the wet grass.

—Jesus, Mollel, says Shadrack. I'd give you my shoes. But you're better off without them.

Mollel unfolds the red blanket and wraps it around his shoulders against the cold dawn. It's a movement which is instinctive, evocative, and which he has not done for years. The last time he wore a *shuka* would have been before he was married, and before he was a policeman.

And right now, he is neither.

—What do I do now? he says, as much to himself as to anyone else.

—Disappear.

Because he is usually so silent, Choma's voice – light, and surprisingly youthful – always takes Mollel by surprise.

—Just disappear, Mollel, Choma continues. You're a Maasai again, now. You can go wherever you like. Walk due south from here and you'll be in Tanzania in a few days. Find yourself a village that needs an elder. Pick yourself a wife.

Shadrack presses an envelope into Mollel's hand. —It's not much, he says. But it's from all of us. Should be enough to buy a few cattle.

—Or a wife, laughs Mungai.

—You'll need these, too. Shadrack passes him a rather fine leather-sheathed dagger. A belt. A yellow walking stick.

—Get word to us when you're settled, continues Shadrack, and we'll arrange for your son to be brought out to you. You'll be together again, Mollel. In a place far from here.

—A fresh start, says Mungai. You were never cut out to be a policeman, anyway.

—And all this, murmurs Choma, waving his hand as though casting a spell, all this never happened.

Money means little to Mollel. Cars, booze, status, women: the things that money can buy, that his police colleagues have always craved, mean even less. He does not drive, he does not drink. He has given up the only two titles that ever meant anything to him – *sergeant* and *elder* – and lost the only woman he ever loved.

Throughout his career, he has always felt himself to be incorruptible. It is part of his identity. His self-worth. His pride.

His vanity.

While all those around him trousered bribes here, *chai* money there, turned a blind eye here, turned a screw there, grafted, gifted, lifted, extorted; extracted *kitu kidogo* here, *Christmas money* there, this and that, give and take, hustling, oiling wheels, greasing palms, lining pockets, soliciting, eliciting, dipping, skimming, creaming a little off the top, earning a little on the side – while they all did that, Mollel stood apart.

Or so he thought.

Perhaps he was not incorruptible. Perhaps he'd never been offered the right bribe.

There is undeniable and intense appeal in the prospect he suddenly finds himself being offered. To disappear; to melt away. To leave it all behind him: Otieno, the department, the danger, the stress, the boredom. And all he'd have to do is walk.

Shadrack offers his hand.

—Goodbye, Mollel. Good luck.

They get into the Toyota, reverse down the lane, swing out into the road and are gone.

Mollel starts walking. He eschews the road in favour of the forest path. As he had anticipated, it is not long before the gaps between the trees ahead begin to glow. Almost before he knows it, the soft pine needles beneath his feet crumble away and he pauses, holding on to a serrated trunk, and looks out at the expanse below. The floor of the Great Rift Valley. A composition in green and gold, flecked by the shadows of clouds which scud high above, yet are still beneath where Mollel stands.

Distant blue mountains rise. Suswa; Longonot. Volcanoes, once. Mountains of God. To the south, Tanzania. To the north, the narrow strip of road which leads back to Naivasha and Maili Ishirini.

How many Maasai have stood, as he now stands, and surveyed this land? There was a time when their possession of it was complete and unchallenged. No border and no road divided it. Even the white man's maps acknowledged Maasailand. No Kikuyu dared pass through this territory without paying homage to the Maasai, lest he find himself bristled with arrows like a porcupine.

Invisible from here, the filaments of barbed wire which segment this landscape. Invisible, the homesteads and farmsteads which now dot it.

After a little searching, Mollel finds a path which zigzags down the escarpment. Every step, it seems, is accompanied by the slightest rise in temperature, a certain thickening of the air. The change in vegetation is stark and remarkable. Where pine forests crested the top of the ridge, the middle ground is clustered with round euphorbia, their candelabra branches studding the steep slope like giant map pins. Between these dinosaurs, voracious lantana billows and spills, narrowing the path to little more than a trail, its tiny, candy-coloured flowers nodding as Mollel swipes past and coating the air with their sticky fragrance.

And before he knows it, Mollel is among Maasai sights and smells again. The red dust on his feet, the fresh, sharp scent of the *leleshwa* bush. With something approaching joy, he snatches a sprig and snaps it off. He crushes the leaves and rubs them across his chest and under his arms, breathing in deeply the healthy smell of sage.

At a division in the track, the chattering of an oxpecker alerts him to company; glistening beads of dung on the track mean that the sound of goat bells is no surprise. The boy, though, who is lying beneath a candelabra tree, jumps out of his skin when Mollel kicks his feet.

—You'll lose your herd, Mollel says, in Maa. Speaking his own mother tongue, usually such a struggle for him, seems perfectly natural and effortless in this setting.

The boy leaps up and sees the wagging tail of a goat picking its way up the cliffside. —*Ashe!* the boy cries in thanks, and he bounds off in pursuit.

Mollel watches him fondly. If he'd lost his herd, he reflects – if he'd lost even a single kid – he'd have received a beating.

And there were such beatings. Plenty of them. There didn't even need to be a reason – any reason, that is, other than the sour smell of honey beer on his father's breath.

Other memories begin to rise like a river in flood.

Of constant migration in pursuit of pasture. Of the lean years, when the grass withered to straw and the animals wore their ribs like zebra stripes.

Of raids – by *morans* from other villages, or by gun-wielding rustlers with lorries in which to carry off the precious cattle they stole.

Of the day the girls were taken into the *boma* and made into women.

Of death, from snake bite, or lion, or simple sickness. Of racking coughs and pus-streaming eyes – none of which was an excuse to avoid herding – then the only cure was a vile-smelling concoction of earth and herbs and ash that was smeared onto the chest, or, in extremis, swallowed.

Of *ukimwi*. That disease of outsiders which so ravaged the Maasai, which no herb or potion could cure. Which killed *moran* and elder, wife and infant alike, leaving them like parched, desiccated skeletons inside a skin of ashes.

—Wait! he calls to the boy, just visible now above him. Where do these paths lead?

—The left one, to the mountain, says the boy. The right, to the lake. So they say. I've never been there.

The shadows have shrunk and lengthened again by the time Mollel reaches Maili Ishirini. The last few miles have meant clambering over barbed wire, or diverting his path to follow high, long electric fences. Eventually he is forced to trudge resentfully along the side of the road, covering his head with his *shuka*, partly against the dust from passing vehicles and partly against recognition.

He approaches the settlement cautiously, ready to avert his face should he see someone he knows. He clings to the close-cropped hedges of the flower farm as though they might shelter him from sight. Like a small animal, he distrusts open spaces.

But his first challenge lies ahead: the gateway to the Lakefront Hotel. He has passed through these gates many times in the last few days. And two of the guards, who he remembers from his visits, are standing chatting at the entrance.

He shucks his shoulders, buries his chin in his chest and quickens his pace. Keeping his eyes firmly fixed on the road ahead, and attempting to exude an air of perfect self-absorption, he strides forth.

He is almost all the way across when:

—*Weh! Mzee!*

He tries to affect that he has not heard, but a falter in his step gives him away.

—Are you deaf, old man? I'm calling you.

Mollel turns slowly, eyes lowered.

Even as he does so, a memory surfaces. Jemimah Okallo, on the road, before her death. He, Mollel, trying to engage her. She avoiding his gaze, ignoring his questions.

In her place, he fully comprehends what it feels like to face authority. He understands the urge to become invisible.

—What are you doing?

—Just passing, murmurs Mollel.

—Are you going into the village?

He nods.

—Well, get me something to eat, won't you? A *mandazi*.

Mollel assents, and turns to leave.

—Wait!

He pauses once more.

—Don't you want some money to pay for it?

The guard holds out his hand with a few shillings in it. —And make sure it's fresh!

The two of them laugh as Mollel continues on his way.

At the little grocery shop, waiting for his *mandazi*, Mollel looks at himself in the spotted mirror which hangs behind the counter.

Now he sees why they called him *Mzee*. Old man. The dust has worked its way into the lines on his forehead, around his eyes and mouth. His cheeks are hollow with hunger and his eyes dim from tiredness. It is several days since he shaved, and the stubble is grey on his cheek.

Any vestige of Mollel, policeman, is gone. Now he is just *Mzee*. Another old Maasai, out of place and out of time.

He need not worry about being recognised. He hardly recognises himself.

Mollel takes a *mandazi* for himself as well as the one for the guard. He chews the doughy snack eagerly as he leaves the shop and squats, bow-legged, under an acacia tree between some market stalls.

This could work out well for him, he muses. He has returned to Maili Ishirini with no real idea of his next move. Yet now he knows he can hide in plain sight, he realises the value of his new persona.

His trek has also helped clarify his thoughts. His mind had

apparently been vacant as he walked the landscape, pondering nothing other than the sounds and smells and where to place his feet. But somehow, along the way, the events of the last few days have become ordered, processed.

He has gained the trust of Rhino Force at the expense of them not wanting him around. Well, that can't be helped. He needs an excuse to turn up again, and Jemimah Okallo will provide it. Shadrack had accused Mollel of being obsessed with that case; it would be plausible for him to want to wrap it up before he disappeared for good.

He rises to his feet, somewhat stiffly. It has been a long time since he sat upon the ground. At least the movement chimes with his new-found old man image. As he stretches, he looks up and sees Beatrice standing at the entrance of her cellphone shop, her ample frame filling the doorway. She raises a hand to shade her eyes and peers at him. He ducks his head down and quickly scuttles away.

—Here, he says, handing the greasy paper bag containing the *mandazi* to the hotel guard.

—Thanks, says the guard, taking it and biting into the pastry with relish. We wondered whether you were coming back.

—A Maasai always keeps his word, says Mollel.

—Oh, we know that! the guard replies with a laugh. You guys got that bond of honour thing going on. Makes life hard for everyone else. You're doing the rest of us out of a job.

The two guards here, wearing the dark blue uniform of a private security firm, are not Maasai.

—What do you mean? asks Mollel.

—We're expensive, chips in the other guard. We have proper training, proper backup. Look.

He pulls a chain out from under his shirt. Dangling at the end is a white plastic device with a small red button at its centre.

—Backup, he explains. Any trouble, we press this. The control room gets the signal, and the patrol van's here in minutes.

—The Maasai don't have anything like that, grumbles the

first guard, through a mouthful of *mandazi*. They just whack the ground with their *rungu* and their mates come running.

Mollel remembers being taught that trick as a boy. The repeated sound of the thump of a heavy wooden club on the ground could travel a long way. If you heard it, it meant someone was in danger. And nothing, not even tending your flock, could excuse a Maasai who failed to answer the call.

—Plus, the bosses don't have to worry about insurance. If a Maasai gets injured on the job, their stupid honour code means it's a badge of shame. He just disappears and is replaced the next day by another Maasai. No paperwork, no training. He's straight on the job.

—They've already virtually taken over the security next door, continues the first guard, with a nod in the direction of the flower farm. It'll be us next.

Mollel's desire for invisibility seems almost to have come true, for despite his presence, the guard adds, in a mutter: —Savages.

Mollel thinks about his theory that Jemimah was attempting to get back into the flower farm. What if the Maasai have decided to deal with an intruder in their own way? It did not ring true. The same code of honour these guards complained about – the code so inculcated in him during his own childhood – forbade attacks on women. But then, he considers, that never stopped his father.

The memory of his father brings the realisation that Mollel, now, must resemble him closely. Self-consciously he pulls the *shuka* around his chest.

Just then, the guards spring to attention. A large, blacked-out Land Cruiser is rumbling down the driveway from the hotel. They each take one of the sides of the double gate and swing it open, standing stiffly with a salute as the vehicle drives past.

It pauses for a moment while the driver checks the road ahead is clear – and then it pauses a little longer. The rear passenger window whirs down and a round, pale face looks out. Chinese eyes scrutinise Mollel.

—You, says the passenger.

Mollel points dumbly at himself.

—Yes, you. Get in.

The door swings open and the passenger moves over to make room for him. Mollel does as he is bid, and to the barely disguised astonishment of the two security guards, he gets into the car and closes the door behind him.

16

It was policeman's instinct that led him to get into the car, and it is policeman's instinct that now compels him to keep his mouth shut. That seems to suit the car's other occupants just fine; the Chinese man by his side and the local driver also remain silent.

He watches the route carefully. There's every chance that, once they find out he's not whoever they think he is, he'll be walking home. Despite their strength, his wiry legs give a twinge of protest at the prospect of a second trek in one day.

They hug the lakeside road until just outside Maili Ishirini, where they strike off on the steep track which leads up to the National Park. They pass the gate to the rhino sanctuary but do not enter; instead, they follow the access road which runs parallel to the high electric fence which bounds it.

Around them, the whispers of dusk begin to settle. This is unfamiliar territory to Mollel; and soon the landscape becomes unfamiliar, too. The car slows and sways on its axle as the terrain beneath the wheels changes from dirt and gravel to something different.

The car crests a rise and a new vista emerges, black and gleaming in the dying rays of the sun: these are the obsidian fields. From cruel, tiny shards to massive, planed boulders, the volcanic glass lies all around, unmoved from where it was spat out through the air millions of years ago. Interspersed with it are tall towers of brown lava, fringed and pitted like dead coral. Once, this must have been a scene of pure hell; today, it is scarcely more comforting.

Mollel's bare feet, leathery as they are, would stand no chance here. Nor, it seems, does anything but the most basic form of life. Here and there an unlucky shrub bursts from a pocket of windblown soil; a glimpse, occasionally, of something like a lizard darting into a prehistoric hole.

The roadway here has been cut straight out of the rock and is unforgiving, even to the high-quality suspension of the Land Cruiser. The driver grips the wheel like a sailor in a storm, and Mollel and the Chinese man both reach for the handles at head height and sway and jolt with each new buffeting.

Up ahead, a tall swathe of gold stands proud against the darkening horizon, billowing like a sail unmasted. As the sun disappears behind the sharded hills at their backs, its colour changes to a suffused, ghostly white. Another crest, and Mollel sees the reason why. A broad chimney, picked out in red and white stripes by powerful spotlights, rises from the land. All around it, pipes worm and writhe and hiss; they rise up toward the chimney as though worshipping some totem, and from its crown pours the powerful jet of white steam.

A gate is before them, its pillars topped with red plastic Chinese lanterns. DOUBLE COIN DRILL CO., the sign reads, alongside a set of Chinese pictograms. They crunch through the gate, which is unguarded, and drive up to a collection of corrugated white boxes – shipping containers, with doors and windows punched into their sides and air-conditioning units attached to them.

A number of Kenyan workers in boiler suits and plastic helmets are sitting on a bench outside one of the units, not talking, eating from bowls perched on their knees. Mollel is reassured by the sight of them, for he knows he is shortly to learn why he has been brought here, and does not anticipate a happy reception should anyone realise they've got the wrong man. At least the local workers provide him with some kind of witness.

The driver cuts the engine and Mollel immediately understands why none of the workers is talking: a curious sight when Kenyans and food are brought together. It's because of the noise. A dual-toned heavy throb and a roaring, hissing whoosh, like a passing jet which does not pass.

The Chinese man gets out of his side and Mollel does likewise. He treads gingerly on the ground, but thankfully the obsidian and lava here have been crushed to such an extent that the gravel is almost comfortable on the soles of his feet. He attracts a few curious glances from the workers, who nonetheless decline to acknowledge him with so much as a nod. The Chinese man, though, beckons to him, and Mollel follows him to the door of one of the converted shipping containers.

A charm, picked out in red and gold, is pinned to the door. The Chinese man turns the handle and holds it open for Mollel, who enters.

Inside, the light is low and yellow, the air thick with cigarette smoke. At a table, a desultory card game is in progress, from which four faces look up. This, Mollel knows, is the moment when his identity will be challenged.

But it is not.

The four Chinese men – five, including the one who brought him here, and who now closes the door behind them, sealing out the majority of the noise – look at this bizarre figure before them. Robed in a *shuka*, barefoot, dusty, a dagger sheathed at his waist, Mollel realises that he is the alien here, in his own country.

—Take a seat, says one of the men.

They shuffle round the table to make space for the two newcomers. As he takes his place, Mollel notices the way the man next to him flinches with distaste, and moves a little further. In contrast, one of the men opposite him, a younger man with glasses and a lively, intelligent face, beams at him broadly.

—So, he says, in barely accented English, you're a Maasai.

—I am, says Mollel.

—Would you like a cigarette? Some whisky?

—No thank you, says Mollel. But he accepts the offer of a glass of water, which he drains in one draught.

—We have people like you in China, continues the young man. Not so many, now. But still, there are some who continue the old ways.

Mollel feels a sense of disappointment. His policeman's instinct has apparently failed him. He has not been brought here for any reason other than to be displayed, exhibited and interrogated – a curiosity, a spot of local colour.

—In many ways, continues the young man, pouring himself a glass of whisky, I see China here in Africa. Not as she is now, of course, but how she once was. That's why we are here. To bring the economic miracle to the dark continent.

The man toasts his own munificence with a flourish, then downs the whisky. The others at the table exchange a look and Mollel feels a flush of pity for the young man, so far from home and evidently out of sympathy with his colleagues.

—You know, he continues, I come from Shanghai. When I was growing up, people still lived in bamboo huts in the swamp. That swamp is a district of skyscrapers now. And you know what made it happen? Energy.

He holds up a finger and smiles. —Hear that? Energy. Unlimited energy. Energy to make roads, and factories, and cities. And you fellows have been sitting on top of it for years! Now, finally, thanks to us, you're getting to use it.

Mollel shifts uneasily. He's not sure whose vision is being shared here. Certainly the other men in the room seem less enthusiastic about the whole project.

The young man's gaze does not move from Mollel. Mollel realises that he is being admired, not for who he is, but for who he could be. He feels like standing up and saying: *I don't wear this, usually. I wear a suit, or a uniform. I live in a block of flats in Nairobi and I have satellite TV. My son plays computer games and I spend my off-duty days in supermarkets and traffic jams. I know what the modern world is like, thank you very much.*

But he says nothing.

One of the other men, the oldest-looking of the five, starts speaking crossly to the young man. Mollel infers from his tone that he has heard these romantic notions before and is having none of it. His assumption is confirmed when the older man turns to Mollel and says gruffly: —Enough talking. Now business.

Mollel is suddenly interested. Perhaps his instinct was correct, after all.

—We've heard, says the young man, who seems to take the lead, perhaps because of his good command of English, rather than his seniority within the group, that you're good at making people disappear.

Good at making people disappear.

When he had been offered the lift in the car, Mollel had immediately assumed that it was a case of mistaken identity. After all, he had to admit, he would find it hard to pick out any of these Chinese workers from a line-up. Why shouldn't it be the same for them? One Maasai must look much like any other. They had seen him at the hotel gate, and had been expecting someone else – perhaps Tonkei, or one of his men.

But now they were talking about disappearances. And that was the local police's speciality.

—Go on, he says, cautiously.

—We have someone here causing us trouble. Someone interfering with our business interests.

Unconsciously, Mollel looks around him, as though taking in the entire drilling operation beyond these metal walls.

—Not this, says the young man, picking up Mollel's reaction. Something else. A sideline.

Mollel raises his eyebrows, but the young man's eyes flicker. —You don't need to know. You just need to tell us whether or not you can do it.

—If the price is good, says Mollel, we can do it.

This causes some amusement around the table.

—There won't be any need for payment, says the young man. She's as dangerous to your operation as she is irritating to ours.

She.

Mollel's chest tightens.

—Who is it? he asks.

—That little ranger from the National Park. Her name is Esther Kibet.

17

At the contractors' suggestion, Mollel gets a lift back to the lake-side in the bed of a pickup carrying some of the local workers. The jolting road makes talk as impossible as it was at the plant, but Mollel is not in the mood for conversation. He is convinced that these workers know nothing of the management's *sideline*, whatever it is, so there is no point quizzing them about it.

Instead, his thoughts are filled with Kibet. The Chinese had warned that she was a *danger* of some sort – if so, could that potentially make her his ally? But she had seen him assaulting Gachui, and Gachui had later disappeared.

And she was an irritation to the Chinese. An irritation which warranted her disposal.

As the truck drives past the ranger's post at the side gate of the park, on impulse Mollel bangs his hand on the cabin roof to ask the driver to stop. He hops out, giving a swift wave of thanks, and heads for the gate.

Even the main public entrance would be dark and silent at this time; this place shows even fewer signs of life. Once the red tail lights of the pickup have vanished down the track, the only light Mollel has to make out his surroundings comes from the stars. He can just distinguish the shape of the main building, and the conical roofs of the metal shacks where the rangers live. But he can hear that there is activity, of sorts. A TV or radio is playing, and gradually he becomes aware of a small square of colour: a curtain drawn across a window, masking a faint light within.

Hoping he is not making a mistake – he does not want his presence here to become common knowledge – he reaches down and picks up a handful of gravel. Carefully, as he knows what brushing against an electric fence feels like, he gets as close as he dares to the perimeter and tosses some stones in the direction of the square of light.

They rattle against the glass and tin, but nothing happens.

Again, he picks up a handful and launches them forward. He pitches a little higher this time, so that the gravel rains down upon the tin roof and rattles against its sides.

This time the curtain twitches. A face appears in silhouette; he recognises Kibet's profile, and raises a hopeful hand. But the curtain falls again with no further sign of acknowledgement.

Wary of bringing the whole ranger station out against him, Mollel holds off repeating the action a third time. He backs away from the fence, wishing he had his cellphone with him. But it was still sitting in a box somewhere deep inside Naivasha Prison.

Then he has an idea. He takes the club which Shadrack gave him to complete his Maasai costume. It's a short *rungu*, about twelve inches long, carved from a piece of solid ebony, as hard as stone and culminating in a heavy bulb: pity the skull that comes into contact with such a weapon.

Mollel crouches down and selects a soft patch of dirt with the fingers of his left hand. Then, raising the *rungu* in his right, he begins to pound the ground.

Thump – thump – thump.

He keeps his eyes fixed on the window. He waits.

Just as he raises the *rungu* to strike the ground once more, he is halted by a sudden flood of white light.

—Drop the weapon!

He almost laughs at the sound of Kibet's voice, but he does not, because he knows she has a gun trained on him. Instead, he lets the *rungu* fall to the ground and raises his hands.

—Mollel?

This time he can't help it. The incredulity in her voice is such that he breaks into a broad smile, and shields his eyes against the flashlight.

—You look *terrible*, she says.

He sits in her little hut, hands wrapped around a mug of *chai*. The radio which he could hear from outside has been turned up even louder to mask the sound of their voices. Kibet explains that, when her colleagues get back from patrol, she does not want to give them the opportunity to gossip about her having a man in her room.

—Although it would certainly surprise them, she adds, with a chuckle.

Kibet's hut, his room at the police post, Jemimah Okallo's bunk in the dormitory at the flower farm. His one-time prison cell. Even the Chinese living out of their shipping containers. So transient, so impersonal. Still, she has done her best with this space. Some KWS posters cheer up the metal walls. A reed rug covers part of the pounded earth floor. A couple of chairs, a trunk with an embroidered cloth covering it, a few photographs in cardboard frames placed on top of it.

—How did you get out of prison? she asks him.

He shakes his head.

—Alright, she continues. What do you plan to do now? Where will you go next?

Again, he shakes his head. She gives an exasperated sigh.
—Well, I hope you're not planning on staying here. Because I might be able to cover for you for one night, but anything more would be noticed.

—I don't need to stay, says Mollel.

—Is it true what they said in court? About your . . . condition?
—It's true.

Kibet gives a long, low whistle. —You've had it pretty rough, huh?

Mollel sips his *chai*. —No one has it easy.

—And this came about ... you got like that ... because of what happened to your wife?

He closes his eyes for a moment. As ever, the images are never far from the surface. Images of rubble, dust and blood.

He kept going back. They called him a hero, because he kept going back. He brought dozens of people out of that blasted building, but he never found his wife.

The hero Mollel, who would have let them all die if only he'd found her.

The incorruptible Mollel, who would sell his soul if only it could bring him some peace of mind.

—We're not so different, you and I, says Kibet.

He opens his eyes. She is wrapped in a thick dressing gown, with the hem of a nightshirt showing beneath, her slim ankles and feet exposed. Her feet are small and delicate, and without her uniform and boots, she looks vulnerable and feminine. Even the curve of her head is girlish without her beret covering her close-cropped hair.

—When I found you laying into Gachui, she continues, her dark eyes meeting his, if I hadn't stopped you ... would you have stopped?

Mollel shrugs. He does not know. There are two truths about that moment. The first, that he was compelled to beat Gachui. The second, that he wanted to. He wants to say both, and dares not say either.

—You know what he did?

—He raped a woman, says Mollel.

Kibet flinches at the baldness of the statement. —Yes, he did, she says. But do you know the circumstances?

—I know it was at the IDP camp.

Internally Displaced Persons. Mollel thinks of the encampment on the outskirts of town. Row upon row of tents behind a high chain-link fence. Another cluster of human lives parcelled out and portioned in a place they did not wish to be.

—It was my people who drove them there, continues Kibet, with a shudder. Kalenjin people. People who had lived with one another for generations. When the Kikuyus and the Luos began killing each other in Nairobi, in Naivasha, the whispering began. *We'll be next.*

—Old resentments about Kikuyu wealth, old myths about Kikuyu land-grabbing came to the surface again. And when a group of Kikuyus started to gather in one of the churches, the whispers said: *It's beginning.*

—It was beginning, of course, but not the way they thought. The people had just gone there for safety. For sanctuary. They never found it.

Mollel closes his eyes once more, but this time the images of fire and corpses come not from his own experience, but from the memory of news reports.

—Those who escaped came here. They came with their children, and what they could carry. And Mdosi and his gang – Gachui, the lot of them – saw it as a business opportunity.

—They were allowed into the camp – did a deal, no doubt, with whoever was in charge – and set up shop. Unlimited credit. And the IDPs trusted them. Why shouldn't they? They were their own people.

—And then the interest kicked in. One hundred per cent a day. And those who could not pay . . .

She tails off. But Mollel has already heard this story. Gachui decided to extract his own payment, and no doubt did so as publicly as possible, to send a powerful message to the rest of the camp.

Mollel recalls his first encounter with Kibet on the steps of the courthouse, protesting at Gachui's release. But he wonders if it really was their first encounter. Something has been nagging at him, something which he feels is just within his grasp.

—You're not afraid of making enemies, are you? he asks.

—I don't need to make enemies, retorts Kibet. I'm a woman.

Despite her attempts to appear otherwise, thinks Mollel. The uniform, the boots, the attitude. And then it strikes him. The person he and Shadrack had been staking out at the brothel in Maili Ishirini. The spray-painter.

That could be cause enough for the Chinese to want to get rid of her. If she was driving away trade from their favourite pleasure house – the only pleasure house in the district.

—Kibet, he says. I came to warn you. Your life is in danger.

Her response is an unexpected laugh.

—You broke out of prison to tell me that? I could have spared you the effort.

She stretches and yawns. The action annoys Mollel.

—You've got to give up your campaign, he says. It's a worthwhile cause, but you're only one person. You can't make a difference.

Even as he says it, he hears echoes of his mother-in-law.

—What if we all thought like that, Mollel?

—Everyone does.

—*You* don't.

She is looking at him intently.

—Who are you, Mollel?

The question takes him by surprise. Who is he? A policeman? Prisoner? Vigilante? Spy?

He deflects the question. —You don't know who you're up against.

—I know perfectly well, she replies. Mdosi and his gang don't scare me.

—It's not just them any more, says Mollel.

He tells her about the Chinese workers. Their plan for her to disappear. Slowly, the complacency drops from her face and defiance is replaced by fear.

—They're not amateurs, Kibet, he says. They mean business.

—I know, she says softly. I know. But it's not just about me. If it were just me, I could give it up. But there's someone else.

The words *someone else* cause a little tremor inside Mollel. He'd assumed she was alone, like him. But then the photographs on the metal trunk tell a different story. There are people in them. He can't see clearly in the gloom of the paraffin lamp, but one image looks like Kibet, with long hair. And a child.

—You see, continues Kibet, you've got it all wrong, Mollel.

It's not about the brothel. They want to get rid of me because they know I'll never allow them to get to *her*.

Her?

The confusion must have registered on his face, because she gives a slight smile and says: —Pass me my boots. It's alright. The other rangers won't be back from patrol for a while.

They step into the cold night air and Mollel feels his tired bones protest at leaving the snug, warm hut behind. Kibet turns on her flashlight and they pick their way across the ranger post. They reach a high gate and Kibet produces some keys and unlocks a padlocked chain.

Everywhere, fences and gates. Locks and chains.

The two of them slip through the gate and Kibet carefully fastens it behind them.

—Be very quiet, she whispers.

Mollel makes no reply. The injunction was unnecessary; the night encourages nothing other than silence.

The flashlight beam wobbles over stony ground, turning clumps of grass into long-fingered shadows which dance at their feet.

They approach a dense area of scrub. A pair of acacias form a natural tunnel through which they pass, dimming the stars above them.

Another gate. Another lock. Another compound within a compound.

Here, Mollel can just make out the form of a building or shed. The flashlight beam bounces across it, and he gets a glimpse of heavily barred windows. But this is not their destination. Onward they press. A clearing opens before them – Mollel senses the space as much as sees it. Kibet then starts sweeping the beam in a wide arc, back and forth. At one point the beam is returned, startlingly, by the brilliant blue eyes of a spring hare, which fixes them with its baleful eyes for a moment, before abruptly turning tail and bounding away.

The beam resumes its passage and, without it at his feet,

Mollel stumbles, stubbing his toe and letting out an unwitting gasp.

—Shh! hisses Kibet.

It's alright for you in your steel-capped boots, thinks Mollel. But then he realises she has caught something in her beam up ahead, and has stopped dead.

Mollel strains his eyes to make out what she's seen. He detects no movement. There is just the hump of a boulder, common enough in this volcanic country. He wonders whether there is something, or someone, hiding behind it.

She takes his hand – in the darkness it feels perfectly natural – and leads him to one side. Keeping the light fixed on the boulder, and keeping their distance, they begin to prowl in an arc around it.

As the angle changes, Mollel sees what appears to be a bird perched upon the boulder. It twitches, as though to preen, then another like it pops up.

—She's heard us, breathes Kibet.

Suddenly, the boulder jerks and lurches. One side rises from the ground and a tail appears, whisking. Below the ear – for this is what the bird-like object is revealed to be – the small, black bead of an eye blinks.

The massive head levers upward, and Mollel sees what he had taken for a broken tree stump swing aloft and become something else. Long, curved and sharp. A horn.

The beast turns and levels the horn at them. Mollel is reassured by the squeeze of Kibet's hand – though he is more reassured by the thought of the AK-47 on her shoulder.

A clicking noise starts to emanate from beside him. It is Kibet. She clucks and coos. The sounds are gentle, caressing. Mother sounds. The rhino snorts, and twitches the great pad of a foot.

—Come on, says Kibet. It's OK.

She leads Mollel toward the creature. When they are a few steps away, she slips her hand out of his and places her flashlight upon the ground. Then, slowly, she stretches out and pats the rhino's shoulder. She rubs its thick hide and tickles its ear, all the time cooing and clicking.

—Don't be shy, Mollel, she says. Come and say hello.

It goes against his every instinct, but the woman's manner is so calm that he approaches. The wide, bristled lips pucker, and almost shyly, the animal moves to meet his hand. Her skin beneath his palm is rough and surprisingly warm.

—You couldn't do this if you weren't with me, says Kibet.

She means that the rhino would not be so docile. But Mollel also understands that his own courage would not be sufficient without the woman by his side.

—Her name is Esme, says Kibet.

—Hullo, Esme, says Mollel, feeling slightly foolish. Maasai seldom even name their dogs.

Esme's ear flicks as Mollel scratches it, and she gives a snort of steamy breath.

—She likes you, giggles Kibet. She usually won't let anyone other than me do that.

The huge bulk of the creature only serves to emphasise its gentle movements. The two massive horns on its nose sway as it turns from Mollel to nuzzle Kibet. The upper horn is dome-like; the lower one more vicious. If this beast wanted to, it could destroy either one of them in moments. If the horn did not impale you, the feet would render you as pulp.

But the hide beneath his fingers, thick as it is, offers no protection from a bullet.

—This, says Kibet, is what they want.

On the way back to the ranger post, they stop at a point facing the deep cleft in the cliffs that marks the entrance to Hell's Gate gorge. Kibet is silent for a while, gazing at the jagged rocks in the moonlight. She gives a violent shudder, then begins to explain. Keeping the animals together had become too risky. As the price of rhino horn soared, attacks on the official sanctuaries became more frequent, and bolder. The poachers were like a small army. They had machine guns. Grenades. And keeping the rhinos together just meant that the poachers could wipe out more of them at a stroke. So a secret programme was launched to disperse the habituated rhinos. They would remain under close protection, but fewer people would know where they were. And, crucially, they would be kept apart.

—It broke Esme's heart, says Kibet, sorrowfully. She was split up from her mate of more than ten years. But it was unavoidable. And in the end, it was for the best. Because they got to him, too.

They reach the door of Kibet's hut and enter.

—So you see, Mollel, it's not about the brothel. And it's not about the rapists. But it's the same thing.

—The same thing?

He collapses into the chair, grateful to be back in the warmth. How long is it since he slept? He closes his eyes.

She shuts the door.

—It's all the same, she repeats. You know how much rhino horn fetches, over in China? What do you think they want it for?

—Some sort of medicine? mumbles Mollel.

He feels her put a blanket over him.

—First thing in the morning, you leave, she says. And no funny business in the night. I'm taking my rifle to bed with me, just in case.

He's vaguely aware that he should feel offended by the implication, but he's too tired to dwell upon it.

For some reason, the thought of that gentle, powerful animal locked away in its lonely compound fills him with immense sadness. He understands Kibet's compulsion to protect it at all costs. And realises that he, now, is compelled to protect her.

When he wakes, sunlight is already pricking through the thin piece of coloured *khanga* which hangs over the window. He stretches his legs and arches his back, before standing. A piece of paper flutters down from his lap to the floor.

Kibet's bed is empty. She, and the gun, have gone. He picks up the note and reads it.

Mollel. I've gone on duty. There is one guard on the gate. You can watch from the window. When he goes to the latrine you can slip out. Good luck. K.

His eyes range around the little hut. The photographs on the trunk catch his eye. He walks over and picks one up. There is Kibet, not in uniform. She has a smile on her face which seems as incongruous as the pretty dress she's wearing. In her arms, there is a little girl. The family resemblance is undeniable.

Another photo of the girl: a couple of years older, in school uniform. Mollel picks it up. As he does so, something falls with a metallic clunk down the back of the trunk. He puts the frame down, suddenly self-conscious about invading Kibet's privacy. He leans over to look for what fell.

In the gap between the trunk and the wall, an object glistens on the pounded earth floor. He reaches down and his fingers make contact with something cold. He picks it up. It is heavy.

Opening his hand, he sees a crescent of gold. A shining, crinkled curve. A smile.

He recognises the upper front teeth. Gachui sneers up at him from the palm of his hand.

18

—Jesus, Mollel, says Kiunga. You don't believe in doing things the easy way, do you?

They are behind Kiunga's cabin at the Lakefront Hotel, hidden from view. Their furtiveness, however, has less to do with Mollel's fugitive status than with Kiunga's desire for a cigarette.

—The only law in this country which everyone seems determined to enforce, grumbles Kiunga, as he drops the stub to the ground and grinds it underfoot, is the one about smoking in public places. And with you around, Mollel, giving up is not an option.

He produces his packet of Sportsman and shakes out another cigarette, which he puts distractedly into his mouth then lights up. A frown is deeply engraved upon his forehead.

—How did you get in, anyway, looking like that?

Mollel is still barefoot, wrapped in his dusty *shuka*. He is only too aware of the fact that he has not washed for days.

—The guards remembered me being picked up by the Chinese yesterday. They obviously think I have influence here.

Kiunga takes a long draw and releases a fan of smoke through his nostrils.

—Let's hope they don't realise that this scruffy Maasai is the same renegade policeman that half the district's out looking for.

Kiunga's phone rings. He takes it, looks at the screen, then flashes a glance at Mollel.

—It's Otieno. What do I tell him?

—Tell him I've made contact, says Mollel. But not that you've seen me. Tell him I've gained the trust of the gang, and we're on the verge of breaking them.

Kiunga raises his eyebrows.

—He's not going to like it.

—Just tell him, says Mollel.

Kiunga answers the phone and before he's even held it up to his ear, Mollel can hear Otieno bellowing down the line. He does not envy his colleague.

Kiunga turns away and wanders off, saying —Yes boss, but . . . Yes, boss. Yes, boss.

Mollel has not told Kiunga about Kibet, or the gold teeth. He's still processing that discovery. And he knows that as far as Kiunga is concerned, Mollel's judgement when it comes to women is questionable. He needs to clarify his own thoughts before he involves anyone else.

He has a sudden overwhelming need to wash the dust from his face and feet. Among these pristine lawns, he feels grimy and squalid. While Kiunga paces up and down, Mollel goes around the corner to the entrance of the hotel *banda* and opens the door.

Inside, the room is like a luxury version of the hut Kibet lives in. Much larger, of course, and with heavy hardwood furniture dotted around. Kiunga's jacket is hung over the back of a chair. An imposing four-poster bed hung with a mosquito net dominates the space, sheets rumpled. The housekeeper has obviously not called yet this morning.

Mollel makes his way to Kiunga's bathroom. He opens the door and pauses. The sound of running water comes from within. He catches the sweet, steamy smell of soap, a momentary image of pink flesh behind the shower curtain and the voice, a female voice:

—Ah, there you are. Are you coming in?

He quickly shuts the door and looks around him in confusion. No, that is definitely Kiunga's jacket on the back of the chair. That is Kiunga's bag open on the dressing table. And, the door to the outside opening now, it is Kiunga who enters. Seeing Mollel, there is no mistaking the sheepish look on his face.

—She doesn't know, he says, urgently.

—Doesn't know what? asks Oberkampf.

Mollel turns back to see her, hair falling in dark, wet strands over her face, shoulders glistening, body wrapped in a towel.

She glares at them both unselfconsciously.

—You didn't know that Mollel was here, says Kiunga hastily, and not entirely convincingly.

—Well, I do now. So I'm going to go back in there and get dressed. And when I come out, the three of us are going to talk.

She sits on the edge of the unmade bed. Mollel is relegated to the armchair and Kiunga stands edgily by the sideboard.

—I don't know where to begin, says Oberkampf. You've interfered with my witness.

—I've not interfered with him, protests Mollel. I persuaded him to cooperate.

—By stabbing him?

—It was a necessary ruse, says Kiunga. He's explained that. Mollel didn't hurt him. At least, not much.

Oberkampf snorts with derision.

Her hair is still damp, but now she is at least dressed. Sitting on the bed, her feet don't quite touch the floor, even in their leather high heels. She is not the tallest woman, about five and a half feet, and utterly unlike the willowy white women who populate the adverts and movies that flick across the small TV screen at the Maili Ishirini Police Post. Her well-cut, expensive-looking suit cannot disguise the size of her breasts and hips. In that respect, she has more in common with the female lead in *Cobra Squad* – which accounts, no doubt, for the attention Shadrack and the others paid her in the hotel bar the other night. Her face, with its small, freckled nose and pert lips, has a captivating quality, despite, or perhaps because of, the flush of anger across her cheeks and the tiny notch of a frown that has appeared between her brown eyebrows.

—Do you know what you're doing? she asks them. You're standing in the way of international justice.

A flash of heat rises within Mollel.

—As I understand it, he says, you're here to investigate the post-election violence. This is something else.

She shakes her head. —This is impunity, Mollel. The system has failed to investigate its own. That's why I'm here.

—No, says Mollel, rising. That's why *we're* here.

—Easy, Mollel, murmurs Kiunga.

—For weeks I've been undercover, replies Mollel. I've left my family behind. I've put my life on the line. I've had my personal history dragged through court. I've been imprisoned, and now I'm on the run. And I'm doing all that to get to a group of policemen who some people might argue are doing society a favour. I'm not doing it for my career, or to make a name for myself. And I'm certainly not doing it for the overtime. I'm doing it for justice. Not international justice, whatever that is. For good, plain, honest justice. *Kenyan* justice.

Oberkampf looks at him with a condescending smile.

—It's our problem, he adds. We'll deal with it.

—Oh, yes? says Oberkampf, still smiling. Is that what Otieno told you?

Mollel looks at Kiunga, who gives a small, embarrassed shrug and averts his eyes. Mollel thinks of Kibet, and decides he is not the only one whose judgement can be impaired when it comes to women.

—Of course your boss has told you that, she continues. He told you that it would be a chance to restore public confidence in the police, right? Did he use the phrase *new broom* at all?

Mollel looks over at Kiunga.

—I didn't tell her that, he says.

She raises her eyebrows at him and the smile on her face shifts, ever so subtly, to a look of triumph. This, thinks Mollel, is why people dislike lawyers.

But his annoyance at her is nothing compared to his anger with himself. Because he knows what she is going to say next, and she is right.

—He wanted you to deal with this secretly, so that it could be covered up. Do you really suppose that once you bust this gang, Otieno's going to want the whole thing dragged through the courts? Or will he just dispatch the murderers to the Somali border, anywhere, to get them out of the way? Of course he doesn't want a show trial, and all the attention that will bring. He just wants a quiet life. That's why he sent you here, Mollel. Because he knew you'd deliver these guys to him, nice and quietly, or die trying. And frankly, he could live with either option.

The raucous call of an ibis in the hotel grounds is the only sound as this sentence sinks in.

—I suppose you two have already talked about this, says Mollel.

Kiunga gives an awkward cough, which Mollel takes as assent, but also as a reminder of his earlier words.

She doesn't know.

No, she doesn't know that you've been assigned to spy on her, thinks Mollel. If she knew that, we wouldn't be having this conversation now. Much less would she have slept with you.

—So, says Oberkampf, clapping her hands together. What are we going to do, boys?

Her frown has gone and been replaced with a beguilingly mischievous smile. Her bare legs swing and she almost wriggles with excitement.

—I've got a feeling you're going to tell us.

—Damn right. We're going to do what we were sent here to do. All of us. You, Mollel, are going to use your new-found trust with the gang to get us the proof you need for a prosecution. But instead of taking it to Otieno, you're going to give it to me. I'll go public. The authorities won't be able to sweep it under the carpet. There will have to be due process.

—Where? asks Mollel. Here, or in The Hague?

She laughs and waves her hand breezily. —Oh, it doesn't matter. We'll leave that to the politicians to argue about. But don't you see, Mollel? There'll be justice. And we'll be the ones who deliver it. What do you say, Mollel? Are you in?

Mollel takes his long-overdue wash in Kiunga's bathroom. To his delight, there is a disposable razor, unused, in the courtesy basket, and he removes the greying stubble from his cheeks and then from his scalp. He splashes cold water over his head and feels the smooth outline of his skull, his jawbone, his neck, his cheeks. He feels more like a human again.

It is with regret that he reties his *shuka* around his body. He would much rather ask Kiunga for the loan of a shirt and trousers. But he is still incognito, and there is work to be done.

Coming out of the bathroom, even though Kiunga and Oberkampf are not talking, and not even close to each other, he has the sense that he has interrupted something.

—As soon as we bust the gang, he tells them, I'm going to be gone from here. Before that happens, I have some unfinished business.

—What? asks Oberkampf.

—The body that was found here. Jemimah Okallo.

—Oh, *her*, says Oberkampf. She has nothing to do with our case, though?

—Does that matter?

—Don't be a fool, Mollel. You're the most wanted man in town, says Kiunga. You'd be better staying in this room all day.

—I don't want this case blown because of some trivial wild-goose chase, Oberkampf adds.

—Trivial? spits Mollel. I thought you were just lecturing me on justice. Doesn't Jemimah Okallo deserve justice too?

—You've got to see the bigger picture, Mollel.

The words *bigger picture* make him think of the small pictures stuck on the wall of Jemimah Okallo's dorm. Which in turn make him think of the pictures of Kibet and the child in the ranger's hut. Which make him think of Gachui's gold teeth – which he still has not mentioned to the other two.

—No, says Mollel. You can think of the big picture all you like. Once you get what you want from Kenya, you'll be gone. Investigating crimes in some other country. Making a name for yourself as the big-shot international lawyer. But we'll still be here. Kenya will still be here. And Jemimah Okallo will still be dead. If we can't bring justice for the Jemima Okallos of this world, what can we do?

19

—I knew it was you! You didn't want me to see you, did you? But I saw you yesterday, outside the shop.

Beatrice is grinning at him, her big, buck-toothed grin. And it's been so long since anyone was pleased to see him that Mollel can't help smiling back.

—I need to talk to you, he says.

—I know you do. Come in.

He enters the shop and Beatrice shuffles her large frame around behind him and shuts the door. She flips around a sign which says CLOSED.

—There. Now we have some privacy.

Mollel appreciates her discretion. All the way to the shop, he had felt every eye upon him, every figure scrutinising him. Yet he had passed, apparently, without being noticed. Just another Maasai on market day.

—Well, Mollel, she says, beaming. Don't you look fine.

He is surprised: fine is the last word he'd use to describe his appearance. But perhaps she has a point. He has shaved and washed. His *shuka* has been shaken out and is now tightly bound around one shoulder. His dagger hangs at his belt. In the seclusion of the shop, he can lose the stoop which he'd been affecting outside to deter attention and hold his head high.

Beatrice does a twirl, which nearly sends a rack of stationery flying.

—Do you notice anything about me?

She is not wearing the gaudy, floral outfit of the last time he saw her but a brown cotton dress, embroidered with lace and studded with tiny cowrie shells.

—You're wearing your traditional gear, and I am too, she says.

This is Kikuyu chic. The brown cotton material is a substitute for animal hide, but otherwise it is smart and, to Mollel's eyes at least, authentic. He wonders what the special occasion is.

Her hair has been braided differently and she is wearing make-up: pink lips and shiny blue eyelids. Mollel feels that a compliment is being solicited, so he murmurs one, and her dark cheeks glow.

—Oh, you, she says, and bats him coquettishly with her heavy hand, causing him to rub his arm.

—Now, she adds. You had something you wanted to tell me.

Mollel nods. He has a disconcerting feeling which he cannot place: an intangible sense of peril which is at odds with the situation. After all, he is locked inside a secluded space with a friendly woman. What possible danger could there be?

—Actually, I was hoping you could tell me.

Her eyes widen. —*Me* tell *you*? You *are* a shy one, Mollel. But I knew that already. Otherwise, why would you have waited around outside the shop so often, pretending not to look?

—Oh, I didn't want him to see me, replies Mollel.

—Him? There is no him, you silly boy! Only you. There's no one for you to be jealous of. And if you're too shy to ask, I'll give you the answer anyway. Yes, Mollel, yes. I will be your wife.

He has grappled with muggers and fought off assassins. He has even, in his youth, had an encounter with a rampant buffalo. But no encounter has caught him as off guard as this one now. Wide arms envelop him, and his face is showered with soft, heavy kisses. He staggers back under the onslaught, hitting a shelf and scattering items to the floor.

—Oh, Mollel, she coos.

The shelf won't take their combined weight and it gives way beneath them. Beatrice gives an excited yelp as she lands on top of Mollel.

—Here? Now? You naughty boy!

Finally Mollel regains the use of his arms and he struggles free.

—You've got it all wrong, he gasps.

Beatrice hauls herself up, adjusting her dress and averting her face. Mollel can see that she is suddenly overwhelmed with self-doubt.

—You're right, she mumbles. I don't know what I was thinking. Look at the mess!

She busies herself collecting the goods which have fallen to the floor. Mollel picks himself up and starts to help her.

—Just leave it, she says.

—Let me help you.

—Just leave it!

He backs off. She picks up the fallen shelf and thrusts it clumsily back into place. Then she gives a long, watery sniff and turns her back to him.

—Look, says Mollel. I'm very flattered . . .

She waves her hand dismissively.

—If things were different . . . he continues, struggling.

—Don't bother, Mollel, she says quietly. I'm just a stupid, fat old woman.

He tentatively puts his hand forward to pat her shoulder, but just as he is about to touch her, she stiffens and turns.

—So, she says boldly. What was it you wanted to ask me?

Her manner is brisk, businesslike. If she betrays her emotions at all, it is in a certain redness around the eyes, a certain vulnerable tremor in the lip. But otherwise, she exudes stoic professionalism.

This is a woman who has known disappointment before, and who has learned to master it. Her transformation is so complete that it is Mollel who feels humiliated. With an absurd sense of rejection, he struggles to regain his composure. It takes him a moment or two to recall what he came in for. The sight of a poster advertising mobile money exchange reminds him.

—It's police business, he manages to say.

She nods. —Of course it is. What do you want to know?

—It's about the man who I was trying to send the money to, begins Mollel.

—Yes. I did some asking around on your behalf, Constable. I wanted to help you out. The police, I mean. I wanted to . . .

For a moment her eyes flash at him with a longing that is quickly blinked away.

—I wanted to do my duty, she finishes.

—And what did you find out?

She gives a slight tut of irritation. —I told the other one all this already. It didn't take long to find out. His name is Boniface Mwathi, and he lives in the next village. He's a guard at the prison.

A guard. That much ties in with what Mollel already suspected. He must be the one on the outside, harvesting the phone numbers from his contacts at the flower farms and elsewhere, gleaning a few details so that he could make the messages authentic and supplying the information to the prisoners who ran the operation.

He is about to thank Beatrice, and compliment her on her detective skills, when something about her earlier words strikes him.

—You said you told the other one?

—Yes, of course. I tried to find you yesterday, but you weren't at the police post. He said you'd got into some sort of trouble. I was – she casts her eyes down – I was worried.

—Who? Who did you tell? he asks urgently.

—Your colleague. The young one. Always acting the know-it-all.

Shadrack.

He recalls Shadrack's words when he read the text message to Jemimah Okallo. *People like this shouldn't be allowed to get away with it.*

Shadrack wasn't the sort to sit on this kind of information. He'd act on it. Him, and the rest of Rhino Force.

Mollel turns, strides to the door and unbolts it.

—If anyone asks, I've never been here, he urges Beatrice.

—I get it, Mollel, she replies, quietly. You were never here at all.

20

—I've checked the police post, says Kiunga. It's locked up, and the car's gone.

Mollel finds it frustrating to be sat like this in the back of Oberkampf's hire car, looking out through tinted windows. But he is still an escaped prisoner, and the one place he'd be sure of being recognised is near his own workplace.

A thump on the dashboard tells him that Oberkampf is frustrated, too.

—Wherever they've taken him, she says, that's where they're doing it. If we get there fast, we can catch them disposing of the body. And then we've got our case.

—If we get there even faster, replies Mollel, we might be able to prevent there being a body in the first place.

—Sure, says Oberkampf. Either way.

—Either way, chimes in Kiunga, we need to know where they've gone. You said they took you up to the clifftop, Mollel. Do you suppose that's where they are?

Mollel shakes his head. —No. That was a test. They weren't going to reveal their secret to me that night.

—What about your little ranger? asks Oberkampf. Mollel looks up sharply. *His* little ranger? He reminds himself that they do not know about his night in Kibet's hut, or his discovery of the gold teeth.

—Yes, continues Oberkampf. She found them last time. Do you think she could find them again?

Mollel knows that it was not chance that brought Kibet to the clifftop. Yet still, somehow, he is reluctant to inform the others of her role in the gang. There will be time enough for that, later. He recalls the horror on her face when she found him kicking Gachui. She was a good actor, that was for sure. She must have taken over once Mollel had left with Shadrack. No doubt he had loosened the teeth in his beating, but perhaps she was the one who had delivered the blow that knocked them out.

She had hated Gachui because he was a rapist. This prison officer, this Mwathi, was not a rapist, but he had used the threat of rape to destroy Jemimah Okallo. And now, unless they got to him in time, his fate would be the same as Gachui's.

Where had she and the others taken Gachui after Mollel had left?

Where, in the vast expanse of this landscape, did they dispose of the body?

He pictures the moonlit view that he and Kibet had taken in after they had been at the rhino sanctuary. And he remembers the shudder she had given at the sight of the deep, riven cleft in the earth.

Hell's Gate gorge.

—Mollel, says Oberkampf again. Do you think Kibet can lead us to them?

He does not reply, but he thinks that perhaps she already has.

Kiunga's police pass is enough to get them through the main gate of the National Park, and Oberkampf's glare is enough to deter any inconvenient questions. Night is falling. If Mollel's theory is correct, nothing will happen in daylight. The gang need darkness to go through with their plan.

The massive cliffs loom red above them in the sinking sun. The car slows as Kiunga reaches a fork in the dirt road. Mollel tries to orient himself by them, first by identifying the spot where he must have stood with Kibet, then by working out where the gorge must be in relation to that point.

—I think it's this way, he says, pointing left.

—I think so too, smiles Kiunga, nodding at a wooden signpost at ground level.

HELL'S GATE 2KM.

Kiunga drives at a pace which Mollel feels to be agonisingly slow. Glancing over his shoulder at the dial, though, he sees that his colleague is sticking scrupulously to the park's 40 kilometres-per-hour limit. It makes sense. If they thundered along, they'd raise a plume of dust that would be visible for miles. If any of the gang were on the lookout, they'd know immediately that someone was coming – and someone speeding with an urgency unlike that of any tourist or regular wildlife patrol.

Apart from the occasional wheeling bird or gazelle, though, the park is utterly deserted. The high cliffs now loom on both sides, and Mollel has that strange sense of experiencing something again, for the first time. Then he realises he is recalling another scene entirely, but one that is eerily familiar: a few months back, in the hours following the disputed election, he was driven down Kenyatta Avenue in the dead centre of Nairobi. There, the empty skyscrapers and deserted streets also seemed something akin to the entrance to the underworld.

They pass under the bulk of the Maasai Bride, who seems at once taller and more slender from the ground than she did from the clifftop, stretching herself up toward the blackening sky, ever yearning, ever lonely.

Another sign for Hell's Gate gorge, and a track leads off the dirt road into what looks like a parking area. They just have time to spot two vehicles parked there – the police pickup and Shadrack's battered old saloon – before Kiunga throws the car into reverse and backs out.

He kills the engine and signals *quiet* to both passengers. He whirs down his window, which had been closed against the dust, and all of them strain to listen.

They hear nothing but the crickets: but that's all they would hear, too, if their sudden arrival had been seen and the gang were now waiting to spring an ambush on them. They would be armed, Mollel knew. Kibet would have her AK-47, Mungai his pistol, Choma his ancient rifle. No one would dispute their version of events: they had been taken by surprise. They thought the newcomers were poachers.

—You go first, Mollel, whispers Oberkampf.

From what he's seen of her, Mollel suspects this is reason rather than cowardice talking. She's right. Although he would be the easiest of the three to justify killing – he is an escaped convict, after all – he's the only one who retains a degree of confidence with the gang.

He opens his door and cautiously steps out.

As he rounds the bushes toward the parked vehicles, he decides to call out rather than risk a hail of bullets.

—*Hodi*, he cries.

No response.

There is no sign of anyone at the cars. He walks around them to make sure. When he reaches the back of Shadrack's old Toyota, he unlatches the boot – there is a trick to it – and looks inside.

Nothing. But lowering his head toward the space, his nostrils burn with the smell of sweat. He looks up at the boot lid, open in front of him. The inside is smeary. He wipes a finger across it. Blood – and fresh, too. Mwathi would have been tied up in here, he assumes. So whether the blood comes from his head impacting on the boot lid as the car was thrown over rocky ground, or whether he was banging his head in an attempt to attract attention or escape, he's going to be in a pretty sorry state by now.

That's if they haven't already executed him.

He hears a low whistle and a movement in the bushes.

—It's alright, he says. They're not here.

Kiunga and Oberkampf appear.

—They've definitely got Mwathi with them, though, Mollel continues, holding up a bloody finger.

—Then there's no time to lose, replies Oberkampf. I presume we follow the signs?

There, just beyond the cars, is a gap in the trees. The gloom within is framed between a pair of tall posts and, suspended between them, above head height, is a sign: TO THE GORGE.

Mollel hears a click and a white circle appears, dancing on the leaves deep beyond the gateposts. Mollel turns to see Kiunga holding a dazzling point of light in his hand.

—One thing I learned about working with Mollel, he says. Always bring a torch.

21

The path down to the floor of the gorge is perilous and, out of some sense of chivalry, Mollel and Kiunga fall into place in front of and behind Oberkampf, so that one of them can always extend a hand. But after the first few offers are dismissed, it becomes apparent that, despite her unathletic figure, she is as nimble as a mountain goat. Mollel is glad to note that she has sensibly ditched her high heels and now wears a pair of scruffy trainers. Moreover, she does not seem in the least bit concerned about her expensive-looking suit, pushing aside thorny outgrowths with her elbows and even, at one particularly precipitous point, sitting in the dirt and slithering down the slope on her backside.

Several times Mollel sees the white disc of Kiunga's torchlight suddenly disappear and looks around to see his colleague scrambling to pick himself up. After the third occasion, Oberkampf extends her hand to him and, grudgingly, Kiunga accepts.

The moon has not yet risen – not that its light would be able to grope far down into this cleft – and only the sound of rushing water below them gives Mollel any real sense of the depth of their descent. But after a time, he begins to feel the ground evening out under his feet. Gaining the stream and entering the gorge proper, the sky becomes visible, sprinkled with stars above them. The edges of this jagged split in the earth are fringed with vegetation and because of the narrowness of the gap between the two sides – at points no more than three or four metres – the gorge looks like it might, on a whim, simply fold in upon itself and seal up without warning. Once more Mollel is reminded of a man-made canyon: this time, it is the winding, claustrophobic passages of Kibera slum. The recollection of being there on election day, with the walls of the shacks around him engulfed in flame and actually falling in upon him, makes him shudder.

Kiunga sweeps the torch beam around them, picking out a swooping vortex: the passage of the river, carved in rock, frozen in time. At its highest point, the torch beam captures striations like bands of cloud on the horizon. Moving down the cavern wall, the circle of light strengthens and shrinks and the stripes become increasingly strident, layer upon layer thrown into swirling contortions by the meandering channel of the current, which has carved and snaked and sunk itself here over millions of years.

This lower part of the gorge – the height of a three- or four-storey building – is sinuous and smooth. The walls are sculpted into shelves and slopes, with the occasional sharp groove or knife-edged ridge. And then, the torch beam dropping still, another change. At approximately six feet from the canyon floor, human height, the names begin.

Kenyan names. European names. Chinese figures. Arabic. Usually with a date – *Wangechi '98, Esteban 2005, Mike + Josie June 04*. The irresistible human urge, when confronted with something startling and beautiful and incomprehensible, to own it.

And at the base of this defile, its maker: the narrow, gurgling stream, at present no more than a few inches in depth, tripping and rushing over pebbles and chicaning through sparkling sand. It is fed by a turbid pool, which in turn finds its genesis in the tall, elongated cascade whose sibilant voice provided the audible landmark which guided their first descent. Mollel is in no doubt: this whisper could turn into a roar without warning. A rotting tree trunk and numerous hefty boulders beached high on the pool's banks are testament to that. He would not like to test the power of this modest stream when it is in the full fury of flood.

Onward they press. The going is easier than descending the side of the gorge, but there is no mistaking that every step forward is dragging them deeper into the earth. Mollel, barefoot, walks in the water, where the bed of silt is more dependable than the smooth rocks which bound it; and when he looks around, he sees that the others, despite their shoes, have followed suit.

His sense of superiority is short-lived. Just as the rotten-egg smell of sulphur began so indefinably that it was hardly noticeable until it became unbearable, so Mollel realises that the water around his feet is as warm as the blood within them – and then it is scalding.

He gasps and leaps out of the stream. Thrown off balance by this sudden movement, he puts a hand out in the darkness and it finds the wall of the cavern. He pulls it away again instantly, shaking it violently in the air. The rock is as hot as the side of a *jiko* filled with coals.

A vicious oath from Kiunga and the sound of scrambling tells him that the others have made the same discovery. Hopping about until the pads of his feet alight upon some blissfully cool, silty mud, Mollel catches his breath and waits for the others to regain their composure.

He is grateful for the fact that the sound of the rushing water is masking their approach, just as the contortions of the passage mean that, until now, he's been relatively relaxed about the light from Kiunga's torch. But now he notices that the steam in the air all around them, which, like the smell and the heat, has crept up on them unnoticed, diffuses the light and scatters it. There is every chance that the glow might be visible now, even around a corner. He voices his concern, and Kiunga reluctantly clicks off the light.

For a moment, the darkness is absolute. And then, slowly, the steam which had threatened to betray them becomes their ally. It refracts the light from the newly emerged moon down into this sightless breach and rises around and above them in a pale luminescence.

The ghostly light heightens the senses. As Mollel listens intently, the strange acoustics of this warped space mean that at times he can't tell whether he's hearing an echo of the stream or his own blood pounding in his head.

But there – he hears something different, as faint as a mosquito's whine and as elusive as its flight. Once more he doubts his own perception, until he hears it again.

Laughter.

Unmistakable now, it drifts and curls around untold corners to reach them. Distant, but definite laughter. Male laughter. More than one person.

Mollel would rather hear a scream. A scream is unambiguous. Its source is pain or fear. Like a scream, laughter is involuntary. But unlike a scream, laughter can come unbidden from more than one place. Mollel has heard laughs of terror and of pain. He's heard men laugh while they're killing, and before dying. He's known laughter accompany the most unimaginable cruelty.

At least with a scream he'd have more of an idea what to expect. At least he'd know Mwathi was still alive.

As cautiously as possible now, the three of them advance. Each curve of the canyon brings the possibility of an encounter closer, so they creep and cling to the walls.

Whatever weird dynamics brought the laughter drifting down to them, there is no further occurrence. Mollel even begins to question whether he really heard it at all, or whether fatigue and fear were playing tricks on his mind.

And then, light. Dim, orange light. Mollel blinks and confirms it: a small, fluttering glow on the wall of the canyon. He approaches it, puts his hand up as though it is the rock itself which exudes this phosphorescence. But as he does so, the light disappears from the wall and plays across his fingers.

He stoops to put his head where the light is falling. The others have seen him and he is aware of them watching breathlessly.

From here, the angle allows him a view around the next bend. The direct source of the light is not visible, but its reflection is: an illuminated wall of rock, flickering in light cast by flames. Just around the corner there must be a fire.

Mollel signals for the other two to hang back. Crouching low, he edges forward, keeping his eyes fixed on the hypnotic interplay of shadows and striations on the side of the gorge. They seem to shift and writhe like the scales of a snake in motion.

And then black against the orange and gold. A silhouette. Massive and distorted, but unmistakably a head, rising on shoulders. The shadow wobbles and grows and a horrifying laugh – the same laugh as before, but amplified – ricochets all around.

Mollel throws himself against the side of the cavern, and hopes that Kiunga and Oberkampf will have the sense to do the same. Whoever is approaching seems not to be bearing a light of their own. They will probably blunder straight past without seeing the newcomers.

That's what Mollel's sense tells him. His instinct, though, screams for flight. The echoes of the demonic laughter still reverberate as a new sound emerges in parallel: an animal sound, somewhere between a whimper and a growl. Mollel's hand fumbles, finds a rock.

His own chest is pounding now, rising and falling frantically, as though in time with the strangulated tones of the approaching figure, whose crashing footsteps fall ever closer.

Mollel stands. He raises the rock above his head.

Edged in flickering gold, the figure staggers out directly in front of Mollel.

Suddenly everything is bathed in white. Mollel's eyes are seared by the blazing light, but he only has an instant for thought. He lets the rock drop to his feet and springs forward, grasping the man around the neck in the crook of his left arm and pressing his hand over his mouth. The pair of them slam into the canyon wall and Mollel slithers down it. He feels the warm wetness of the stream on his legs and the sensation is matched in his hands by the warm, wet blood on the man's skin.

—Turn out that bloody light! he hisses at Kiunga.

The torch snaps off, but for Mollel its shape remains, a floating blot which he attempts to blink away.

—Is it him? whispers Oberkampf.

A peal of laughter drifts toward them, but it does not sound any closer than before.

—I don't know, replies Mollel. I didn't get a chance to see.

He brings his lips in close to the man's ear. —I'm going to ask you a question. Don't try to speak. Just nod your head. Are you Boniface Mwathi?

The head jerks up and down.

It doesn't make sense. Why would they have let him go? Are they playing with him? Giving him a false chance at freedom before hunting him down like an animal?

The man in his grasp starts to shiver. Mollel becomes aware, from the recollection of what he saw in the brief moment before Kiunga's torch blinded him, that the man in his arms is naked.

—I'm going to let you go. You're not to make a sound. Understood?

Another nod of the head. Mollel releases his grip and they both struggle to their feet.

The blotch in front of his eyes is fading now, and Mollel can make out Mwathi in the misty, refracted moonlight. The man can barely stand. Kiunga slips off his jacket and places it around Mwathi's shoulders.

—He's in a bad way, whispers Oberkampf.

Even as she says this, Mwathi stumbles. He's obviously taken quite a beating. His tormentors can afford to be relaxed. There is only one way out of this canyon. Even giving him a head start, there's no chance they would fail to catch their quarry. Not unless he had assistance.

—Get him out of here, says Mollel. Get him as far away as possible. Carry him out if you need to. Don't take him to hospital. Hide him at the hotel if you must, but make sure you get a statement. We need this on paper, before he changes his mind.

Before he realises that witnesses don't last long in this town, thinks Mollel.

—Oh, and Kiunga, urges Mollel. See if you can get out of him what the connection is with Jemimah Okallo.

Kiunga nods and throws one of Mwathi's arms over his shoulder, giving an unbidden grunt as he takes the strain.

—What about you, Mollel? breathes Oberkampf. You're coming with us, right?

A chilling laugh floats down from the direction of the firelight.

—When they decide to come this way, says Mollel, they'll catch up with us in minutes. There's only one thing to do. I've got to stall them.

He feels the touch of Oberkampf's hand upon his shoulder.

—Good luck, Mollel, she says.

22

He adopts a posture of submission; a shambling, exhausted walk. Feet dragging in the stream, shoulders bowed. Cowed, defeated. A walk of terror. The steps of a man meeting his executioners.

It is not altogether feigned.

He rounds the corner and holds up a hand against the light. The fire is low and its orange flames flicker within a long, deep, glowing cavity in the canyon wall. Sitting and squatting within – the roof of the cave is too low to allow anyone to stand – are four figures. The sand around them is littered with crumpled beer cans.

The now familiar laugh rings out, proximity robbing it of the mysterious acoustic which carried it to Mollel's ears before, and also removing its mystery, if not its threat.

The laugh is Shadrack's. And it halts abruptly as his eyes rise and meet Mollel's.

—Oho! Look who's back! Shadrack calls out. What's the matter, Mwathi? Wasn't that little lesson enough for you?

—It's not Mwathi, says Mollel. It's me, Mollel.

Figures spring to their feet, crouching under the cavern roof, scrambling to come out. The unmistakable bulk of Munene with a gun swinging in one hand. As soon as he steps into the gorge, he raises it directly at Mollel.

—What are you doing here, Maasai? he barks. Who's with you?

—No one, says Mollel, throwing his hands upwards. I came here alone.

Shadrack splashes past him, torch in hand. He gains the corner and cautiously puts his head around, shining the torch up and down the space.

—He's right, says Shadrack. No one here, at least.

A rustling noise, like the slightest breeze which has mistakenly found itself inside this dank and airless canyon, reaches Mollel's ears. He realises it is coming from within the low, long cave.

Choma is sitting there, cross-legged by the fire. He remained in place while the others leapt out to confront Mollel. And now his shoulders heave. The rustling sound is his laughter.

—They might be surprised to see you, Mollel, he chuckles. I'm not. I knew you'd be back.

Of course he did, thinks Mollel. No doubt Kibet had been in touch to warn him about Mollel's re-emergence in Maili Ishirini.

So where is she? Justice was being meted out to a man who'd threatened a woman with rape, causing her death. Mollel doubts she'd want to miss this.

He peers into the darkness. Beyond the cave, the canyon winds on, the stripes melt and twist and the sulphurous mist reflects the lowering fire.

But there is no sign of Kibet.

—I suppose you met our little blackmailer on the way out, Mollel, Choma wheezes.

—We had a minor run-in, says Mollel.

—Sorry we had to go ahead without you. By rights he should have been yours. But we thought you'd be halfway to Tanzania by now.

—Give me the gun, suggests Mollel, holding out his hand toward Munene, I'll go finish him off myself.

Silence.

Shadrack, who has come back from the edge, places his hand on Mollel's shoulder, exactly as Oberkampf had done a few minutes before.

—Listen to this guy. *Cheesy kama ndizi!*

Shadrack roars with laughter. Munene and Mungai join in. Munene is shaking so hard that he lowers his gun to wipe a tear from his eye. Only Mollel and Choma remain impassive. Slowly, the old man beckons to him. As the peals of laughter ebb away, he says:

—Come, Maasai. Sit.

Mollel bends low, steps into the scooped-out space. He puts his hands up to protect his scalp and his fingers walk along the smooth, warm stone. The fire is hardly necessary, due to the mellow heat of the rock, but its shimmering light illuminates the low ceiling and emphasises the sensation that this is a cocoon, safe and dry.

Choma sits in the sand. Munene and Mungai take their places beside him. Shadrack brings up the rear, crouching by the fire, holding out his hands toward it as much in tribute as for warmth.

Mollel is reluctant to sit down in any way that might hinder him springing up, should he need to. After his long walk, that means no squatting in the sand. Instead, he sees a likely place on a long, flat stone near the fire.

He moves to sit, and immediately a chorus of protest rises up from the other four policemen. —No, no! Not there!

Their cries are so alarmed that he has to pivot away from the stone, his weight already committed to sitting. In the low space, he fails to execute any kind of elegant move, and instead slumps down into the sand.

He holds out his hands toward the stone, the way Shadrack had to the fire, expecting it to be radiating intense heat. That, he assumes, must be the reason why they all warned him off – like those steam pipes running across the terrain with their signs warning DANGER. HOT. NO SITTING.

But his palms feel no heat. He looks around for clarification.

—Don't you know where you are, Mollel? creaks Choma.

He shrugs. —Hell's Gate gorge.

—Here. *This* place.

Choma casts his fingers around in a curve which describes the swoop of the rock above them.

Mollel shakes his head.

—I thought everyone around here knew about the Devil's Bedroom, says Munene in his low, deep voice.

—I'm not from around here, says Mollel.

—That's for sure, mutters Mungai.

—Perhaps not, continues Choma. But even in the big city, you must know the power of a good myth.

Mollel has an image: an image of his hands in the rubble and dust, in the minutes and hours that followed the bombing of the American embassy. He had pulled at the broken concrete and twisted metal so hard that his hands ran with blood, which caked black in the dust and the sun.

So many years ago, now. A lifetime – almost the entire lifetime of his son, just turned ten with Mollel not around to celebrate.

It was a photograph of Mollel, streaked in black and white, which made the front pages the following day. And even though it took a while for journalists to identify and track down the figure covered in ash, the stories had already begun to circulate – and escalate.

He pulled out a dozen people. He pulled out fifty. He rescued a hundred or more. He was tireless. They tried to stop him, but he kept going back. They couldn't hold him back.

But Mollel alone knew why he kept going back. He'd have let them all die, every one, if he could have held his Chiku in his arms once more.

By the time an opportunity came for him to refute the myth, he found he needed it. He was half crazed with grief. He spoke, unguarded and at length, to these reporters who sought him out – to anyone who'd listen – but not about the bombing. Instead, his thoughts ran fugitive along other lines: trivial things. Things that had irked him but about which he had never had the courage to speak about before. And now, in the face of this – well, what did it matter who knew about the dirty little secrets which

200

kept the pockets of the Nairobi policemen so handsomely lined? It was a relief to get it off his chest.

And so Mollel the whistle-blower was born. Mollel the incorruptible, who happened also to be unsackable – because he was the hero of 7 August 1998.

So yes, he knows the power of a good myth. His entire career has been based upon one.

—The Devil's Bedroom, continues Choma, his voice as dry as a distant cricket's call. That's what the guides here call it. They say the myth has been around as long as the Maasai, but personally, I reckon they made it up for the tourists. From what I've heard, you Maasai don't believe in the devil.

Mollel does not comment. He's seen enough in his time to remain open-minded on that matter.

—So, along with every good myth, you need a curse. Something to make the flesh prickle and the blood run cold. Something for mamas to tell their *totos* to keep them in bed at night. Given the layout of this place, there's not much mystery about how they came up with this one.

Mollel looks once more at the long, low stone. Its surface is eroded smooth by water, sand and time. He frowns. It's difficult to tell in the firelight, but he has more than a suspicion that what he had previously assumed was discoloration in the stone is, in fact, smears of blood.

Munene's deep voice picks up the story, vibrating in the hollow and stirring the smoky air.

—He who lies on the Devil's Bed, dies soon after.

Mollel recalls the wet, sticky skin of the naked man. The patches on the stone could well conform to someone being held down upon it.

Mollel looks from face to face.

—So what is this? he asks. Magic?

A moment's pause. And then, hearty laughter breaks out once more.

—There's no such thing as magic, Mollel, scoffs Shadrack.

No, thinks Mollel. Unless you believe in it. And then it's real enough. Real enough, combined with the mysterious setting and the doling out of a good beating, to instil terror into the likes of Boniface Mwathi, or even a hardened case like Gachui. The message was straightforward and unmistakable: change your ways, or see the prophecy fulfilled.

So, in a way, there was magic at work here. These four rogue policemen were using the power of the legend to effect change. And, whatever they professed, part of them believed it, too: their superstitious reluctance to allow Mollel to sit on the Devil's Bed had proved that.

What this did not prove, however, was that the policemen were murderers. Quite the opposite. If their intention was simply to eliminate their foes, why go through this elaborate charade?

—Does it work? he asks.

—Never failed yet, replies Shadrack, with some measure of pride. Mollel gets the feeling the youngster takes particular relish in this ritual. They either change their ways, or they disappear.

—Disappear? asks Mollel.

—They go, replies Choma. They get the message and they hit the road. We don't see them again. Maybe they've gone back to where they came from, or decided to strike out somewhere new. Either way, they're not our problem any more.

—And Kibet? asks Mollel. What's her part in all this?

—She's the real magician, says Choma with a laugh. We let 'em run back through the gorge, after we've terrified them half to death. Kibet's job is to meet them once they've made their way out. She makes it look like chance. As though she's on a regular night patrol. She picks them up, drives them to the road. But on the way, she fills their head with dire warnings. About what has happened to those who went before. She acts sympathetic, but gives them no time to think. They've got to get as far away as possible, she tells them. Then, at the roadside, she gives them some clothing – some old things she keeps in the back of the truck – and some money. Makes it look like charity. But it also prevents them from going home, or seeking support from friends. It's usually daylight by then, and they're on the first *matatu* headed anywhere away from here.

—So Kibet is the one who sees them last?

—And first, interjects Shadrack, his admiration for her evident in his voice. She's the one who identifies who's suitable for this treatment.

Of course she would have selected Boniface Mwathi. She and Shadrack were close, and he would have told her about the blackmail plot against Jemimah Okallo. And Shadrack, in his eagerness to impress her, would have told her as soon as Beatrice had identified the prison officer to him. No doubt she was looking forward to collecting him, bloodied and terrified, and taking him on to ... where?

Where did she take them? These others might believe that she simply sent them on their way, but Mdosi certainly didn't, and his network was better informed even than the police. He'd know if his men were simply leaving town, or departing this world more permanently. And whatever their fate, Kibet was the one delivering them up to it.

—Strange, says Mollel. I didn't pass her on the way down.

—There's plenty of time yet, replies Shadrack. That one'll be clawing his way out of the gorge for an hour or more.

Which gives Oberkampf and Kiunga time to get him out before they run into her, thinks Mollel, with relief. So far, they don't know about her involvement in the gang. He wants it to stay that way – for now.

Ruefully, he recalls the last time he allowed himself to get close to a woman. She ended up deceiving him. He never managed to bring her to justice. He isn't going to make the same mistake twice.

His thoughts are interrupted by Choma's rasping voice. —I hope she's not going to leave it too late, the old man wheezes angrily. He'll find it pretty cold once he emerges from the gorge. I don't want him dying of hypothermia on us.

As though sensing the irony of such apparent concern for

their victim, Choma adds: —The whole point of this is that we don't have any awkward bodies to explain.

As ever, Shadrack leaps to Kibet's defence. —She said she had a friend in trouble. She wanted to be there for her.

—As long as she gets here in time for *him*, mutters Choma.

A friend in trouble? From what Mollel saw, she has no friends. Certainly no one she cares about enough to keep her away from meting out justice.

And then he realises. There is one friend she cares about that much. Now he knows exactly where to find her. With what he's learned from the policemen here tonight, he is sure he has enough evidence to get out of her exactly how the missing men are being killed, where their bodies end up and who – if not she herself – is doing it.

—Is there any quicker way out of this gorge than the way we came in? he asks.

—Yes, says Shadrack. But it's a bit tricky. I wouldn't want to tackle it in daytime, let alone in the dark. It's an escape route the guides use in case of flash flooding.

—Just show me, says Mollel. I'll go up top and wait for our friend until Kibet gets here.

Choma nods his assent in the firelight, and Shadrack says: —OK. But you'd better be sure of your footing.

—I'll be perfectly safe, replies Mollel. After all, I never sat on the Devil's Bed.

23

Mollel is grateful for the darkness as he creeps on his hands and knees, and sometimes his belly, along a ledge halfway up the face of the gorge. The moonlight is strong enough for him to make out the next handgrip or toehold, but not quite bright enough to reflect off the stream which echoes below. That sound alone is reminder enough of the fall which would await any slip on this dusty, treacherous climb.

Several times he fears he has struck out on a false route, the prospect of a shuffling, feet-first retreat filling him with dread. But then he makes out the fallen tree Shadrack had told him about, stark and black, and forked like inverted lightning. It had once grown tall on the bank of the gorge, and indeed its roots still lie up there, but now claw blindly at the starry sky. The long, straight trunk runs down toward the opposite side, Mollel's side, at a near-perfect forty-five-degree angle. There it has lodged, forming a bridge, of sorts, albeit one which ends in a sheer rock face.

It's only a matter of time before termites chew the remaining roots, or rain erodes the soil around them, and the tree crashes into the gorge far below. Mollel just hopes that it won't be taking a middle-aged Maasai along for the ride.

Someone has made an attempt to clear the way to the sturdiest central members of the tree, where they have gouged their way into the cliff. Knuckles of hacked-off branches point accusingly downward, as though in warning. Mollel places a tentative palm onto the thickest limb and tests it.

Even this slight weight brings movement, but he gauges it is the natural springiness of the wood rather than a shift in its position. He begins to edge out.

Just a few days previously, he had ventured forth like this along the pipeline into the lake. A slip now would be less forgiving than those black waters, or even the hippos which inhabit them. Although a proficient climber in his youth, it is years – decades – since Mollel scaled a tree, and even then it was never an upside-down one, where the Vs of branches point the wrong way and provide no holds. He is forced to squeeze the trunk with his knees and shins and haul himself up, fingers scrabbling for grip, envying the leopard its claws and its equal ease in ascending or descending face first.

It is with a long-suppressed shudder and a sigh of relief that he gains the security of the upturned root ball and jumps from it onto hard, firm earth. After his long climb from the canyon floor it feels like reaching a mountain's summit, and for a moment Mollel relishes the sight of the wide, star-strewn sky stretching in all directions above him. Then, as his eyes fall upon moonlit peaks and cliffs not far away, he realises with a strange, anticlimactic feeling that all he has succeeded in doing is drag himself up to ground level.

At least those hills provide him with a point of orientation, as does the solitary bulk of the Maasai Bride, just visible over the dense black treetops.

—What took you? Mollel says, stepping out into the moonlight as the panting forms of Kiunga and Oberkampf, the bloodied and naked Mwathi shuffling between them, emerge from the entrance to the gorge.

—Jesus, Mollel! cries Kiunga. Then, in more hushed tones: Are you trying to frighten people to death?

—Not me, says Mollel. But others are.

They get back to their car. Kiunga points the key fob and the car chirps, clunks and flashes. Mollel winces. These luxury four-wheel drives were never designed with stealth in mind. Nothing to be done about it. They bundle Mwathi into the back, Mollel, for decency's sake, opting to sit beside the naked man while Oberkampf gets into the front passenger seat and Kiunga takes the wheel.

—What did you mean, asks Oberkampf, turning in her chair to address Mollel, they're frightening people to death?

—Look at him, replies Mollel. At his side, Mwathi sits hunched and shivering, the vibrations of the moving vehicle barely disguising the chatter of his teeth. He stares blankly ahead. The beating he received was the most lenient part of his ordeal, Mollel feels sure.

—They had an elaborate ritual laid out for this guy. One they go through every time. Why would they bother to terrify their victims, if they were going to execute them immediately afterwards?

—They're sadists? suggests Oberkampf. I don't know. You tell me, Mollel. They're your people.

It's the early hours of the morning, and she's just helped haul a wounded man up from the bottom of a treacherous gorge. So Mollel is prepared to overlook the obvious irritation and contempt which rings so thickly in her voice. He can't escape the conclusion that she would rather have found Mwathi dead and witnessed the policemen in the process of disposing of the body. Then her case would have been wrapped up.

But that throwaway comment. He can't let that pass.

—*Your people*? he repeats.

Kiunga groans. —Please, Mollel. Not now.

—I just wonder what you mean by *your people*. Because none of them is Maasai. But perhaps you mean Kenyan? The world knows we're savages, right? Because that's what the news networks showed them. Kenyans killing Kenyans. Thank God you're here, Justine Oberkampf of the International Criminal Court, to show us the error of our ways. To punish us. Because *my people* are obviously incapable of solving our own problems.

Kiunga hunches his shoulders and conspicuously focuses on his driving.

—Actually, Mollel, says Oberkampf slowly, measuredly, when I said *your people*, I meant the police.

Police. He's never felt like one. Even in uniform, he has always been an outsider. Maasai in a force dominated by Kikuyus, an honest man in a profession where honesty is a sacking offence. He has spent the last few days as a prisoner and a fugitive. But it's only now that he realises that, whatever happens, he'll never escape what he is.

Police.

—They're not sadists, he responds. They're not getting a thrill out of torturing people before they execute them, because they're not executing them. It's all an act. A pretty inventive one, for that matter. They can't deal with criminals properly because of corrupt judges and clever lawyers.

He can't resist adding: —*Your people*.

Despite his reputation as a whistle-blower, Mollel has never been a great believer in rules. Justice, he has always felt, is self-evident. It is something eternal, more powerful and more significant than the human society which attempts to define it, and bind it with rules and laws.

They have taken the sky and bound it.

Tonkei's words resurface like a mantra. Fitting that he should be reminded of the Maasai now, for this is a very Maasai attitude. Time was – no, even now, if they could get away with it – the Maasai would deal with a problem in their community this way. In the swiftest and easiest way possible, and without involving outsiders.

Perhaps, reflects Mollel, he is more Maasai than he likes to think.

And more of a policeman, too. There's no doubt that Oberkampf's slight against his profession stung him. The truth is, the discovery that the police were not behind the killings has somewhat restored his faith in his colleagues. He even admires their ingenuity. The cocksure Shadrack, the cynical Choma, the unsubtle Munene. They are, in their way, trying to do their best in the face of a hostile system. For the first time, he thinks of the men with a certain degree of warmth.

—Well, sighs Oberkampf. This has been a waste of time.

—A waste of time? asks Mollel, incredulously. The killer, whoever it is, has a habit of picking up these men shortly after the police squad is done with them. We've saved this wretch's life.

The slightest shrug from Oberkampf tells Mollel that that doesn't figure highly with her.

—So what now? asks Kiunga, chipping in for the first time. If it's not the police running the death squad, who is it? And how do we find them?

Mollel is saved from having to name Kibet by Oberkampf's interjection.

—*We?* This has nothing to do with us, Kiunga.

For a while, they had felt like a team. But, realises Mollel, this was just an illusion.

—I'm here to investigate the post-electoral violence – and possible government collusion, continues Oberkampf. If it's not the police wiping out these criminals, it's probably just a rival gang. In which case—

—In which case, you're not interested, says Mollel.

—In which case, it's beyond my mandate.

And that, thinks Mollel, *is why law and justice are not the same thing*.

Apart from the rumble of the car over the bumpy ground and the faint wheezing that emanates from Mwathi, there is silence. A few lights ahead show the entrance to the park and the ranger's post there.

—Let me out here, says Mollel.

—Mollel! protests Kiunga. Where are you going?

—To see a friend, he replies.

24

Kibet had told Shadrack that she had to go see a friend. She only has one friend, as far as Mollel knows.

Esme.

He lingers at the roadside while he watches the red lights of the car approach the ranger station. He sees the car's headlights pick out a pair of armed rangers who flag it down, and chuckles to himself as he imagines how Kiunga and Oberkampf are going to explain the bloodied, naked man in the back seat.

The rangers occupied with the car and its unusual cargo, Mollel edges past the buildings at the park gate and through the cluster of metal huts which house the workers, alert to movement at the illuminated windows. He moves swiftly, silently, though the reassuring sound of a television drifting from one of the huts would mask any unwitting noise he might make.

He continues up the track which leads to the ridge. His journey this night – from the depths of the earth to the high peak which crests the entrance to Hell's Gate park – has his heart pounding. Or is it the prospect of confronting Kibet?

A shape against the stars resolves into the familiar arch of acacia branches guarding the entrance to the rhino sanctuary. Mollel passes under it, and almost at the same moment in which the stars are extinguished, a sudden scream makes him stop dead.

It is no human scream: the sound quickly drops in pitch,

revealing a guttural, growling undercurrent. But this is no animal.

The sound ends as suddenly as it arose, but lingering like an echo, the faintest whiff of exhaust fumes confirms its source: a chainsaw.

The re-emergence of the stars after the arch shows Mollel that the gate is closed. Testing it, though, he feels it move under his fingers and hears the chain rattle and slide through the loop and fall slack. There is space enough for him, ducking, to squeeze through the gap. Whoever shut this gate behind them was in a hurry, or unfamiliar with how to fasten it properly. Which means Kibet, if she is here, is not alone with Esme.

A glimmer of light appears ahead. Mollel instinctively crouches. But the light is not moving. He draws closer, rounding a clump of bushes, and sees its source. The single high window of the shed which stands within the compound. From here, the rafters are all that are visible. Shadows play across them, and for the first time, he hears voices. Without making out the words, he can tell that they are urgent, and businesslike. He creeps forward.

One voice rises above the others, both in volume and pitch. He recognises it as belonging to Kibet.

—You do that again, she is saying, and I'll turn that damn machine on you.

—I had to test it, a man's voice protests. I know what I'm doing.

—But you don't know *her*, replies Kibet.

Mollel wants to see what is happening inside the shed, but he dare not pull himself up to the window. He has an idea: he has already climbed one tree this night. Why not another?

Retreating some distance from the shed, he gropes in the darkness for the smooth bark of an acacia. Leopard-like, he springs up, grasping the trunk between his knees. He hauls himself up once, twice, before feeling a branch which he can pivot himself up onto. He does so gingerly, feeling vicious thorns brush against him but not allowing his weight to settle until he has ascertained that the portion of the limb beneath him is smooth. He places his feet on the branch and crouches there, one hand against the trunk. From this position he has a clear view of the golden rectangle of light which marks the open, glassless window of the shed. He can also make out the form of Kibet addressing another uniformed Wildlife Service ranger, who has a chainsaw hanging in one hand.

—Don't even think about starting that thing up again until I say so, she admonishes him.

The ranger casts her a resentful nod. Without warning, an intense crashing, akin to a wrecking ball hitting a house, shatters the night air. Kibet, alarmed, looks at something beyond Mollel's line of sight.

With the people inside the shed distracted, Mollel gambles on being able to approach closer. He lowers his hands to the branch, swings himself down and drops to the ground. Through the window, he had seen a wide pair of double doors on the far side of the shed, and they were open slightly. This will be his vantage point.

He moves stealthily around the shed to where the doors stand a little more than a man's width apart. The tremendous crashing continues, accompanied by a curious snorting sound.

Peering around the doorway, Mollel can see for the first time that the interior of the shed is dominated by a crate-like structure, considerably taller than the camouflage-clad people who are now clustered around it. No risks were taken in its construction: the edges seem to be made from steel girders and the sides from thick timber planks. Even so, the crate is shuddering violently.

At the side of the crate closest to Mollel, a raised ramp, somewhat akin to the tailgate of a lorry, is bolted fast in place. But the ranger closest to it is looking at the heavy iron bolts with increasing nervousness as every additional crash leaves the door rattling precariously on its hinges.

Kibet runs into view, carrying an aluminium stepladder, which she quickly unfolds and climbs. The top of the crate must be open, because she looks over the side. Mollel sees her swerve away as the tall, craggy point of a horn sweeps perilously close to the woman's face.

—She's panicking! cries Kibet. She's going to injure herself!

Another ranger, this one armed with a long, slim rifle, runs over to the ladder. He tugs Kibet's trouser leg to get her to descend and takes her place on the steps.

Kibet turns away. Her face is utterly distraught.

The ranger, now at the top of the ladder, raises the rifle to his shoulder and points it down into the crate. He rests his head along the stock and draws a bead. It's close range: he's virtually touching the top of the crate with the muzzle of the rifle.

There is a crack of gunshot. At the same time, the rear door of the crate bursts open and slams down onto the concrete floor with an explosion of wood. The ranger closest to it barely has time to spring away – had be been any closer, he would surely have been crushed. Like the others, he turns and runs. Even the man with the gun has leapt from the top of the stepladder and flown. Only Kibet remains. She has rushed in the opposite direction, toward the danger.

Mollel sees a huge, wide, grey bulk backing out toward her, stubby tail flicking furiously, two massive feet like tree stumps bucking and kicking. The shape moves from side to side, rocking the crate as it eases out toward the doors where Mollel stands, and toward Kibet.

The rhino's shoulders, narrower than its hips, glide out and the beast is free. It sways and turns, a tiny black eye rolling around in confusion and fear. Mollel can see a minuscule red dart, like a discarded feather, hanging precariously from the animal's neck. It looks like it has barely penetrated the skin. The head thrashes up and down, the mighty horn waving like a huge broadsword. And right in front of it is Kibet.

The creature spies her. Its ears flick. It stamps its front feet and lowers its head.

—Esme, says Kibet. She opens her arms wide.

The rhino charges.

Mollel flies forward, grabbing Kibet by the waist and pulling her away from the thrust of the horn. He feels it swish past him, feels the cold air accompanying the swipe and prepares to dodge the next attack.

But it is not necessary. The rhino's head, as though unable to bear any longer the weight of its weapon, wobbles and then starts to sink. The forelegs fold under the body and the huge bulk slumps to the floor.

Kibet rushes forward and throws her arms around the rhino's neck. —Oh, Esme, she coos, and tenderly plucks the dart from the creased skin behind the ear.

Like a child fighting sleep, Esme's eye flickers and blinks. Then, without shutting, it transforms, from bright black to glassy grey. Kibet gently passes her hand over the eye and lowers the eyelid before leaning across the now harmless horn and doing the same on the other side.

Slowly, cautiously, the other rangers approach.

—Who the hell are you? one of them asks, raising a gun at Mollel.

Kibet stands and takes Mollel's hand.

—It's OK, she says. This is my friend.

The others seem too shaken up to challenge this assertion, and the man who fired the dart goes over to the prone figure.

—We haven't much time, he says. Let's do this.

The chainsaw-wielding ranger steps forward.

—Oh, Mollel, cries Kibet, and turns away from the scene, burying her face in his shoulder.

The ranger pulls the starter cord and the chainsaw growls into life. Mollel hurries Kibet away from the impending act. Feeling her fall weakly against his body, he clutches her to him and together they stagger out of the doorway of the shed.

Mollel can feel Kibet shaking in his arms. It is not fear, he feels sure, or even the cold night air that is making her shiver.

—What are they doing? he asks.

—It's horrible, she replies. So horrible. But we had no choice.

The growl of the chainsaw changes into a searing howl.

—Once you told me the poachers were targeting me, Kibet continues, tearfully, I knew they were after Esme, so we had to act. We could keep transferring her from place to place, always hoping to keep one step ahead of them . . . or we could do this.

An acrid smell begins to burn Mollel's nostrils. Combined with the fumes of the chainsaw exhaust, it is at once alien and yet familiar. He tries to place it.

—We're taking away their reason to kill her, says Kibet. With no horn, there's a chance – a slim one – they'll lose interest. It doesn't always work. The stump goes right down into the skull. They can always find a market, even for the remaining amount. And to extract it . . .

She shudders. Mollel recalls what she told him, the day he first met her, about the elephant poachers and how they had taken the whole face from the animals they slaughtered in their greed for the tusks.

—But hopefully, it won't be worth the risk. We've mutilated Esme. She'll never be the same again. But at least she'll be alive.

And you too, thinks Mollel, holding the woman close to him. In that moment, her involvement with the disappearances – with the murders – is pushed to the back of his mind, replaced with an overwhelming sense of admiration. She has risked her life to protect this creature, even when she knows the Chinese gang want her dead. It is the same selfless dedication which has led her to protect the women of this town, when the law and the system has failed. Whatever she has done, she has done it out of compassion.

Her bravery humbles him. And then he finds himself feeling a torrent of conflict. If doing what's right means stopping this woman from doing justice, however arbitrary that form of justice may be, he wonders if terms such as *right* and *justice* even mean anything any more.

The noise stops abruptly, and at the same moment, Mollel identifies the familiar scent which has stung his nostrils: it is like burning hair.

The same smell he had detected on Jemimah Okallo's clothing in her dormitory.

The thought is interrupted by the emergence of two of the rangers from the doorway. Between them, they bear the long, curving horn, and they lay it on the ground before Mollel and Kibet like some kind of trophy.

Kibet, horrified, turns her head sharply away.

Mollel understands her revulsion. This horn is no inanimate object, but a severed member. It's like having a human head or a hand tossed at their feet.

Mollel is the only one who knows that Kibet is involved with the disappearances. He has no doubt about the nobility of her motives. Her tactics may be unacceptable, but – he considers – does that really mean she was wrong? All that's important is stopping her doing it.

He has a decision to make in Hell's Gate.

25

It seems only appropriate that it is Kibet who is elected to take the horn to KWS headquarters in Nairobi. The whole operation has something of a ceremonial air about it – like a funeral – and this final stage is the equivalent of committing the body to the earth.

But the horn is not to be buried, nor burned. It is to be placed in a vault pending possible scientific research. But, Kibet confides to Mollel as she drives him out of the National Park, the horn wrapped in a blanket on the back seat, many suspect that the rhino horns – along with other valuable items, such as confiscated ivory – are being held as a kind of foreign reserve hedge, the way some states hold gold: to be dipped into in time of need.

—Of course, I don't believe it myself, she adds.

Mollel is not so sure.

He asks her to drop him on the roadside near the police post, and watches the tail lights of her truck disappear into the distance. Then he crosses the road and heads for the entrance to the flower farm.

He has followed his nose: not toward the sickly mixture of rose perfume and fertiliser which hangs low over this place, but toward the more elusive memory of a scent. The scent of burning hair.

It's not an unusual smell. You get it every time you walk past a salon where women are being primped and pampered.

Perhaps that was all this was, too. Jemimah Okallo, or one of her room-mates, had been straightening their hair with an iron. But somehow Mollel feels that the workers in this place have had more on their minds than beauty treatments.

He is expecting to be challenged at the gate, and has some words prepared about being a police officer – after all, he is out of uniform, and has no identification – but to his surprise, the guards simply nod and swing open the wicket for him. As he passes through the small inner gate, he realises that it is precisely because of his garb that he has been granted access, and he recalls the words of the guard at the hotel next door, who, seeing him in Maasai dress, had said:

—*He's one of us.*

Following his nose, still – or at least, the memory – he makes his way toward the dormitories. He expects to find them shut up and dark, but even as he rounds the corner, he is surprised to hear raised voices – female voices – and movement.

The doors are thrown open, lights blazing, and women come hurrying all around, pulling on their work overalls and aprons. As one of them passes by him, Mollel grabs her arm. She turns and glares into his eyes.

—We're going as fast as we can! she protests, her eyes still bleary with sleep. Can't you give us a bit more warning next time? These night-time shipments are killing us!

—What is happening? asks Mollel. At this question, the woman scrutinises him more closely.

—I don't know you, do I? she asks in return. Are you new?

—Get on with your work, he answers gruffly, releasing her arm. Just at that moment, he has glimpsed the silhouette of a Maasai warrior, *rungu* held threateningly in hand, at the far side of the dormitory block. He is talking to a security guard. It could well be one of the ones from the gate.

Mollel leaves the dormitory area and walks along the outside of one of the polytunnels. The curved skin beside him seems to have captured the daylight of hours before and is slowly releasing it. There is even a glow of warmth which he can feel upon his skin. There is nothing natural, however, about this place.

Inside, he can see vague shapes moving. The plastic is too opaque to be able to make out anything in detail, but there is a lot of activity for this time of night.

He crouches and feels around in the dirt. Eventually his fingers alight upon a small stone, a piece of gravel with a sharp edge. It is not the keenest point in the world, but he hopes it will serve. He picks up the stone and presses it, hard, into the yielding flesh of the glowing plastic sheet. After a moment's resistance, the sheet gives in to the pressure and a tiny hole remains.

He puts his eye to the hole and looks inside.

The long, wide blocks of colour which are the rose beds are largely undisturbed. No pickers are visible there. Instead, all of the activity appears to be focused upon a long, central table. Workers hurry in with tall stacks of white polystyrene boxes, which they drop, teetering, onto the table. These are immediately snatched by other workers, who start flinging them down the production line.

The next stage is the packing. Great piles of cut stems sit at intervals along the table, and gloved women grasp handfuls and drop them into each box, before passing it on to be sealed.

A woman carrying a basket of flowers runs up and tips it onto one of the rapidly diminishing piles. As she comes away from the table, she wipes her brow and pauses. Another woman, passing, stops and rests her hands wearily on her knees.

—Mr De Wit's not going to like this, says the first woman. Roses being packed uncounted, colours being mixed. Bad blooms going in with the good ones.

—De Wit's not going to know about it, is he? replies the other woman. Haven't you noticed how this only happens when he's away? Here, better hurry up. One of those Maasai bastards is coming.

They scurry back to their work, and Mollel sees a flash of red in front of him. The red chequered cloth of a Maasai *shuka* fills his vision. And then:

—Seen everything you need to, Mollel?

He leaps up with a start. Turning, he sees Tonkei and another two *morans* directly behind him. They all hold *rungus*.

—I'm glad you came back, Mollel, says Tonkei. There's some-one who wants to meet you.

The two *morans* grab him and march him toward the roadside end of the polytunnel. He hears the hum of a diesel engine and sees a large container lorry waiting there, idling. Its back doors are open and inside are two men. As the sealed white boxes of flowers are thrown up to them, they catch them in their arms, pivot and toss them into the gloom, presumably to be stacked by other workers further within.

A shove on the back propels Mollel through the entrance of the polytunnel and he blinks in the artificial light. He is being pushed toward a closed-off area: a construction of painted ply-board much like the office in which he had sat with De Wit and the snivelling Jemimah Okallo when he first came here. But, as Tonkei opens the door and Mollel comes in behind him, he sees that, unlike De Wit's office, this space is completely enclosed. There is a ceiling above, and no windows. It is an en-closure within an enclosure.

At a workbench in the centre of this cramped space, two women sit. The only light comes from an angled lamp which points down on to the bench, a pool of light illuminating a machine. At first glance, Mollel takes it to be an industrial sewing machine. It is the same size. But instead of a spool and needle, it possesses a gleaming, fine-toothed circular saw. Between the saw and where one of the women sits – the ma-chine's operator, presumably – there is a small Perspex shield. Both women are wearing protective goggles and paper masks.

In the air is a smell. A somewhat stale smell. It fights for dominance with the perfume of flowers, but it is recognisable nonetheless.

The smell of burned hair.

*

Tonkei nods at the two *morans* and they leave, closing the door behind them. He unclips his cellphone from his belt and punches in a number.

—Guess who I've got here? he says into the phone, in Maa.

He glances over at Mollel. —The very same. Sure.

Tonkei takes his phone and places it on the workbench. —Mbatiani wants to speak to you, he says.

Mbatiani.

A Maasai name. But not just any Maasai name. The name of one of the greatest ever Maasai warriors. *Laibon* Mbatiani, a witch doctor and leader who so impressed the British invaders he fought against that they named a peak of Mount Kenya after him.

It was said that Mbatiani would return, in time of need, to lead the Maasai people back to possession of their rightful home.

And now Mollel was about to talk to him. Or at least, to someone bearing his name. Tonkei presses a button and the phone's speaker gives out a crackle.

—Mollel? asks a voice.

It's a distant, tinny voice. Distorted and crackling, but familiar. So familiar that, for a moment, Mollel has the surreal impression that he is talking to himself.

—Yes? he replies.

Mbatiani gives a low chuckle. —It *is* Mollel. I've been reading about you, Mollel. You've been making headlines.

Mollel does not answer. He is still trying to place that voice.

—I guess you'll be looking for a job, now you're out of the police force? To be honest, I'm surprised you lasted as long as you did. I never thought you'd end up as a prisoner on the run, though. By the way, it sounds like Mdosi's going to pull through. Bad luck, but well done for trying. You got a lot closer than I ever did. We've been trying to eliminate him for a while now. We got most of his gang, one way or another. But not the big guy.

Another chuckle. So it was the Maasai gang who were behind

the disappearances, after all. Presumably Kibet's role was to deliver the victims up to them.

—So I have a proposition for you, Mollel. Come and join me. We need a man like you. I think you'll find it more rewarding than the police.

—I'll think about it, says Mollel.

—You can think about it, replies Mbatiani. But don't take long. I think you'll come to realise very soon that you have very little choice in the matter.

The tone of Mbatiani's voice changes. —Tonkei! he barks. Is that shipment ready yet?

—Not quite, replies Tonkei, the usual cocky confidence in his voice replaced with a degree of fear.

—Well, get a move on. We can only delay the plane for so long.

The door of the cubicle opens and Tonkei lets out a sigh of relief. —Ah, it's here now. We'll be on our way shortly.

—Good. See you soon, Mollel.

The phone blips and the strangely familiar voice is extinguished.

Mollel turns to see the newcomers. They are his two *moran* guards, and they bear something heavy between them. Something wrapped in a blanket.

They open the blanket and place the rhino horn on the workbench. The two women immediately set about their work. At the flick of a switch, the circular saw whirs into life. One woman expertly manoeuvres the horn across the bench while the other starts guiding its tip toward the circular saw.

With the ease of a chef chopping vegetables, a set of fine discs begins to appear next to the saw. They are all of equal thickness, but each one is slightly larger than the previous.

—*Pht*, spits Tonkei. I hate this smell.

He leans across and scoops up a handful of the rapidly mounting pile of discs. —Here, he orders one of the *morans*. Take this lot and start putting them in among the roses. Remember, only in the boxes marked Black Champagne. Right?

Mollel feels dazed. Any thought of identifying the voice on the phone is forgotten. All he can think about is Kibet.

How could he do it? How could he be duped, again?

Her love for the rhino was as false as any hint of feeling she may have had for him. She had rendered up the horn to the the Maasai gang, led by this Mbatiani. Her indignation at the rapists was no doubt false, too. She was involved in the disappearances of Mdosi's men as part of her role in some turf war that was ongoing between Mdosi and Mbatiani – presumably for control of this trade in animal parts.

And to think that he had been covering for her all this time. Not revealing her role in the whole affair, even to Kiunga.

It is not just the acrid smell of the horn being sliced which tastes bitter in Mollel's mouth.

All this time, the *morans* have been coming and going, taking sections of horn. As the two women approach the end of their strange task, Mollel remembers them once more. This must have been Jemimah Okallo's job, too. Desperate for money to pay off the person who was threatening her, she had attempted to sneak back into the flower farm at night. Why? To plead for her job back? To find Tonkei and threaten him with revealing their operation? This was more likely. It would certainly explain why she would not be allowed to leave this place alive. And rather than simply disappear her, as they did with Mdosi's men, it was a smart touch to leave her body in the water right here. That way, she would serve as a warning to others.

Tonkei grabs the last few discs of horn, the size of dinner plates now. The job done, the two women sit back, raise their goggles and mop their foreheads.

—Come on, says Tonkei to Mollel.

They exit the cubicle and once more Mollel finds himself blinking in the brightness. The scene has changed. The main table, where the packing was taking place, is now devoid of workers. Piles of roses and boxes lie scattered, abandoned. The loaders of the truck have gone, too. Only Tonkei and the two *morans* remain. Beside the truck is a stack of six polystyrene boxes, the height of a man. On each of them is a sticker with the words *Black Champagne*. The topmost box is open and a gush of green foliage and black petals is just visible over the side.

Tonkei takes the discs in his hand and reaches up, slipping them inside the box and giving them a good shove down among the foliage. Then he lifts up a lid, places it atop the box and uses a tape gun to seal it.

—Get into the truck, will you, Mollel?

He makes it sound like a request, but Mollel has no doubt that it is an order. He mounts the rear step of the lorry and stands above Tonkei in the doorway. A chill comes over him. The air in the container is refrigerated. He feels the vibration of the truck's engine through his feet.

Tonkei passes up the boxes of Black Champagne roses two at a time. Mollel stacks them against the side of the truck, alongside the rows of white boxes which continue, canyon-like, into the darkness beyond him.

—Make yourself comfortable, says Tonkei with a sneer, as soon as Mollel has finished. You're riding back here.

Mollel looks down. He could leap onto the young warrior now, and knock him out. But as though reading his thoughts, the two other *morans* close in. One of them now bears a spear. The weapon glints incongruously in this modern, industrial setting; Mollel has no doubt it is lethal, just the same.

As the doors swing shut upon him, Tonkei says: —Sorry about the cold, Mollel. Not much we can do about that. But we promise not to pump the container full of carbon dioxide. That's what we'd do if this were a regular delivery. Good for the flowers, you know. Not so good for snooping Maasai.

The three of them laugh, and the door shuts.

In the darkness, Mollel runs his hands up and down the door, searching for a handle. There is none.

The truck roars into life and there is a jolt. Mollel sways on his feet and is thrown against some of the boxes around him. He steadies himself and senses the motion. A set of rapid jerks, and then the vehicle turns sharply and gains pace. Smoother now. They must be on the road.

And then a different noise. Closer. A muffled cry.

Mollel cautiously moves toward the noise, feeling his way along the stacks of boxes. There is light in this space – a dim bulb at the far end glows just enough to allow Mollel to see the stacks swaying around him. He nearly stumbles as he reaches the far end of the container and something soft bristles against his shins. The crying becomes louder. Crouching down, he touches a warm, round head. His fingertips locate a band of cloth over the wet face. He gropes, finds a knot, struggles and loosens it. The cloth comes away in his hands.

—Mollel, she cries. Thank God, Mollel. I was driving . . . they just came out of nowhere. I thought they were going to kill me.

Kibet's voice collapses into sobs.

—They knew, Mollel, she gasps. They knew all about the horn.

26

As soon as Mollel has freed Kibet from her bonds, she flings her arms around him. In the cold, it seems only natural to remain that way, as he comes to her side, and they huddle against the wall of the container.

He is being forced once more to revise his conclusions about Kibet. If she were an accomplice to the Maasai gang, why would they bind her in this way?

—Tell me, he says. Tell me about the disappearances.

She tells him. She confirms the story he's already been told by Shadrack and the others. After Mdosi's men kept being freed by Judge Singh, they grew frustrated by their inability to do anything about it. So the police decided to exact their own judgement.

But it was never murder. The four officers would take the men down into Hell's Gate gorge and give them a good beating, scare the wits out of them. Then they'd be released. Kibet would appear, seemingly by chance, and urge them to make themselves scarce. Most of them leapt at the opportunity.

—But Gachui? asks Mollel. I found his gold teeth, Kibet. I found them in your cabin.

Kibet is silent for a while. Mollel feels her stiffen. Eventually, she says:

—You're the one who knocked them out, Mollel.

Deep down, he knows that. It is not exactly a moment he is

proud of. But he persists: —What were you going to do with them?

—I wasn't going to keep them, if that's what you're thinking. I don't need to justify myself to you, you know. But just so you understand, he raped a woman, if you remember, over a debt the husband owed to him.

He feels her shudder. The two of them are still together, but whatever warmth existed between them has been lost since Mollel voiced his suspicions.

—Well, it's a poor form of compensation. But I was going to give those teeth to the family. I felt it was the least they deserved.

Mollel knows Kibet is telling the truth. He also knows that she is angered by his distrust of her.

His arm is already around her against the cold, and he squeezes. There is no knowing how long they may be trapped in this refrigerated space. Perhaps the plan is to let them freeze to death. The alternative – execution in some remote spot – is hardly more attractive.

Kibet shivers against him, and he hears her breath coming in short, shallow sobs.

—It will be OK, he whispers.

To his amazement, what he had taken for sobs turns into a laugh.

—I was just thinking, she gasps. What with the roses, and the low light, it's pretty romantic in here.

That dark humour is typical of Rhino Squad. Mollel has never been one to crack jokes when his life is in the balance – but he admires those who can. And then, much to his own surprise, he makes a joke of his own.

—Don't forget the rhino horn.

Kibet immediately pulls up.

—The rhino horn? Esme's horn?

—Yes, replies Mollel. It's here.

Kibet stands and looks about her in the gloom.

—In the flower boxes. These ones, marked *Black Champagne*.

Kibet takes the uppermost box and rips off the tape. The lid falls to the floor as she rummages among the foliage, hands oblivious to thorns, and pulls out a smooth, thin disc.

—What have they done?

—It's been sliced up and distributed between these boxes. All set to be smuggled out of the country.

Kibet holds the disc up to her face, and inhales deeply.

And then she is a flurry of activity, rummaging further in the box to pull out another disc. She hastily shoves the discs, which are too wide for a pocket, down the front of her ranger's shirt.

—What are you doing? asks Mollel.

—They won't get away with this, Kibet spits. I won't let them.

Mollel is about to warn her that it won't make any difference, that their only chance of survival depends upon not angering the gang – but just at that moment they hear the engine change pitch and the floor underneath them rumbles and judders while the boxes rock and sway all around.

The lorry comes to a halt with a whoosh of air brakes, and after a moment, the doors swing open.

—Get out.

Mollel and Kibet rise stiffly. He helps her along the length of the container, between the boxes, and extends his hand to lower her down to the ground.

The night air feels warm after the refrigerated container, and Mollel can just make out the first traces of dawn on the eastern horizon. He recognises the spot. They are on the Nairobi road, close to the start of the escarpment, but still firmly down in the basin of the Rift Valley. Tonkei is waiting beside a pickup truck with a driver inside.

—Get in the back.

Mollel and Kibet get into the back of the pickup and Tonkei and one of his *morans* sit opposite them. The *moran* still has his spear.

—Be careful with that thing, says Mollel. The *moran* replies with a blank stare.

The flower lorry and the pickup both move off at the same time, the lorry continuing on the tarmac road toward Nairobi, the pickup lurching onto a rough track leading straight into the bush. Soon the road is far behind them, and Mollel, head swaying from the movement of the vehicle, hunches his shoulders and allows, for a moment or two at least, his weary eyes to close.

The next thing he is aware of is a glowing beyond his eyelids and the warmth of sunlight on his face. He opens his eyes. Tonkei and the *moran* are watching him. Neither gives any sign of emotion.

Grass, golden in the low sun, stirs around the side of the pickup, giving the impression of a bow wave as they move through it, as though they are riding in a boat. Progress is steadily uphill. Beyond, a blue peak rises. Mollel does not know this country, but thinks he recognises the profile of the Kikuyu escarpment in the distance.

They pass a bare patch on the ground, the earth wet and a fine wisp of vapour curling up from it. *Ol Doinyo e-Puru*, thinks Mollel. The mountain of smoke. They must be on the other side of Hell's Gate, now.

The journey continues and the grass becomes sparser, the patches of steaming earth more frequent.

Eventually, the smooth ride through the grass ends and they encounter rocky ground. It's too much for the pickup. At one particularly steep point, the driver ratchets up the handbrake and kills the engine. Tonkei leans over and drops the tailgate.

—We walk from here, he says.

They pick their way through sharp-edged rocks like shattered foam. A frozen sea. Slopes rise before them, only to be supplanted by another once they gain the ridge. The rest of the world seems to have disappeared into a wide, flat blur.

Eventually the trail levels out, and Mollel notices that they are no longer climbing up the peak, but along its side. A small, wild clump of thorn bushes, unexpected in this landscape of rocks, comes into view in front of them. Something in the way that Tonkei and the *moran* modify their step gives Mollel the impression that their journey is reaching its conclusion.

A figure, clad in a red shawl, steps out from a gap in the bushes.

This, thinks Mollel, must be Mbatiani.

At the sight of him, the two other Maasai pause and adopt a reverential pose, bowing their heads slightly. Mist swirls around the figure standing before them. The vapour is thicker here, and the strong smell of sulphur is heavy in the air.

—*Supai*, Mollel, says Mbatiani.

And a stir of wind on the mountainside whips the vapour away from the figure's face. Now Mollel knows Mbatiani's identity. He finally knows who he is facing.

It was a year or more after the discovery of their uncle's body that the Samburu people passed by Mollel's village once more. As before, they were invited to overnight their camels – fewer, now – in the *boma*, in return for some of the delicious milk.

But they refused. They just wanted to get back north, to a land they still called home. Mollel maintained a certain contempt for them, but he was no longer so convinced of the Maasai's superiority. The Samburu were a sorrier group even than before: the Maasai of Tanzania had not been welcoming to the newcomers. They did not like the strangers, their clothes, their accent or their camels. More importantly, they had made it plain that their land was not for sharing.

—Where's the little guy? asked one of the Samburu *morans* when he saw Mollel.

Mollel had little idea. After a short period of amiability following Uncle's death, he and Lendeva had drifted into antagonism and competition once more. Lendeva had decided that herding goats was beneath him, and demanded an equal share of the cattle duty. Mollel knew well that this was against the rules of family seniority and the two of them had fought bitterly. Mollel had won – for now. But he saw the rate at which his brother was growing, and suspected it would not be long until the elder of the two was the smaller in stature. Then, victory in a physical fight would not be so assured.

—I wondered if he'd got himself killed, said the Samburu.

—What makes you say that?

—He was so determined to learn about our arrows. We showed him how to identify the *ol morijoi* tree. How to select one that looked as though it were nearly dead from drought. I did it with him myself. I taught him how to chop up the branches, ten or more, and boil the chips for two days. Then I showed him how we mix the tar with sand and roll the tips of the arrows in it.

—You taught him all that? asked Mollel, with a growing sense of unease.

—He was a good student. He wanted to start making batches of the stuff straight away. That's why I thought he'd end up killing himself. He didn't just want to learn our ways, you see. He wanted to experiment.

—Experiment? How?

The Samburu laughed. —Oh, he had an idea about not using the poison on arrows, as we do. He brought a load of thorns one day, started going on about making them into darts. Thought he could blow them from a reed. I told him, darts would be useless. They'd simply bounce off most animal hides. If he were to prick himself, though, that would be a different story.

—*Supai*, Lendeva, Mollel greets his brother.

Tonkei raises his head in surprise at the unknown name. Lendeva nods and gives a wave of his hand.

—Take this woman to enjoy the view for a while, he says. Mollel and I have some catching up to do.

When the *morans* are out of earshot, Mollel asks: —Where have you been, Lendeva? The last time I saw you was in Nairobi. Just before ...

A frown – pain? pity? regret? – passes across Lendeva's brow. He knows what Mollel is referring to. Just before the American embassy bombing. Just before Mollel lost his wife.

—City life didn't suit me, Lendeva replies.

—But you didn't return to the village. Mother never saw you again, either.

—Oh, don't play the dutiful son with me, Mollel, scoffs Lendeva, the familiar contempt rising in his voice once more. You abandoned her, too.

—At least I saw her before she died.

Lendeva raises his eyebrows. —She's dead? I assumed she would be by now. Was it . . . peaceful?

—No, says Mollel angrily, spitefully throwing the words at him like weapons, it was horrible, and painful, and she was frightened. She cried out for you, Lendeva. She called your name. It was the last thing she said.

Lendeva turns away. Distractedly, he puts his hand out to one of the thorn bushes and twists off a barb.

He holds it in his hand. The long thorn has a small, round gall at the end. From a hole in the gall, a steady stream of ants is emerging. Mollel sees that they are crawling onto Lendeva's palm, his thumb, sinking their jaws into his skin. But Lendeva is unmoved. He turns his hand over and raises it, looking at the furious creatures with a mixture of curiosity and amusement.

—The red ant, he says to Mollel. You know, the only tree it won't eat is the whistling thorn. The tree that grows a home for it. The whistling thorn houses the ants, and in return, they protect it. Any animal that comes along to try to strip the leaves off this tree, they sting it. They look after their home, and their home looks after them.

Now, realises Mollel, it is not Lendeva speaking. It is Mbatiani. This is the person he has become over the years when Mollel no longer knew him.

—We, the Maasai, are the red ants. The others, the farmers, the city folk, the Europeans – they are the black ants. There may be more of them, but we will fight fiercer than they do when it comes to protecting our home.

He drops the thorn and shakes his hand. A smile plays upon his lips – the smile of a boy Mollel once knew so well.

—Vicious little bastards, aren't they?

—What are you trying to say, Lendeva? Mollel asks. That you're protecting Maasai land? That's not what it looks like to me. You're running a smuggling operation, sending poached ivory and rhino horn out of the country. That might make you wealthy, but you're no Maasai hero. You're no Mbatiani.

Lendeva's brow furrows. —Do I look wealthy? he spits. This is not about money, Mollel. At least, not for personal gain. Those elephants, those rhinos. Whose land do you think they're on? It doesn't belong to the government, or the Kikuyus, or the whites. It belongs to us! This, Mollel – he sweeps his hand wide – this land, under this sky, is ours. Everything in it is ours. And I will use our resources to get back what belongs to us.

—So you're going to raise a private army?

—I already have one, replies Lendeva. There are more of us than you think. And once word gets out, there will be a million or more of us. Every Maasai in Kenya, and beyond, will agree with us. Maasailand will be restored, one way or another.

Maasailand. That nation which spread from the Indian Ocean to the great lake, encompassing Africa's two highest mountains. Its borders remained unmarked yet undisputed, all other tribes deferring fearfully, choosing between vassalage to, or destruction by, their Maasai masters, until the British came with their trains.

—So why not do it politically? Why turn to violence?

Lendeva laughed. —Mollel, this is Kenya! Did you learn nothing from the last election? Who were the most violent factions? And who is in power today? No, we Maasai sat that one out. And look where it got us. It will be different next time.

—Even if you get what you want, protests Mollel, what will it be worth? With your poaching there will be no elephants, no rhinos. That's not the Maasai way.

Lendeva rolls his eyes. —Oh, Mollel. You sound just like *her*. Well, you're not going to take our ivory away, and nor is she. Bring her forward!

Tonkei and the *moran* haul Kibet toward them.

—You're about to find out, Mollel, what happens to people who get in our way. The Mdosi gang found out when they tried to muscle in on our business. We found they were easy to pick up, one by one, once this woman and her police colleagues had softened them up for us. Come.

He parts the thorn bushes before him and Mollel sees why this clump of vegetation exists here on this otherwise bare mountainside. Its life force is drawn from the vapour which rises from a wide hole, sunk into the side of the mountain. It is almost perfectly round, reminding Mollel of the nest of the baboon spider. He remembers how Lendeva, as a boy, would lower a twig into those holes and tease the creature until he felt a pull, then he would pluck out the twig once more with a plump, hairy spider clinging to it. Mollel remembers his revulsion at the sight.

Like the spider's hole, this chasm is not man-made: it is a lava tube. Mollel has seen them before, but never this wide. A car could easily be swallowed into it. And approaching closer, he realises that its depth is barely comprehensible.

Lendeva picks up a heavy rock and tosses it in.

They wait. And wait.

There is no sound.

There is no bottom.

—Her first, says Lendeva to Tonkei. Then my brother can tell us whether he's going to join us, or die.

Tonkei drags the struggling ranger forward, while the other *moran* lowers his spear at Mollel's face.

Released from Tonkei's grasp, Kibet stands at the very edge of the lava tube. The steam rises in wisps around her. She looks wildly at Mollel, and then back at Tonkei, who has raised his spear to her ribs.

—No! gasps Mollel. I'll join you. Whatever you want, Lendeva – Mbatiani – I'll call you whatever you like.

Lendeva smiles.

—Oh Mollel, he sighs. I thought you'd have learned by now,

that once I've made up my mind, no one stands in my way.

And the tortured, rictus grin of Uncle flashes up in Mollel's mind.

—You know, the older you get, Lendeva, the more you remind me of him.

—Shut up! barks Lendeva.

—This is just the sort of thing he would do. And you look so alike. You always hated him for taking our mother. But you didn't know the half of it.

—Don't talk about our mother! Lendeva warns, his voice taut. But Mollel ignores him, pushing on.

—I was the elder brother, Lendeva. I knew he had designs on her long before father died. And I knew something else, too. When our father used to disappear, drink, for days at a time, Uncle used to come to our hut. She fought him, but she did not always win.

The tip of Lendeva's spear wobbles in Mollel's face, and he thinks for a moment about grasping it. But Tonkei still has Kibet at the mouth of the lava tube, and the risk is too great. He looks into Lendeva's eyes. They are furious, gleaming with tears.

—You killed my Uncle, Lendeva, when you shot him with that poison dart. But you killed *your* father.

—Do it! screams Lendeva, and turns to Tonkei.

Tonkei hesitates a moment, takes a deep breath, and plunges the spear towards Kibet's stomach.

She folds forward, grasping her gut. Then she raises her head again. She is smiling.

Slowly, she puts her hand into the fold of her ranger's shirt. Tonkei and Lendeva watch in astonishment as her hand reappears, holding a wide, shiny grey disc.

—I have a load more of these, she calls out. What are they worth to you? Thousands of dollars? Hundreds of thousands?

Nonchalantly, she tosses the disc over her shoulder. It disappears soundlessly into the chasm below.

—Wait! shouts Mollel. Tonkei stops himself from pouncing, and looks back for further orders, a frown crossing his face as he realises it was not his leader, but his leader's brother, who had spoken.

Kibet, meanwhile, is drawing another of the discs of rhino horn from her shirt.

—Let us go, says Mollel, and you can have the horn.

Lendeva's lip curls. But the answer comes from elsewhere.

—No, Mollel.

It is Kibet.

—I'm not going to give it to them. It doesn't belong to them. And it never will.

Tonkei, frustrated, takes his chance. He leaps forward to grasp the disc from Kibet's hand, but she throws it behind her as he does so. Steam whirls around the tall Maasai and the ranger and they seem, for an instant, to be shrouded in it.

Mollel takes his moment. He grabs the end of the spear, just below its leaf-shaped tip, and levers it from the *moran's* grasp. Gripping it in both hands, he gives a warning swipe. The *moran*, caught off-guard by the loss of his weapon, is nonetheless alert enough to spring back instinctively as the blade whisks past his face.

Looking up just as the steam parts, Mollel sees Kibet and Tonkei still struggling at the lava tube's edge. Tonkei has his arm firmly around her neck, but Kibet twists and sinks her teeth into his flesh.

Tonkei gives a yelp of pain and reflexively releases her, realising too late his mistake. His feet slide on the loose scree of the lava tube's edge. He tries to compensate, crouching and throwing his weight forward. His arms wheel helplessly as he teeters and his eyes throw out a panicky cry for help.

Mollel, still holding off the other *moran*, knows he cannot get to Tonkei in time. Kibet is the only one who can save him. Tonkei reaches out to her, but it is too late.

A strange throbbing sound seems to rise with the steam from the lava tube. It is as though the gaping maw is rumbling to be fed.

Is it the reverberation of Tonkei's body, finally hitting bottom? Or something else?

Something else, decides Mollel. For the throbbing sound is growing, strengthening. And now Lendeva and the *moran* seem aware of it too, for they exchange a concerned glance.

An earthquake? An eruption?

It sounds as if something has awoken in the bowels of the Earth.

The rumbling from the hole turns into a roar at that moment, and a sudden burst of wind and dust flattens the bushes around them. The sound, Mollel realises, was not coming from the depths of hell, but from the sky, the weird acoustics of the lava tube sucking it up and spitting it back out. The dark belly of a helicopter hovers above them.

Mollel sees the barrel of a gun bristling from the side of the craft. Behind it, leaning out of the open doorway and holding on to the side, is Kiunga. Oberkampf is just visible over his shoulder.

—*Don't shoot*, screams Mollel, his voice whipped away by the wind and the din of the helicopter's blades. But he sees Kiunga's rifle lower on its strap. Mollel's red *shuka* flies around his body as he lifts his arm to shield his eyes. He looks up the mountain, and down. Kibet is there, slumped exhaustedly on her knees. The other *moran* has his hands raised. But Lendeva is gone.

27

They circle several times in an attempt to spot Lendeva, but they see no sign of him.

The pilot taps the fuel gauge and points at the horizon. The message is clear. They have to return to base. In a way, Mollel is not disappointed. It seems wholly appropriate that, having sprung back into his life from nowhere, his brother should disappear again.

—We'll catch him, shouts Kiunga. But Mollel knows they will not. Having so nearly made the transition himself, he knows how easy it is for a Maasai to merge into the landscape and be gone.

The great crater rises below them, as though bidding farewell, and then sinks as they climb for the flight back to Nairobi. They pass over Maili Ishirini, little more than a jumble of squares and flashing metal roofs clustered around a road junction, the harsh white polygons of the flower farm and the glittering lake. Mollel sees the cliffs of Hell's Gate, almost laughably low from here, and the great plume of steam from the geothermal plant. Between the two, the solitary figure of the Maasai Bride and the deep winding gorge, visible only as a trail of green in the dusty plain.

And then the whole place is gone. The Rift Valley itself is behind them, and the knuckled ridge of the Ngong Hills approaches, bristling with the wind turbines that power the great city beyond it.

Nairobi. His home.

Its suburbs and slums emerge like smudged fingerprints of paint over the earth. A faintly visible pall of smoke and smog hangs over the city like a low veil. And there, the towers of the centre stud the scene, a bold punctuation marking their destination.

The journey has taken only a matter of minutes, but Maili Ishirini seems a world away. Mollel strains as the helicopter begins to descend and skims fast over the northern outskirts of the city. Somewhere, down there, is Kawangware, his mother-in-law's home, and home, too, to his son. He wonders whether Adam, perhaps kicking a ball around Faith's yard, might look up at that point and see the speck carrying his father. Soon, Mollel realises, with a longing so profound and long-repressed that it almost makes him gasp, he will be reunited with his boy.

The helicopter's engine changes pitch and they begin to veer away. The city's towers, larger now, rotate as the final approach is made. Dense clusters of houses give way to larger, flatter warehouses and godowns, and individual vehicles are distinguishable – and people too now – as they near the airport, that vast swathe of concrete and strips of grass with its white aircraft serried at the side, or gathered nose forward at the terminal building, like animals around a trough.

The helicopter slows and hangs in mid-air, a sensation far more unnerving than motion over the ground. Then slowly, it begins to descend. Mollel has a glimpse of a great, whale-like cargo plane being loaded with crisp white pallets, and he imagines the flowers therein adorning the dressing tables and dining rooms of European homes some twenty-four hours from now.

A pair of black saloon cars gleam, impossibly clean, on the concrete below them. Government cars. Some men stand beside them, and as the distance to the ground narrows between them, Mollel is able to recognise the tall, stocky form of Otieno.

Touchdown is gentle: a tender kiss. Then the roar of the

engine gives way to the powering down of the blades, which gradually change from a blur above them to visible, rotating strips, which slow further then come to a halt.

The silence is almost startling. And in that moment, the passengers of the craft – Kibet, Kiunga, Oberkampf and Mollel – exchange glances, but no words. Words, it seems, would shatter something that the three of them, in that instant, share.

And then the door of the helicopter opens. Oberkampf is the first out then Kibet. The two policemen follow.

A KWS pick-up is beyond the black saloon cars. Kibet looks over at it, then turns to Mollel.

—There's my ride

Her eyes meet his only fleetingly then she walks towards her waiting vehicle. She does not look back.

—Sergeant Mollel, booms the familiar voice of Otieno.

It is a moment before Mollel realises his rank has been reinstated.

—Sergeant Kiunga, Otieno is continuing. He shakes Kiunga's hand, then Mollel's. Good work out there, Sergeants. I'm sure that the Naivasha police can take over the rest of the job from here. Now that we've firmly established it was Tonkei's gang of Maasai responsible for the disappearances, there's no need for HQ to take such a close interest. Thank you, Sergeant Kiunga, for your interim report. Sergeant Mollel, I assume you'll be able to write it up formally, once you've had a rest?

—Kiunga? asks Oberkampf, staring at the young sergeant. Kiunga lowers his head.

—Oh, I see, she says, turning to Otieno. So he was reporting back to you all along. I had assumed someone would be. I just hadn't realised it would be him. Well played, Collins. I really trusted you.

—Sorry, Justine, mutters Kiunga.

—And what will happen to the Maili Ishirini police? demands Oberkampf to Otieno. They may have proved themselves not to be executioners, but they still played judge and jury. I have enough material for a damning indictment of your force.

—Miss Oberkampf, interjects Otieno, turning to her with a grin. Please don't worry about those four troublesome individuals. They'll be sent to retrain somewhere, far out of harm's way. I'm thinking of the Ethiopian border. And as for your report ... well, there are a couple of gentlemen here from the Interior Ministry who'd like a little word with you about that.

Two heavyset men step forward, their suits and sunglasses as expensive and pristine as the government cars that brought them.

—Justine Oberkampf, one intones, under the terms of your visa you were allowed to investigate the post-election violence. We have reason to believe that you have overstepped the terms of your investigation, and therefore, by order of the Minister of the Interior, your visa is revoked. There is a flight to Amsterdam in two hours. We're here to see you're on it.

Oberkampf casts Kiunga a rueful glance.

—Sorry, Kiunga mutters again.

She is led away.

—You know, I've had my problems with the Diplomatic Police before, chuckles Otieno. But when it comes to removing undesirables from the country, they have no equal. We'll be doing the same with your Chinese smugglers too, Mollel, never fear. We'll just have to be a bit discreet about it, that's all. No point upsetting our investment partners.

—See if they will name names before they're kicked out, says Kiunga. Tonkei was obviously their contact point for the ivory. But I've got a feeling he must have been reporting to someone else.

Mollel ponders a moment how to describe Lendeva in his report. Should he call him Mbatiani? Should he call him his brother?

And then he wonders: should he mention him at all?

—So, Maasai, says Otieno, putting his arm around Mollel's shoulder. Does it feel good to be back?

For a fleeting moment, Mollel recalls the sense of peace he felt when all he owned was the *shuka* he wore and the dagger at his waist.

And he thinks of Lendeva, striding across the Maasai plain or shattered in the depths of Hell, and he hopes that some kind of peace has come to him.

And then he remembers his son, and realises that in less than an hour – Nairobi traffic permitting – he will be reunited with him once again.

The report can wait.

—Yes, says Mollel. Yes. It feels good to be back.

Reading Group Notes

In conversation with Richard Crompton

— Mollel is a complex and contradictory character: a fierce detective with a tragic past; a former Maasai warrior living in the city; a rule breaker who strives for justice. Where did your idea for Mollel come from?

Mollel is an amalgam of different people I met in my research. As you say, he combines two worlds, yet is not truly of either. He's turned away from his Maasai heritage, yet it continues to define him in the police force. It's very important that Mollel, as the reader's eyes and ears in these complex and layered worlds, remains somewhat an outsider. He needs to see afresh so that the reader can too.

— When you write a novel, is it an evolutionary process or do you know exactly where you want it to go from the first page?

I always have a very strong feeling for the texture of the novel. I know the tone I want to strike and at which point certain tensions or emotions will arise. That's set in stone right from the start. Then it's a question of how I strike those notes. Quite often the plot will have to change to accommodate the feeling I want to get across.

— *Hell's Gate* is the second book in a series featuring Mollel. Have you mapped out Mollel's journey? Or are you on the lookout for cases and crimes that may interest your hero?

Again, I know very clearly where Mollel will go in terms of his character development, and that of those around him. I'm always on the lookout for stories to provide the backdrop to his journey, and I scour the papers daily. There's never any shortage of material.

— **You've been living in East Africa for several years now. Do you consider Nairobi to be your home, or do you ever pine for England? What impact has living in Africa had on your writing?**

I love Kenya, but still feel (like Mollel) an outsider. Increasingly I feel the same when I return to Britain. I think it has sharpened my understanding of the country I grew up in, and this is coming to the fore in some of my writing which is set in Britain.

— **What's your opinion of the Kenyan justice system, and how has this influenced your vision of Mollel?**

On paper, the Kenyan justice system is a good one. In reality, it is crippled by underfunding and corruption. Mollel is supposed to be a good man in a bad system – but I hope I portray the fact that even many of those we may consider corrupt, believe themselves to be motivated by good intentions. There are very few absolutes in human nature.

— **As a former BBC journalist, how does reporting on a story compare to writing a novel? Which form of writing do you prefer?**

I love the immediacy of news reporting and the economy of writing to pictures. I miss the daily and hourly deadline. But in terms of the autonomy of truly expressing oneself free from editorial control or managerial diktat, there is no substitute for the novel.

— Who are your favourite authors and how have they influenced your writing?

Georges Simenon: Mollel is, in part, a homage to Maigret. I hope I have captured some of the humanity and rich characterisation of those wonderful novels. As for the classics, I would truly love, one day, to write a work with the ambition of *Middlemarch* or *Bleak House*. Let's see.

— What are you working on right now?

Mollel 3. I also seem to spend a lot of time changing nappies and reading stories.

Discussion Points

- *'They have taken the sky and bound it.'* Discuss.

- 'You can take the Maasai away from the village, but you can't take the village out of your heart.' How important are ideas of home and land in *Hell's Gate*? Where does Mollel feel most at home and why?

- Mollel believes that Kenyans can identify a stranger's tribe from 'the way they speak, the way they look or dress, the gestures they use . . .' Do you think the same is true of the communities in which you live?

- 'Nairobi doesn't need the law right now. It needs order.' Do you agree? How is justice brought about in *Hell's Gate*?

- Although Mollel still seems to possess a sense of pride in his Maasai culture and heritage, he has in many ways turned his back on his people. Can you attempt to explain this conflict? What do you think Mollel wants for his son, Adam?

- What lessons can you take away from the myth of the Maasai Bride? Do you think there is any value in looking back? Why was she turned to stone?

- At one point in *Hell's Gate*, Mollel points with his lips, a Kikuyu trait. How much does one's environment affect behaviour? Can you discern any development in Mollel's personality or character during the course of the novel?

- Kibet risks her life to protect the rhino in Hell's Gate national park. Have your ideas about poaching and the ivory trade changed after reading the novel?

- 'I'm never off duty.' What motivates Mollel?

- 'Is this what it means to be Kenyan today? To constantly squabble over language and tribe and land.' Discuss the ways in which Richard Crompton portrays Kenya and its people. What do you think the future holds for the country? Are you hopeful that political divisions can be resolved?

Further Reading

The Constant Gardener by John le Carré

Out of Africa by Karen Blixen

Maigret on the Defensive by Georges Simenon

Devil on the Cross by Ngũgĩ wa Thiong'o

A Good Man in Africa by William Boyd

White Mischief by James Fox

The State of Africa: A History of the Continent Since Independence by Martin Meredith